Dear Reader,

The editors at Harlequin and Silhouette are thrilled to be able to bring you a brand-new featured author program beginning in 2005! Signature Select aims to single out outstanding stories, contemporary themes and oft-requested classics by some of your favorite series authors and present them to you in a variety of formats bound by truly striking covers.

You may notice a number of different colored bands on the spine of this book. Each color corresponds to a different type of reading experience in the new Signature Select program. The Spotlight books will offer a single "big read" by a talented series author, the Collections will present three novellas on a selected theme in one volume, the Sagas will contain sprawling, sometimes multi-generational family tales (often related to a favorite family first introduced in series) and the Miniseries will feature requested, previously published books, with two or, occasionally, three complete stories in one volume. The Signature Select program will offer one book in each of these categories per month, and fans of limited continuity series will also find these continuing stories under the Signature Select umbrella.

In addition, these volumes will bring you bonus features...different in every single book! You may learn more about the author in an extended interview, more about the setting or inspiration for the book, more about subjects related to the theme and, often, a bonus short read will be included.

Watch for new stories from Vicki Lewis Thompson, Lori Foster, Donna Kauffman, Marie Ferrarella, Merline Lovelace, Roberta Gellis, Suzanne Forster, Stephanie Bond and scores more of the brightest talents in romance fiction!

We have an exciting year ahead!

Warm wishes for happy reading,

Marsha Zinberg

Marsha Zinberg
Executive Editor
The Signature Select Program

Signature Select™

COLLECTION

JACQUIE D'ALESSANDRO
JULIE KENNER
SUSAN KEARNEY

THE HOPE CHEST

HARLEQUIN®

TORONTO • NEW YORK • LONDON
AMSTERDAM • PARIS • SYDNEY • HAMBURG
STOCKHOLM • ATHENS • TOKYO • MILAN • MADRID
PRAGUE • WARSAW • BUDAPEST • AUCKLAND

ISBN 0-373-83645-7

THE HOPE CHEST

Copyright © 2005 by Harlequin Books S.A.

The publisher acknowledges the copyright holders
of the individual works as follows:

YESTERDAY'S MAGIC
Copyright © 2005 by Jacquie D'Alessandro.

TODAY'S SECRETS
Copyright © 2005 by Julia Beck Kenner.

TOMORROW'S PROMISE
Copyright © 2005 by Susan Hope Kearney.

CONTENTS

This book is dedicated to my mom and dad, Kay and Jim Johnson, for buying me my beautiful hope chest, then showing me how to fill it with dreams. And, as always, to my wonderful husband Joe, who makes all my dreams come true; and my terrific son Christopher, aka Makes My Dreams Come True, Junior.

Acknowledgments

Thank you to Brenda Chin and Marsha Zinberg
for giving me the opportunity to participate in this wonderful
venture. Thanks also to Damaris Rowland, Steve Axelrod,
Kathy Guse, Lea and Art D'Alessandro, Jenni Grizzle
and Wendy Etherington for their unfailing support.

YESTERDAY'S MAGIC

Jacquie D'Alessandro

For Brenda Chin and Marsha Zinberg.
Thanks for encouraging me to write a story that was really "out there."

CHAPTER ONE

Cardiff, England 1820

LADY AMANDA PRATT strode quickly along Cromwell-on-Sea's main road toward Gibson's Antiques and Curiosities. *Botheration,* it was already twenty minutes past two, and the sign posted on the shop's door when she and Aunt Lydia had passed by earlier indicated the store was temporarily closed and would reopen at two o'clock. Amanda had wanted to return promptly at two, but what with all the fascinating wares Cromwell-on-Sea's shops had to offer, she'd completely lost track of time. When she'd noted the hour and realized Aunt Lydia was nowhere near ready to depart Hobson's Millinery, Amanda had told her aunt to take her time. She'd simply nip back to Gibson's to purchase that extraordinary box displayed in the window.

Just thinking about the treasure quickened her step. She'd never seen anything remotely like it, not even in London's grand shops on Regent, Bond and Oxford Streets where she regularly hunted for pieces to add to her collection of unusual boxes. The shop owners in

London were well acquainted with her finely honed bargaining skills, and her lips curved at the prospect of this unexpected opportunity to put her expertise to use here. She certainly hadn't anticipated seeing something so outstanding while visiting her aunt in this small village just outside Cardiff. The instant she'd seen the rectangular box, which was about the size of a loaf of bread and made of intricately inlaid, glossy wood, she'd wanted it. She'd nearly pressed her nose to the shop window, admiring the treasure.

But it was more than the unique gleaming surface that had fascinated Amanda. It was the image on the curved lid that had so thoroughly captured her attention. A silhouette of a woman with long hair that appeared to be blowing in the breeze. She wore a flowing, Grecian-style gown that clung to the front of her form and billowed behind her from that imaginary wind while she seemingly walked into the distance, her arms stretched upward, as if reaching for something above, beyond her. Her upturned face was turned in partial profile, her pose simultaneously mysterious, beseeching and seductively teasing. Yet the woman also struck Amanda as being somehow…lonely. And searching for…something. *I know precisely how you feel…*

Amanda shook off the thought and hurried on. She passed rows of well-kept shops lining both sides of the wide, busy street crowded with early-afternoon pedestrians purchasing items ranging from freshly caught fish to fragrant bread to embroidered linens. Children scampered about, the sounds of their laughter rising above the squeak of carriage wheels and the calls of entrepreneurs hawking their wares from a group of stalls set up at the far end of the street next to the smithy. Normally she would have strolled leisurely, allowing her senses to absorb the scenery, to savor the newness of sights and scents so different from London or her family's country home in Kent. Then she would have engaged in one of her favorite activities—watching people and wondering about their lives, who they were, where they lived, what sort of personalities they possessed, whether or not they were happy, what secrets they hid. But all that would have to wait. Right now she was a woman with a mission.

A refreshing, brisk, salt-scented breeze, courtesy of the Bristol Channel, ruffled Amanda's forest-green spencer, and she breathed deeply, enjoying the contrast of the warm sun and cool, fresh early summer air. London's air definitely did not smell like this. No, this sea air was scented not only with the tang of salt, but with more intangible fragrances. Peace. Tranquility. Freedom. When Aunt Lydia had issued an invitation to join her in Cardiff, Amanda had instantly pounced upon the opportunity.

Would the answers she so desperately sought be found in this modest seaside village, far removed from the pressures of her mother's incessant demands that she quit dawdling and choose a husband? She prayed that would be the case. In all fairness she supposed she was dawdling, but only so she could search her heart, which for reasons she did not understand, required searching. Heavens, with the success of her Season, she should be the happiest girl in all of England, after being declared "an Incomparable," and blessed with four serious suitors, all gentlemen from fine families.

So why wasn't she happy? Dancing on air? She'd always dreamed of falling in love, marrying a man who made her heart race, having a family. In her mind's eye she'd clearly envisioned herself surrounded by several laughing children, half a dozen rambunctious dogs, a litter of kittens, a fragrant abundant garden, and...*him.* That nameless, faceless gentleman whose identity remained a mystery other than to know that he was kind, loving, generous. Made her laugh. And loved her to distraction, as she loved him. Why was determining which of her four suitors was that man proving such a daunting, depressing task? Surely it should not be so. Well, once she'd decided which of her suitors to marry, this feeling of malaise and frustrated confusion that had plagued her all during the Season would evaporate.

Gibson's Antiques and Curiosities lay just ahead, and Amanda nearly ran the last few steps, then halted in front of the window. And stared. The velvet perch upon which the box—*her* box—had rested was now empty.

Dismay flooded her. Surely someone couldn't have purchased the box in the past twenty minutes since the shop reopened. Smothering the unladylike word that rose to her lips, Amanda quickly entered the shop. She vaguely noted the two gentlemen in the shop. Instead her attention was riveted on the glossy wooden box that sat on the glass-topped counter separating the men.

The middle-aged man behind the counter said to her in a tremulous, reed-thin voice, "Welcome. I'm Wallace Gibson, the owner. I'll be happy to assist you in just a moment."

Hoping she wasn't too late, Amanda swiftly approached the counter then pointed at the box. "Actually, that is the piece I was interested in."

Mr. Gibson swallowed, bobbing the prominent Adam's apple in his pencil-thin neck. He appeared nervous and flustered, and his gaze flicked to the other man. "I'm afraid I've just sold the piece," Mr. Gibson said, "to this gentleman."

Amanda pressed her lips together and strove to swallow her disappointment. Not to mention her annoyance—at herself for being late and at this stranger for buying the box she'd already mentally added to her hoard of treasures. Vexing man. Not that she could fault him his discerning taste, but really, with all the other objects crowded into this shop, why did he have to choose *her* box?

She turned to look at him and found herself being studied with arctic-blue eyes that lived up to their shade as they held no warmth whatsoever. Something she could not decipher flickered in those chilly depths, but then the curtain fell once again.

The afternoon sun slanting through the front window highlighted the uncompromising stark angles and planes of a face far too forbidding to be called handsome. His hair was an unremarkable dark brown and mussed, as though he'd plunged his fingers through it, one lock falling over his forehead. His mouth was well formed, but did not look as if it smiled often, if ever. He looked stern and uncompromising and Amanda had to fight the urge to take a hasty step backward under his frigid scrutiny. Good heavens, no wonder Mr. Gibson appeared jittery. And how utterly unfair, irksome and distressing that the lovely lady on the box now belonged to this cold man.

Undeterred by the gentleman's chilly demeanor—indeed, she'd dealt with her share of difficult men this past Season—Amanda offered him what she hoped passed for a warm smile. "I admired the box through the window earlier today when the shop was closed. As the piece has not yet been wrapped, would you mind if I looked at it?"

He studied her in that unwavering, oddly unsettling way for several more seconds, then asked, "Why would you want to continue to admire something that you know can never be yours?"

Unlike his eyes which gave away nothing, Amanda detected a wealth of underlying emotion in his deep voice. Loss. Pain. Regret. All of which piqued her curiosity, and she briefly wondered if he realized his voice revealed so much. Probably not, she decided, as those cold eyes surely did not belong to a man who'd willingly share his feelings.

"I suppose I'd like to admire the box for the same reason that I love visiting galleries and museums," she said. "Although I cannot bring the items home, I still enjoy looking at them, find pleasure in appreciating them, if only temporarily." She favored him with her best dimpling smile. "After all, I cannot own *everything*. Where would I put it?" When he offered no reaction to her jest, she continued doggedly, "May I look at the box?"

A muscle in his jaw jerked, then he gave a tight nod and stepped aside. Amanda took immediate advantage of his silent consent.

The piece was as lovely as she'd thought. Lovelier even. She ran a single fingertip across the glossy, curved lid. "The texture is so unusual," she murmured. "How did you acquire this piece, Mr. Gibson?"

"Oddly enough, I recently discovered it in my very own attic. I was searching for a volume of Shakespeare's sonnets I'd recalled tucking away years ago when I happened upon it."

"So it is a family heirloom?"

Mr. Gibson frowned and shook his head. "I suppose it must be, although I'd never seen it before. Of course, it *was* nestled in the bottom of a trunk set in the far corner of my admittedly overcrowded attic."

"I'm surprised you would wish to part with something so unique."

"As a businessman, I cannot afford to become sentimentally attached to things."

"No, I suppose not." She ran her hands over the box, searching for a latch to open it, but couldn't find one. She then carefully lifted the piece. "How does it open?"

"I'm afraid it doesn't," Mr. Gibson said. "I spent hours looking for a clasp or hinge but there's nothing of the sort. While at first glance it appears to be a box, it's clearly just a solid piece of dense wood. I'd place it as late-sixteenth or early-seventeenth century, most likely intended for use as a doorstop. The perfect, unmarked condition of the wood however indicates it was used purely for decorative purposes—based on the female figure, most likely in a lady's bedchamber."

Another fissure of annoyance trickled through Amanda. *Yes, and it would have, should have, decorated my bedchamber along with all my other trinkets if I hadn't been late in getting back to the shop, allowing this cursed man the opportunity to buy it.* A profound sense of disappointment and loss washed through her.

Inexplicably feeling as if she were saying farewell to an old friend, she set the box back on the counter, then gently traced her index over the length of the silhouette. As she touched the edge of the box, a soft click sounded. Then, to her amazement, the lid slowly opened about an inch, moving up on unseen hinges attached to the back.

She heard Mr. Gibson's sharp intake of breath, and

sensed the other gentleman's sudden attention, but her gaze remained affixed on the box.

"I thought you said it didn't open, Gibson," the man said sharply.

"I would have sworn it didn't. How did you do that?" Mr. Gibson asked Amanda.

Bemused, she said, "I simply ran my finger down the length of the silhouette."

"Obviously she touched some hidden spring," the man said. He reached out then slowly opened the lid the rest of the way. Three heads bumped as they all leaned forward.

Amanda turned her head toward the stranger, intending to apologize, and found herself nearly nose to nose with him. She stilled out of sheer surprise at his sudden, unexpected closeness, and for several seconds they simply looked at each other. Her breath caught, and she illogically pondered why a man with such chilly eyes would be gifted with such thick, dark eyelashes. Her inquisitive nature instantly reared its head. Who was he? Did he live here, or was he a visitor as she was? What was his life like? She suspected he was not a happy man. Why not? What secrets lurked behind those eyes?

When her breathing resumed, her head filled with the scent of him—a pleasing fragrance of sandalwood, mixed with the clean smell of freshly laundered linen. For the second time, something she couldn't decipher flickered in his eyes, then he straightened. "I beg your pardon," he said, his voice a soft rasp. Definitely not the chilly tone he'd used earlier.

Amanda quickly straightened as well, cursing the heated blush creeping up her neck. He returned his attention to the box. Amanda did likewise, surreptitiously lifting onto her toes and craning her neck.

A series of intriguing, carved curlicues adorned the inside edge of the box, and what looked liked random silvery dots marked the inside of the lid. Before she could see anything else, the man closed the lid. Amanda barely suppressed the *No!* that rose to her lips.

He looked at Mr. Gibson who appeared to pale under the gentleman's steady stare. "If you'll please wrap this now—I'm in a hurry."

"Of course. I'll just fetch the paper and twine from the back room." With a nod, he scurried from around the counter then strode toward the rear of the shop.

A heavy silence descended between Amanda and the stranger, broken only by the ticking of the enormous antique grandfather clock in the corner. *Damnation,* she wanted that box. Now more than ever. Her intuition told her the man would not part with it. Still, she had to try.

She turned to him, but before she could speak, he said, "My thanks for discovering how the box opened."

"You're welcome," she replied, although what she really wished to say was, *She who opens the box should own it.* "Would you consider selling me the box?"

He did not so much as blink. "No."

She heard a faint tapping sound and realized it was her foot rapping out her irritation against the wood floor. After forcing her toes to remain still, she drew a calming breath. She couldn't give up. Not only did she want the box for her collection, but for reasons she couldn't fathom, she did not want this forbidding, cold-eyed man to have it.

"What if I were to offer you double what you just paid for it?" Every antique merchant in London with whom she'd ever relentlessly haggled would have fallen into a slack-jawed stupor at her unprecedented, extravagant offer.

He leveled an assessing look upon her that made her feel as if she were pinned beneath a microscope. "You make such an offer without knowing how much I paid? Are you normally so rash, madam?"

His question startled her. Rash? Her? Lady Amanda Pratt, who was well-known not only for her circumspect behavior but her keen eye for a bargain? A woman who put careful thought into all her decisions, even the most mundane? "No one has ever described me as such."

"Indeed? What if I told you I'd just paid five hundred pounds for the box?"

She stared at him steadily for several heartbeats. "Did you?"

"What if I did?"

Hideous man. She did not believe for an instant he'd

paid such an outrageous sum. But she surely wouldn't help her cause by accusing him of lying. Yet if she could get him to agree to sell it for double what he paid, she could then demand that Mr. Gibson produce the bill of sale to verify the amount.

Raising her chin a notch, she said, "As I am a woman of my word, I'd then have to say I just purchased an exceedingly expensive box."

"Why do you want it?"

"I collect boxes. Have since I was a child when my grandmother gave me an unusual piece of Sèvres. I'm especially fond of pieces depicting women."

"Yet your attraction to the piece seemed undeterred even when Mr. Gibson explained it wasn't a box at all, but rather a doorstop."

"That did not lessen the beauty of the outside."

"So you based your judgment strictly on its outward appearance."

Amanda raised her brows at his tone—accusatory, yet laced with an unmistakable trace of disappointment that allowed heat to creep into her face. "As did you, sir. Mr. Gibson said he'd told you the box did not open, yet you purchased it anyway—obviously basing your judgment strictly on its outward appearance. Tell me, why do *you* want the piece?"

"I, too, have a collection. Not specifically of boxes, but of…unique objects. The box will be a nice addition."

Amanda's gaze drifted down to the box and she

studied the image of the woman for several seconds with a longing she couldn't explain. The woman's features were not defined, yet she somehow seemed vaguely, inexplicably familiar…the way she was reaching for something unseen, just beyond her grasp.

Practicality ruled nearly every facet of Amanda's life, yet there was a streak of the fanciful, of the dreamer in her nature that, in spite of her best efforts to subdue it, she could not completely suppress. And that fanciful streak imagined the woman on the box reaching out to Amanda, as if she desperately wanted, needed to tell her something.

Raising her gaze back to the man's, she said, "I offer you three times what you paid."

"No." The harshly spoken word hung in the air between them, extinguishing any lingering hopes she'd harbored. "Nor would I accept four or fives times the amount," he continued. "She—the box—is not for sale."

She was saved from making a reply when Mr. Gibson rejoined them. Her mind commanded her feet to move away, to busy herself in another section of the shop, but she remained rooted to the spot, watching in silence, feeling as though she were in mourning, while the shopkeeper carefully wrapped the box that should have been hers, then secured the wrapping with string.

She couldn't help but notice that Mr. Gibson's hands weren't quite steady and he kept furtively peeking at the box's new owner, a fact that tickled her already piqued curiosity—another facet of her character she tried, often unsuccessfully to her mother's deep chagrin, to keep in check. It was almost as if Mr. Gibson was afraid of the man. She supposed she couldn't blame him, what with the man's large size and intimidating manner. His demeanor almost seemed to dare a person to say something untoward to him. Perhaps she would have feared him as Mr. Gibson so clearly did if she hadn't been so overwhelmed with the desire to cosh him.

Although the man stood still as a statue while Mr. Gibson secured the wrapping with sturdy twine, Amanda could sense his impatience. The instant Mr. Gibson cut off the excess twine after tying the last knot, the man snatched up the package. With a curt nod to no one in particular, he strode from the shop.

The instant the door closed behind him, Mr. Gibson seemed to wilt with relief. "Egad," he murmured faintly, slipping a handkerchief from his pocket and dabbing at his damp brow. He offered her a faint smile. "His lordship's visit was very…unexpected."

Amanda's brows rose. That rude, irritating man who hadn't even possessed the manners to bid them farewell was a *peer*? "His *lordship?*"

"Why, yes." Mr. Gibson's eyes widened. "Do you not know who that was?"

"No. This is my first visit to Cardiff, and I only arrived several days ago. Who—?"

The door opened and Aunt Lydia walked swiftly

into the shop, cutting off Amanda's question. Her aunt's flushed face bore an excited expression Amanda well recognized. It was the expression that always preceded the words, *you'll never guess...*

"You'll never guess who I just saw," Aunt Lydia said in a breathless voice. She reached the counter, her ample bosom heaving beneath her peacock-blue gown. Before Amanda could answer, Aunt Lydia turned to Mr. Gibson. "I see you've met my niece."

"Not formally, Lady Lydia."

Aunt Lydia performed a cursory introduction, then said, "It looked as if he exited your shop, Mr. Gibson."

"If you mean who I think you mean, then yes, he did."

"Never say so!" Aunt Lydia said, snapping open her fan and waving it vigorously under her chin. "Amanda, did you see him?"

"If you mean that insufferable man who just left the shop, yes, of course I saw him."

"And did you not recognize him?"

"No. I'm positive I've never seen him before." *And equally positive that I never wish to see him again.*

"Understandable, as I'm certain you've never met. But did you not recognize his *name?*"

"I fear he didn't deign to introduce himself," Amanda said with a sniff. "Who was he?"

Aunt Lydia touched the backs of her fingertips to her forehead in one of the dramatic poses she was so fond of striking while imparting momentous news. "That, my dear girl, was none other than Maxwell Wolford, the earl of Dorsey."

"Or, as he is more commonly known," Mr. Gibson intoned, "the Crazed Killer of Cardiff."

CHAPTER TWO

"THE CRAZED KILLER OF CARDIFF?" Amanda repeated. An involuntary shiver ran down her spine. She wasn't certain what sort of behavior would prompt such a grisly sobriquet but clearly it wasn't anything benevolent. Still, her sense of curiosity all but tingled. "Why is he called that?"

"Because of *The Incident,*" Aunt Lydia said.

"Incident?" Amanda asked. "Is this a bit of local lore?"

"More like the most scandalous, most talked about occurrence in decades," Aunt Lydia said, the feathers in her turban swishing in tandem with her animated words. "Even after two years have past, the chatter still hasn't completely died out."

"Indeed it hasn't," Mr. Gibson said. "The Incident is still rehashed regularly, with much of the speculation fired by the sudden way Lord Dorsey retreated to his estate. His withdrawal, combined with his refusal to in any way refute or address the rumors, continues to lead most people to view him as secretive and suspicious. Not to mention odd."

Aunt Lydia waved her hand in a dismissive gesture. "Oh, but many people considered the poor boy odd well before The Incident, what with all those scientific experiments of his."

"Experiments?" Amanda repeated, slow horror dawning in her mind. "Surely you don't mean—I've heard tales of men who conduct experiments on cadavers in the name of science. Men who sometimes procure the bodies by arranging…untimely deaths." A chill ran down Amanda's spine. "Is this Lord Dorsey such a man? Is that why he is called the Crazed Killer of Cardiff?"

"Good heavens, what a gruesome imagination you have, my child," said Aunt Lydia with a visible shudder. "No, the unfortunate name became attached to the gentleman when he inherited his title upon the sudden death of his older brother, Roland."

"Lord Dorsey killed his brother?"

"Speculation to that effect arose almost immediately," Aunt Lydia said. "Nothing was ever proved, however."

"How did his brother die?"

"A carriage accident—which also took the life of Roland's young wife, Countess Dorsey, who was expecting their first child."

"How horrible," Amanda said. "I'd then guess that the current Lord Dorsey was suspected since the accident not only allowed him to inherit the title, but erased any possible male heir that might have been born?"

"Precisely," Aunt Lydia said with a nod. "Apparently the brothers had engaged in a terrible row before the accident. It was rumored that Roland banished his younger brother from the estate. That, coupled with the fact that many people already considered the younger brother odd, gave way to the speculation that he'd somehow planned and arranged the accident to do away with Roland."

Although she normally did not indulge in idle gossip, Amanda found herself fascinated by the tale. Had she looked into the eyes of a *killer?* "Why was the younger brother considered odd?"

A frown furrowed between Aunt Lydia's brows. "Even as a child, he was of a very serious, scientific nature—a complete contrast to Roland who was gifted with the devil's own allure and the face of an angel. There wasn't a person in the village, from the youngest child to the oldest curmudgeon, Roland couldn't charm. While other boys were wild for horses and the hunt, Maxwell's interests were astronomy and stargazing. He wasn't given to fits of laughter and frivolity as most lads are. Spent his time trudging about in the woods looking for insects, peering at heaven knows what under microscopes, working in the laboratory he constructed himself by refurbishing an abandoned, ramshackle barn on the estate's property—much to the distress of his father, who made no secret of the fact that Roland was his favorite son. Indeed, Roland was well liked by the entire village. His death was a loss to everyone."

"Lord Dorsey worked on that laboratory for years," Mr. Gibson added. "Was his pride and joy—some say, his whole life. The accident occurred after he'd been ordered to leave the estate, which meant leaving his laboratory. 'Twas the main reason suspicion fell upon him, although many believed he also secretly coveted the title."

Aunt Lydia turned to Mr. Gibson. "The last I heard, Lord Dorsey had not ventured off his estate since The Incident."

"Haven't seen him in the two years since. Not until he entered my shop today." Mr. Gibson lowered his voice and leaned forward. "Gave me a bit of a start, as you can imagine."

"Oh, I'm certain it was a very great surprise."

"I'd wager that today's visit will have the entire village talking of nothing else."

"Yes, I'm sure you're right. Tell me, Mr. Gibson, how did he look?"

"In appearance, much the same. Indeed, I recognized him instantly. However, his demeanor struck me as… weary."

Aunt Lydia made a tsk-tsk noise. "As I recall he was always very robust. Of course, with all the speculation surrounding The Incident, 'tis no wonder the man would appear fatigued. What was his manner of dress?"

"Fine clothing, as one would expect, albeit his jacket was a bit wrinkled."

"Yes, he always had a bit of the rumpled look about

him. Rather as if he'd taken a nap in his clothing." She swiveled her attention back to Amanda. "And you, dear. What was your impression of Lord Dorsey?"

"I thought him rude, cold and abrupt," she answered. She didn't bother to add that she particularly disliked his deplorable timing. Botheration, if the man hadn't ventured into the village for two years, why couldn't he have waited one more day? Or even one more hour?

"Rude, cold and abrupt..." Aunt Lydia pursed her lips then nodded slowly. "Yes, I suppose circumstances understandably would have rendered him as such, although I assure you he was not always that way." She again looked at Mr. Gibson. "Did he purchase anything?"

"Yes," Amanda broke in. "The box I wished to buy. He'd already paid for it by the time I arrived."

"Oh, dear." Aunt Lydia patted her hand in a show of sympathy. "How utterly vexing. This is precisely why men should not be permitted in shops—they always foul up the works. They should simply give money to their wives and allow them to handle all purchasing matters. Of course, Lord Dorsey doesn't have a wife."

"Indeed?" Amanda said, her voice ripe with sarcasm. "I cannot fathom why."

"Oh, it's because of The Incident, my dear," said Aunt Lydia, who, as Amanda had learned, was quite immune to sarcasm. "He was engaged, but his fiancée cried off after The Incident."

"Lord Dorsey bought the betrothal ring from me,"

Mr. Gibson chimed in. "Beautiful antique piece with a square-cut emerald. Was the last time I saw his lordship until this afternoon."

"Did he purchase anything else today, Mr. Gibson?" Aunt Lydia asked.

"No. He seemed in a hurry to be gone." Mr. Gibson raised his brows in a significant manner. "Lord Dorsey paid the full asking price of the box without the least hesitation."

The haggler in Amanda blanched at this bit of news. Aunt Lydia pressed her hands to her bosom. "Never say so! The gentleman used to be quite the bargain hunter, much like my niece. Clearly he's much changed since The Incident."

Amanda digested the information for several seconds, then asked, "Do you believe he killed his brother, Mr. Gibson?"

Mr. Gibson scratched his head, then said, "Can't say I'm certain what I believe. It always struck me hard to credit that the same man who visited my shop several times a month, a man who possessed such a love for the unusual and who took such care when handling delicate antiques, would be capable of murder. But I've lived long enough to know that people aren't always as they seem."

Amanda turned to her aunt. "And what is your opinion?"

"I think the entire thing is stuff and nonsense, and I wrote to Lord Dorsey shortly after The Incident telling him as much. I'll grant you, Lord Dorsey has always been…different, which often made him a target for ridicule and, sadly, suspicion. As I've summered in Cardiff for two decades, I've been acquainted with the Wolford family for years, and have had enough dealings with the man to say without hesitation that no, I do not believe he killed his brother. I've always known him to be kind, even to people who did not deserve such consideration from him." She drew herself up and fixed her steeliest glare upon Mr. Gibson. "And I must say, I'm surprised that you, sir, who have known him since he was a child, would give credence to such cruel and unsubstantiated gossip. He is a *scientist*. He coveted his brother's title and responsibilities about as much as you would a frilly pink silk bonnet."

A dull flush crept up Mr. Gibson's neck. "You can't deny that it's suspicious—the way he abruptly withdrew from polite society, turned himself into a complete recluse."

"I most certainly can deny it," Aunt Lydia retorted, leveling a withering, down-the-nose look upon the shopkeeper the likes of which Amanda hoped never to have leveled upon her. "There is a word for such behavior, Mr. Gibson. It's called 'mourning.'" She tugged Amanda's arm. "Come, dear, let us take our leave. I find I've lost my appetite for shopping." She departed the shop like a ship under full sail, and Amanda followed, leaving a red-faced Mr. Gibson in their wake.

Once outside, Amanda fell into step alongside her aunt who continued to mutter under her breath about the sad state of affairs that society was populated by persons who insisted upon spreading gossip. Amanda decided it would be most imprudent to point out that her aunt and her aunt's friends had been among the worst gossipmongers during the entire Season. Of course, Amanda knew her aunt would argue that gossip during the Season was *essential*. After all, how else could one gain the necessary information that led to advantageous matches? And to be fair, Amanda had never known her aunt to engage in maliciousness.

While her aunt continued to mutter, Amanda's thoughts strayed to Lord Dorsey. She recalled the frigid blast of those icy blue eyes, but then remembered his voice and the underlying pain she'd sensed. Was it the result of his being wrongfully suspected and subsequently scorned? Or was it his conscience eating away at him for committing murder? Aunt Lydia believed him innocent, and Amanda had always trusted her aunt's sound judgment. And even though Amanda had thought Lord Dorsey irritating and abrupt, she found it difficult to cast him in the role of killer. Those flashes of pain and loneliness in his eyes…

To be falsely suspected of a crime, and the devastating effect that would have on one's life, aroused Amanda's sympathy. His words echoed through her mind: *So you based your judgment strictly on its outward appearance.*

Had he merely meant the box? Or had he been referring to something deeper, such as the way many of

Cardiff's citizens had judged him? Had he wondered if she was judging him as well?

Before her curiosity could completely run amok, she pushed the questions aside, as well as the image that rose in her mind's eye of the box that would never be hers. She'd accompanied her aunt to this seaside haven to solve the troubling dilemma of which of her suitors to marry. Indeed, to determine why the decision posed such a puzzle to begin with. She'd always assumed her heart would lead her directly, unerringly to *him*, but her heart had remained frustratingly silent thus far. She had neither the time nor the inclination to dwell on the enigmatic Lord Dorsey. And given his reclusive nature, surely they would not cross paths again.

MAXWELL ENTERED Dorsey Manor's black-and-white-tiled marble foyer where he was greeted by Sutton.

"A fine day you chose for an extra long walk in the gardens, my lord," the butler said, relieving Maxwell of his silver-tipped walking stick. His sharp gaze dropped to the package under Maxwell's arm. "Did we receive a delivery?"

"No. Actually, I did not walk in the garden today. I ventured into the village."

Pure astonished bewilderment crossed Sutton's normally impassive features. "The *village*, my lord?"

"Yes," Maxwell confirmed, feeling inexplicably amused at this uncommon ruffling of Sutton's feathers.

"I had a yen to—" *relieve the solitude that I find unbearably suffocating of late* "—visit the shops."

"The *shops,* my lord?"

"The horror in your tone would indicate I'd expressed a desire to strip naked and prance through the village bare-arsed, Sutton."

"I beg your pardon, my lord. I was merely surprised by your words." Their eyes met, and there was no mistaking the concern reflected in Sutton's. "You were... treated well, I trust?"

Snatches of whispers echoed through Maxwell's mind. *It's him. Yes, I'm certain...would recognize him anywhere...he's not been seen in the village in two years...heard he's not left his estate's grounds in all that time. He always was an odd, reclusive fellow...not like his brother who was so dashing, handsome and charming...surely only guilt would force him into such seclusion... They say his brother's death wasn't an accident...*

Maxwell shoved aside the snippets that had floated around him during his walk through Cromwell-on-Sea and offered Sutton a half smile. "Treated well enough. As you can see, no one slapped chains about my ankles and dragged me off to the gallows."

Maxwell instantly regretted his attempt at humor when Sutton's thin cheeks paled. "You shouldn't have gone alone, my lord. If I'd known you planned to venture off the grounds, I'd have arranged for a footman to accompany you." He drew himself up straighter. "Or I'd have walked with you myself."

A combination of sympathy, affection and gratitude suffused Maxwell at Sutton's fierce show of loyalty. Good God, the poor man's arthritic knees would have made the walk unbearable. Yet Maxwell knew Sutton would have gone with him just the same.

"A kind and much appreciated offer, Sutton, but I needed to step out of the shadows by myself. Perhaps if I'd done so sooner the rumors would have settled down."

"Doubtful. People have long memories." Sutton's lips tightened. "And they can be very cruel."

"Yes, I know." *All too well.* "I'll admit I was tempted more than once this afternoon to plant someone a facer." He pursed his lips in an exaggerated fashion, as if giving the matter deep consideration. "Hmm, yes, perhaps I should have done just that. Then, I might come to be known as the Deranged Pugilist of Dorsey Manor rather than the Crazed Killer of Cardiff, although you must admit that the latter has much more of an alliterative ring to it."

Sutton's lips didn't so much as twitch at Maxwell's jest. Indeed, his concerned expression grew more pronounced. Before he could speak, Maxwell placed a hand on the older man's shoulder. "Fear not, Sutton. I've no intention of engaging in fisticuffs or allowing the village gossipmongers to tread upon my tender feelings. Indeed, all turned out well." He held up his package. "Found myself a new treasure in Gibson's shop."

Sutton's expression softened a bit. "Well, that's excellent, my lord. It does my heart good to see you in good spirits."

"Thank you. And now I'm off to my study to unwrap and admire my purchase." After instructing Sutton to arrange for tea, Maxwell strode down the corridor toward his study, filled—for the first time in two years—with anticipation about something other than his laboratory.

Once seated behind his mahogany desk however, his gaze drifted across the room, as it so often did, to the grouping of oval-framed miniatures gracing the white marble mantel. Father, Mother, Roland's wife, Marianne, Roland. All gone.

Normally he ruthlessly bludgeoned back the plethora of images those paintings evoked, but this time he did nothing to stop the memories from bombarding him. His gaze touched on his father's stern features. Father…so filled with disappointment and disapproval when it came to his younger son, if he bothered to pay attention at all. He studied the face of the man who had never understood him, but then Father had never tried. He'd had his heir in Roland who was everything Father wanted in a son, a fact that had hurt deeply, but one that had been buffered by Maxwell's mother's love.

His gaze moved to Mother's image and emotion clogged his throat at the sight of her warm, tender smile. She'd never looked upon him with anything other than acceptance and love, and even though fifteen years had passed since her death, he still missed her warmth and subtle wit and infinite wisdom.

His gaze shifted to Marianne, a dazzling, flawed beauty from London who'd been sadly unprepared for a quiet life in a small village with a man she'd found out too late she did not know as well as she'd thought. And Roland…

Maxwell's gaze lingered on his brother's handsome face. The remorse and guilt that always struck hit him hard, and he sucked in a sharp breath at the blow. He squeezed his eyes shut and forced himself to take slow, steady breaths, as painful images of their last moments together flashed through his mind. Images that no amount of research or work or brandy could erase. Images that in spite of the passage of two years continued to steal his sleep and haunt his waking hours. Images he'd hoped a change of scenery might temporarily erase, thus his walk into Cromwell-on-Sea.

A humorless sound passed his lips. Based on the whispers, and the glares he'd felt boring into his back, he shouldn't have ventured beyond Dorsey's borders. But the sense of desperation—and, damn it, loneliness—plaguing him had compelled him to risk the inevitable reaction his presence would produce. In the past he'd always found solace in his laboratory, amongst his glass beakers and microscopes, his only connection to the outside world the floor-to-ceiling windows that glittered with shafts of sunlight during the day and silvery fingers cast by the moon and stars at night.

But lately the sense of peace he craved was proving frustratingly elusive. Today even his beloved Hershel telescope pointing toward the bright afternoon sky, awaiting darkness to reveal the mysteries of the starlit summer sky, had failed to ease his discontent.

He'd paced all morning, then stared down at his verdant lawns and beyond, to where a slice of sparkling dark blue capped with white foam was visible above the trees. He'd tried to will away the unrelenting restlessness prowling through him, but to no avail.

In spite of learning long ago that lying to himself was a fruitless exercise, he'd indulged himself lately, reluctant to put a name to the feeling pervading him, but he could fool himself no longer. The simple, inescapable truth was that he was…lonely.

At first he'd scoffed at the notion. How could a man with a houseful of servants be lonely? But it was indeed loneliness that had prompted his ill-conceived walk to the village.

Maxwell swallowed around the lump that lodged in his throat. He'd sought only peace, and perhaps a friendly smile, but that was not to be. Gibson had been clearly discomforted to have the Crazed Killer of Cardiff in his establishment. Bloody hell that hurt. Over the years, he'd spent many happy hours exploring Gibson's shop. He loved the smell of the place—that musty scent of aged items whose histories held promises of long-forgotten secrets.

With a sharp pang he recalled the last time he'd entered the shop before today. He'd purchased the antique emerald ring he'd given Lady Roberta the day he'd asked for her hand. A ring she'd accepted, only to return a fortnight later with a terse note as his entire world had unraveled around him. Just when he'd thought he'd already lost everything, Roberta had delivered the final blow. *Due to the circumstances in which you now find yourself, I can no longer consent to be your wife.*

Maxwell tore his gaze from the image of Roland's face and looked down at the package sitting on his desk. At least something good had come out of today's outing. This lovely treasure.

He quickly unwrapped the package, then studied the unusual piece which had captured his interest the instant he'd laid eyes upon it. Although he'd never seen the likes of the wood's glossy shine, it was the image of the woman on the box that truly intrigued him. Looking at her now, she continued to fascinate. Although the image was a featureless silhouette, she somehow appeared to be looking back at him, beckoning him, even as she reached out for something in front of her. He could almost hear her whisper, *This way...come with me...I want to show you something...*coaxing him to discover the secrets she guarded, to discover what mysteries lay beneath the lid upon which she dwelled.

Maxwell ran a single fingertip over the glossy, curved lid, lightly brushing over the woman's hair. If he'd been a fanciful man, he'd have sworn he felt the silky softness of those dark tresses. He couldn't wait to see the inside of the box again. To examine the fascinating markings around the edge and gracing the curved inside of the lid. Odd that the young woman in the shop had figured out how to open the box when Gibson hadn't been able to.

An image of the young woman raced into Maxwell's mind. He hadn't recognized her—no doubt she was one of the many people who traveled to Cardiff during the summer to enjoy the seaside atmosphere, a theory supported by the fact that she hadn't appeared to recognize him. No fear or speculation had glimmered in her golden-brown eyes when she'd looked at him, a fact which had surprised him. Indeed, the only emotions toward him he'd been able to detect were mild curiosity and not so mild annoyance.

Her unexpected arrival had greatly disconcerted him. Just before she'd entered the shop, he'd been fantasizing that the woman on the box was a dark-haired beauty. Then suddenly, as if he'd conjured her from his imagination, in walked a dark-haired beauty.

She'd clearly been as enamored of the box as he, and had obviously not been pleased to find he'd purchased that which she'd set her heart upon. His conscience pricked him as he'd once been in a similar situation and well knew that sense of frustrated disappointment, but he quickly quieted his inner voice. Based on the fine cut and material of her gown, she was clearly wealthy. And no doubt spoiled. Certainly a woman as attractive as she was accustomed to getting what she wanted. Probably only needed to flutter her eyelashes at a man to get her way. Or look up at him with those big, expressive brandy-colored eyes, which really were quite extraordinary…

Not that he'd been tempted for an instant to relinquish the box to her. No, he was quite immune to fluttering lashes and pouts—not that she'd resorted to either, which had rather surprised him. As for her figuring out how to open the box, clearly that was just a bit of luck. He'd have discovered the secret spring himself given time.

With an effort, he pushed the woman from the shop out of his thoughts. After all, it wasn't as if their paths would ever cross again.

CHAPTER THREE

THE FOLLOWING AFTERNOON, Amanda and her aunt sat on Tufton Manor's flagstone terrace enjoying a light repast of tea and biscuits. Amanda loved Aunt Lydia's home, especially this elm-shaded outdoor retreat. While she sipped her fragrant brew, she watched a pair of playful squirrels frolic on the lawn. The pair seemed perfectly suited, chattering at each other, dashing about, and Amanda found herself envying them their compatibility and freedom.

"Oh, there you go, looking so wistful again, my dear," said Aunt Lydia.

Amanda pulled her attention away from the squirrels and looked across the wrought-iron table. Her aunt's pansy-blue gaze rested upon her with a concerned expression that trickled guilt through Amanda.

"I was simply absorbed with the scenery." Forcing a smile, Amanda reached across the table and patted her aunt's hand. "Thank you for bringing me to this delightful place. I never realized the sound of the sea was so comforting. I've experienced more tranquility in the three days since we arrived than in the previous three months."

"I knew you would enjoy Cardiff, my dear. So much more restful than Bath, what with all the crowds that gather there, and a nice change from your usual summers in Kent." Aunt Lydia didn't add *away from your mother,* but the sentiment hung in the air like a rain-filled cloud. After clearing her throat, Aunt Lydia continued, "I didn't doubt for a moment that the village and fresh air would cheer you up, although why you should be unhappy is a mystery to me. 'Tis a blessing that you shall have a choice of husbands, my dear. Few young ladies are so fortunate."

Amanda kept her smile in place. "A blessing indeed."

"And you are even more fortunate that your father is letting you make the choice yourself rather than choosing for you. Of course, my brother has always been very wise."

Yes, her father had generously allowed her this time in Cardiff to examine her heart, although convincing Mother had been no easy task. Amanda well knew both her parents would expect, nay demand, she make her choice when she returned to London. Yet she was no closer to choosing now than when she'd arrived.

"Your father wants you to have the man your heart desires, dearest," Aunt Lydia said, her voice turning pensive. A faraway look stole into her eyes. "Trust me when I tell you that many fathers do not bestow such consideration upon their daughters."

Amanda gently squeezed her aunt's fingers in a silent show of sympathy. Although Aunt Lydia rarely discussed the circumstances, Amanda knew her aunt's father had forbidden her to marry the man she'd loved, citing that the third son of a baron—a man who dabbled in trade, no less—was completely unsuitable for the daughter of an earl. Aunt Lydia had honored her father's wishes, marrying a man of his choosing, Viscount Tufton, who had passed away five years ago.

Aunt Lydia's sad expression cleared, and she smiled. "But you shall have the man you want, Amanda, and I am very happy for you. Tell me, have you divined yet in which direction your heart leans?"

"No, I've not yet had much opportunity for serious reflection."

Amanda's conscience pricked her at that statement, which definitely skirted the truth. While she'd had little time for introspection since arriving in Cardiff, she *had* given the matter of her suitors a great deal of thought since the Season had ended a fortnight ago. All four of the gentlemen seeking her hand were excellent candidates. Handsome, wealthy and charming. Yet in spite of the fact that she looked forward to getting married, none of them…thrilled her.

She smothered the same impatient frustration that lately seemed to be her constant companion. What on earth was wrong with her? Given her suitors' eligibility, clearly the problem rested with Amanda herself. 'Twas the only way to explain why none of those gentlemen filled her with that heart-fluttering madness her imagination longed for. That she'd always thought, expected, *dreamed* would seize her.

But how to solve this problem? Mother insisted that affection required cultivation, like flowers in a garden. Amanda found that analogy rather deflating as she'd never possessed her mother's talents in the garden. She could only hope that this time away would enlighten her as to which gentleman would eventually best…thrill her.

"Of the four gentlemen, I'd say Lord Abbott is the handsomest," Aunt Lydia said, her tone musing, "although Lords Branton, Remington and Oxmoor are all attractive."

"Yes," Amanda agreed, wondering for the hundredth time why her heart did not perform the slightest flutter. "Indeed, Lord Abbott is easily the handsomest man I've ever encountered. From his perfect, artfully arranged blond curls to his perfectly tailored clothes, to his perfect manners, the man is quite…perfect." And her mother's definite favorite. "He'd no doubt make an amiable husband—an easy man to live with."

Aunt Lydia's eyes filled with distress. "Oh, but my dear, you do not want to choose the man you think easy to live with."

"I don't?"

"No." Leaning forward, Aunt Lydia grasped Amanda's hands tightly. "Choose the man you think it impossible to live with*out*. *He* is the man who will fulfill you. Who will make your heart sing. Who will bring you happiness. Who will make you look forward to each new day." Her voice lowered and became almost fierce with urgency. "And once you determine which one of your suitors is that man, do not hesitate. Do not waste a moment of your lives together. Grasp it with both hands and cherish the time you have—before something, or someone, or circumstances wrests it from you."

Before Amanda could fashion a reply to her aunt's surprising words, Mortimer stepped through the French windows and approached them with unprecedented speed.

Aunt Lydia regained herself and raised her brows at her butler. "Heavens, Mortimer, is something amiss? You're practically galloping."

The normally sedate butler halted then extended a silver salver upon which rested a cream-colored card. "You have a caller, my lady."

"Hardly unusual," Aunt Lydia murmured as she plucked the card from its highly polished perch. She glanced down and her eyebrows shot upward. "But in this case…"

"Are you in, my lady?"

"Oh, most definitely. Our guest may join us here, Mortimer. Please arrange for another tea setting."

"Yes, my lady." Mortimer withdrew, and Amanda studied her aunt over the rim of her china cup, recognizing her expression, anticipating the inevitable next words—

"You'll never guess who's come to call, my dear," Aunt Lydia said in a breathless voice.

Amanda pretended to ponder carefully, then teased, "Based on your reaction, I'd have to venture it's one of your handsome gentleman acquaintances bearing flowers and an ostentatiously large piece of jewelry."

She'd expected her jest to float above Aunt Lydia's head. Instead her aunt surprised her by saying with a cryptic smile, "You're correct about the handsome gentleman, but I suspect 'tis *you* who prompts this visit, not I."

"Me?" Amanda laughed. "I sincerely doubt it as I do not know anyone in Cardiff, save you, and most certainly not any handsome gentlemen." A sudden sinking feeling assailed her and she sat up straight. "Good heavens. Don't tell me one of my London suitors has turned up here?"

"No, my dear. 'Tis clear you've made *another* conquest."

The French windows opened and Amanda's head snapped toward the sound. Mortimer stepped through the entrance, followed by a solemn-faced man Amanda instantly recognized as her box-purchasing nemesis, Lord Dorsey.

What on earth was he doing here? Whatever it was, it could only have to do with Aunt Lydia as she had not so much as exchanged names with the gentleman. Their eyes met, and even from across the terrace Amanda felt the impact of his unsettling regard. She could not recall anyone ever looking at her so…intently. Her imagination fancied him seeing right into her mind, reading her thoughts. An odd tingle worked its way down her spine, and she forced herself to look away. But when she lowered her gaze, it fell upon the wrapped package he held. It was just the size of the glossy wooden box.

Her heart leaped. Had he decided to sell it to her after all? He certainly could have found out who she was from Mr. Gibson.

Lord Dorsey halted near the table, then made a formal bow. "Good afternoon. Thank you for seeing me, Lady Lydia."

"Lord Dorsey, I'm delighted you've called."

"The pleasure is mine, my lady."

Aunt Lydia indicated Amanda with a wave of her hand. "I believe you met my niece, Lady Amanda Pratt, at Mr. Gibson's shop yesterday."

Lord Dorsey turned toward Amanda and she was once again struck by the impact of those vividly blue eyes. "Although we spoke, I'm afraid we were not properly introduced." He made her a bow. "How do you do, Lady Amanda?"

Something—perhaps in the speculative, intent way he looked at her, or maybe in the way he said her name, in that slightly husky tone—sent another odd tingle through Amanda. But surely the strange feeling was simply the thought of seeing the wooden box again. "Lord Dorsey," she murmured, inclining her head.

"Please join us," Aunt Lydia said nodding toward the empty chair beside Amanda. "Mortimer is arranging for another setting for tea—unless you'd care for something else?"

"Tea is fine, thank you." He lowered himself into the ornate wrought-iron chair, then set the wrapped package on the table in front of him.

Aunt Lydia raised her quizzing glass and unabashedly looked him up and down. "You're looking well, Dorsey—very much the same." Her lips twitched. "And clearly still employing the same valet as when I saw you last."

First surprise, then unmistakable amusement flashed in his eyes, followed by a quick grin. Amanda blinked at the transformation that smile wrought upon his stern features. In fact, his entire stiff posture appeared to relax a bit.

"Randolph does the best he can with me," Lord Dorsey said with a sheepish expression, "but I fear I'm not the best subject. I'm grateful—and astounded—he's remained with me all these years, although he does his fair amount of grumbling, I assure you."

"Yes, I'm certain he does," Aunt Lydia said with a twinkling smile as she lowered her eyepiece. "Yet somehow those rumples suit you. Always have. Make you appear, well, scholarly, which as everyone knows, you are. As I recall, astronomy was your particular favorite area of study. Is it still?"

"Yes. I've always found the sky fascinating. So full of

mystery. Silent with secrets just waiting to be discovered."

"Well, given your dedication, I'm certain that if anyone can find those secrets, it is you, Dorsey."

He again appeared surprised by her words, as if he was not accustomed to people complimenting him, and, Amanda realized, he most likely was not, a realization that unexpectedly tugged on her heart.

"Thank you, Lady Lydia," he said. There was no mistaking the sincerity and gratitude in his voice. "And though it is unforgivably late in coming, I hope you will accept my thanks for the kind note you sent me after…my brother's death. Although my silence might indicate otherwise, it was very much appreciated."

"You're welcome. I'm sorry for the hardships you've endured. People can be very unkind. And foolish." She nodded toward the package. "Now, are you going to tell us what you have brought, or are we to expire from curiosity?"

"I must confess that this package is the main reason I called." He turned toward Amanda. "It's the box from Gibson's shop. In an attempt to locate you, I called upon Mr. Gibson before coming here. He informed me you were Lady Lydia's niece and staying with her."

Amanda's heart jumped. He *did* intend to sell her the box! Aunt Lydia shot her a smug "I told you so" look, then said, "Ah, so you've come to call upon my niece."

Amanda offered up a silent prayer of thanks that any significance Lord Dorsey might have attached to that statement clearly sailed over his head.

"Yes," he said, sounding almost relieved. He leaned closer to Amanda, and she instantly recognized the same masculine scent she'd smelled yesterday—sandalwood and fresh linen. "I spent all of last night and all of this morning trying to figure it out, but I could not," he said, his voice taking on an urgent tone. "I couldn't sleep. The entire puzzle has rendered me utterly frustrated and confounded."

Amanda stared, unsettled by the thought that her sudden befuddlement was due as much to his nearness as to his cryptic words. "I'm afraid I don't understand. Figure what out?"

"How you opened it." He unwrapped the box, then slid it closer to her. "In spite of all my efforts, I have been unable to do so. Will you show me what you did?"

Amanda stared at the box, then lifted her gaze to his, as understanding dawned, bringing with it acute disappointment along with a healthy dose of annoyance. "So you didn't bring the box here to accept my offer to buy it?"

His brows raised. "No. As I told you yesterday, I've no wish to sell it."

"You merely brought the box here so I could show you how to open it?"

"Yes."

"Because, in spite of hours of trying, you couldn't

figure it out for yourself?" she couldn't help but add, a twinge of smugness filtering into her voice.

Irritation flashed in his eyes. "Correct."

Silence stretched between them for several long seconds while Amanda's annoyance simmered.

Finally he jerked his head toward the box. "Well? Will you show me how you opened it?"

"Are you always so abrupt, my lord?"

He blinked. "Abrupt?"

"You do not preface your request with even the hint of polite conversation—questions regarding the weather, my state of health, whether I'm enjoying my visit, that sort of thing. Since you were equally terse in the shop yesterday, I was merely wondering if you were always so abrupt, or if it was just me who brought it out in you."

For several seconds he looked completely nonplussed. Then he raked a hand through his hair. "Forgive me. I've not had occasion to spend much time recently in polite society. Apparently my manners have suffered as a result. In my own defense, I can only say that it did not occur to me that you'd wish to partake of small talk with me."

Those words, which sounded so…lonely, spoken in that quiet, straightforward way, squeezed the area surrounding Amanda's heart. They stared at each other for several seconds, then he cleared his throat, and a whiff of mischief flashed in his eyes. "The, er, weather is particularly fine today, is it not?"

Good heavens, the effect of just that bit of deviltry was nothing short of...dazzling. "Very fine indeed," Amanda replied, forcing herself to answer in her most prim voice.

"And your health, Lady Amanda? It is good?"

"Very well, thank you."

"No dyspepsia or vapors or anything unpleasant I trust?"

"I am blessed with a most robust constitution."

"Excellent." He leaned back in his chair, folded his arms over his chest—his very broad chest, she noted—and looked at her with such exaggerated earnestness, she was hard pressed to decide if she was more annoyed or amused. "And your journey to Cardiff went well, Lady Amanda?"

"Exceedingly."

"No difficulties with brigands or highwaymen or anyone of that ilk?"

"None."

"Brilliant." He again leaned forward, pinning her with his gaze. "*Now,* will you please show me how to open the box?" he asked in a very polite, somber voice.

A sound that distinctly resembled a smothered laugh that was quickly turned into a cough came from Aunt Lydia, and although she should have been outraged, Amanda couldn't deny her own amusement, which she firmly tamped down. Not to mention her curiosity, which she allowed free rein. Why hadn't he been able to open the box?

"If I show you how to open it, will you permit me to examine the inside, or will you scurry away as you did yesterday?"

"Did I scurry?"

"Like a sand crab along the shore."

Instead of taking offense, his lips twitched with clear amusement. "Egad. Not the most flattering comparison. Are you always so blunt, Lady Amanda, or is it just me who brings it out in you?"

"I always endeavor to be honest."

"Hmm. Well, I cannot deny that's an admirable trait. Still, I believe your simile was inaccurate as crabs scurry sideways, and I distinctly recall moving *forward*."

"Very well. Then you scurried like a rabbit—"

"Not to put too fine a point on it, but I believe rabbits *hop*."

She pressed her lips together to contain the smile that threatened to break through. Why on earth was she finding this exchange exhilarating rather than aggravating? When she remained silent, he raised a single dark brow in a gesture Amanda interpreted as a clear challenge—something she'd never been able to resist.

She cocked her brow right back at him. "In truth Lord Dorsey, you scurried away like a thief who knew he was in danger of being coshed by the woman he'd just stolen from."

"Surely a woman would swoon rather than cosh."

"I sincerely doubt it. Especially a woman who possesses a most robust constitution."

After studying her for several seconds, he inclined his head. "I see. In that case, I can only reply that it was not my intention to *scurry*. Although if I'd actually suspected I stood in danger of being coshed, I'm certain scurrying would have ensued. I meant only to *hurry* as I was anxious to return home."

"With your treasure," she said.

"Yes. But I'd also had enough…shopping for one day."

His words and dry tone left no doubt that his venture into the village hadn't been entirely pleasant, and her conscience slapped her for baiting him. "Do I have your word that after I've shown you how to open the box you'll allow me to examine the inside?"

"You'll accept my word, Lady Amanda?"

His softly spoken question, accompanied by his steady gaze gave Amanda the distinct impression that he was asking about more than the box, and that her answer was important to him. She barely knew this man, and although he'd irritated her, he'd also managed to arouse both her curiosity and sympathy. She'd always considered herself a good judge of character and her every instinct told her he was honorable. Certainly not capable of the horrible act about which the villagers gossiped.

"Yes, Lord Dorsey. I'll accept your word."

There was no mistaking the surprise and gratitude that flickered in his eyes. During the heartbeats of silence that followed her statement, Amanda swore something passed between them—an unspoken camaraderie, but also something else she couldn't name. She only knew that it caused an unprecedented warmth to seep through her.

With an effort, she looked away from him, only to notice Aunt Lydia. Aunt Lydia whom she'd forgotten all about. Aunt Lydia who'd remained uncharacteristically silent during Amanda's exchange with Lord Dorsey. Aunt Lydia whose avid gaze bounced between them with a *very* speculative gleam in her eye. *Oh, dear.*

Amanda hastily pulled the box closer to her, then took a moment to admire the glossy surface she hadn't thought she'd ever see again. "In truth, I'm not certain precisely what I did to open it other than run my finger over the image of the woman then gently press here…" She dragged her finger downward, then exerted a bit of pressure when she reached the edge of the box. Just as it had yesterday, a faint click sounded, and the lid rose an inch.

"Astounding," Lord Dorsey said. Reaching out, he pressed the box closed. "Again, if you please. Slowly, so I can see exactly what you do."

Amanda repeated the action and again the box opened.

"I see now," he said. He closed the box and mimicked what Amanda had done. Nothing happened. He tried again. And again. With no luck.

"You seem to be pressing the right place," Amanda

said, as confused as he. "Here." She touched the edge
of the box and it opened instantly. Lord Dorsey tried
again to no avail.

"Maybe I'm not exerting enough pressure—or perhaps too much," he said, his voice tinged with confusion and frustration. "Perhaps if you pressed my finger
to the spot." He rose and moved to stand next to her.
Placing his left hand on the back of her chair, he leaned
forward and held out his right hand. "Would you
mind?"

Amanda was instantly inundated with warmth and
the heady, masculine scent emanating from him. He
seemed to surround her body like a blanket. She shifted,
and her shoulder brushed his hip, his nearness firing
heat through her, much as it had yesterday. Not willing to risk turning her head to find her nose inches
from his body, she fastened her gaze on his extended
hand. His large, strong hand, poised directly in front of
her. It looked fascinating, and she was hit with the unsettling realization that she wanted very much to touch
him.

"Lady Amanda?" he said softly.

Amanda jerked her chin upward and found him
looking down at her with an undecipherable expression. Whatever was reflected in her own expression
prompted him to say, "In spite of what you may have
heard to the contrary, I do not bite. Or worse."

Amanda's face flamed. Obviously he referred to the
rumors surrounding him, and she was piqued with both

annoyance and shame that he clearly thought her to be the believer of idle gossip. "Nor, obviously, are you clairvoyant, my lord, as I was not thinking anything of the kind."

"Indeed? I'm well aware of what is said about me, Lady Amanda." His features remained impassive while he spoke, but there was no mistaking the shadows of pain and hurt in his eyes. He slowly lowered his hand and straightened, and a sense of loss she could not explain hit Amanda.

Looking him directly in the eye, she said, "I am not in the habit of indulging in, or giving credence to, idle gossip, Lord Dorsey, especially when the subject is someone else's character. I much prefer to form my own opinions. Now, do you wish for me to assist you? If so, I shall need your hand. And I hope you do, for I am as mystified as you that you cannot open the box."

A furrow formed between his brows, and his gaze searched her face. Then, with a nod, he again extended his arm. Reaching out, she clasped his broad hand in hers, and was immediately taken by how small and pale her hand looked in comparison. His skin was firm and warm, his fingers long and strong. A scar cut diagonally across the length of his index finger and she wondered what had caused the injury.

Curling her fingers around his, she led his hand to the box. Settling her index finger over his, she pressed it to the exact spot she'd touched, using the same amount of pressure. Nothing happened. She tried several more times before he slowly slipped his finger from beneath hers. Her finger landed on the spot and the box clicked open.

"How extraordinary," Aunt Lydia murmured. "May I try?"

Amanda felt Lord Dorsey's start of surprise at her aunt's voice, and she wondered if he had forgotten her presence as Amanda had.

After a dozen unsuccessful attempts, Aunt Lydia admitted defeat. Mortimer arrived with the tea, and when asked, he attempted to open the box, but was also unable to do so. Several footmen were summoned as well, yet all were unsuccessful.

"It appears that Lady Amanda is the only one who can open it," Lord Dorsey said after the servants had all been dismissed. "'Tis a phenomenon for which I can offer no explanation."

"It seems a simple enough explanation, my lord," Aunt Lydia said, eyeing him over the rim of her teacup.

"And what is that?"

"Clearly my niece has the magic touch."

He frowned. "I meant a logical, scientific explanation."

"My dear Lord Dorsey, some things simply defy logic, science and explanation. They just…are."

With those words echoing through his mind, Maxwell pulled his gaze from the box and looked at Lady Amanda. Their gazes met and he stilled, searching her face, seeking some clue as to why this woman, and apparently only this woman, could open the box.

He studied her closely, but instead of an explanation, he noticed the porcelain texture of her skin. It looked incredibly soft, and he imagined it would feel like silk beneath his fingers. Rather than an answer, he discerned a pale smattering of freckles on her pert nose that he could only describe as…fetching.

His gaze traveled downward and settled on her mouth. While he instantly knew it offered no reason for her ability to open the box, he could not seem to look away from those full, moist lips. They beckoned like a siren's call, enticing him to taste, filling him with a sudden, fierce hunger that clenched low in his belly. Then he noticed another freckle…a single golden dot near the corner of her lovely mouth. His fingertips instantly itched with the overwhelming desire to reach out and touch that beguiling spot. Indeed only clasping his hands together on his lap prevented him from doing so.

Bloody hell, he was losing his mind. He needed to rein in his runaway thoughts before they galloped out of control. A fine plan, but one that went totally awry the instant he forced his gaze upwards.

She was staring at his mouth. His lips tingled as if she'd actually caressed him there, firing an unmistakable heat through him. Even though it had been a long time since he'd felt desire, there was no forgetting how it felt—especially when it gripped him with such intense force.

She looked up and their gazes collided. Her eyes, with their flecks of gold, reminded him of fine, aged brandy, and, he was quickly realizing, they were just as intoxicating. Surprise and what appeared to be confusion were reflected in their golden-brown depths, and Maxwell wondered if she was experiencing the same reaction as he.

She blinked several times, then lowered her gaze to the box, breaking whatever odd spell had been cast over them. With a touch she opened the box, then asked, "May we look at the inside now?"

"Of course." Maxwell opened the lid the rest of the way and they both peered inside. Lady Lydia rose and moved to stand behind him, looking over his shoulder. The interior was finished with the same unusual, enamel-like gloss as the exterior.

"It's empty," Lady Lydia said, her voice filled with disappointment. "I was halfway expecting, or at least hoping, it would be filled with jewels or gold coins." She returned to her seat and proceeded to freshen her tea.

Lady Amanda shifted her chair nearer to his and he caught a hint of a delicate scent. Her scent. Under the guise of peering deeper into the box, he leaned closer to her and breathed in. She smelled like…sunshine. And flowers. His eyes drifted closed and he instantly pictured her, standing in a bloom-filled meadow illuminated by slender skeins of golden sunlight. A gentle breeze murmured, catching her hair and gown, flowing them behind her while she reached upward, as if to capture a dazzling, gild-kissed ray. She looked lovely and alluring and—

Exactly like the woman on the box.

His eyes popped open. Good God, he really had taken leave of his senses. The woman on the box had no features—she didn't look like anyone. Still, he found himself turning to stare at Lady Amanda's profile, and the similarities immediately hit him. The curve of her cheek, the sweep of her forehead, the tilt of her chin—

"Do you think these carved curlicues lining the edge might be something more than merely a decoration?"

Her question yanked him from his brown study, and he quickly shifted his attention back to the box. "More than a decoration? Why do you ask?"

"Because they don't appear to follow any sort of pattern as you'd expect on a decorative border."

He studied the swirling black lines, then reached out to trace them with a fingertip. "You're right," he agreed, impressed by her quick observation. "I wonder if it could be some sort of writing, although I've never seen anything quite like this. It looks a bit like Arabic, but based on my knowledge of the language from my alchemy studies, this isn't it." He tipped the box onto its back, and with heads bent closely together, they looked at the curved inner lid.

"These dots do not appear to be in any sort of pattern either," he murmured.

"No, they don't," she agreed. She leaned closer to the box. "Could you tip it up a bit more please, so it's in the sunlight?"

Maxwell complied, and she leaned closer still, until her nose was practically buried in the box. Then she abruptly straightened and turned toward him. "I don't think they're dots, Lord Dorsey," she said, her voice filled with a note he well recognized from experience—the excitement of discovery. "Look at their shape. They appear to be tiny *stars*."

Maxwell leaned closer and peered at the miniscule markings. "You're right," he said, impressed again, his voice taking on the same excited tone as hers. He studied the pattern for several seconds, then frowned. "It is not a pattern I immediately recognize, but with further study and comparison to my constellation charts I may be able to identify it."

"What initially looked like nothing more than a spattering of dots might be a map of the heavens," she said softly. "How fascinating."

Maxwell turned toward her. When their gazes met, she smiled—a beautiful smile that displayed even, pearly teeth and made her eyes glow.

His entire body tensed with a yearning, a sense of longing and want unlike anything he'd ever before experienced and if he'd been free to do so at the moment, he would have laughed at his unprecedented reaction to this woman. "Fascinating," he agreed, his voice coming out in a husky rasp.

"Well, it certainly appears you made quite a find, Lord Dorsey," Lady Lydia said.

With a start, he turned toward his forgotten hostess. "I beg your pardon?"

"You've made quite a find. And clearly it is even more captivating than you'd originally thought."

Something in her tone made him wonder if she was referring to more than the box, but her expression was innocence itself. "Indeed it is." He turned back to Lady Amanda and he was struck by the overwhelming need to know more about this intriguing woman who opened the mysterious box, seemingly by magic, and whose beautiful smile, astute observations and expressive eyes bewitched him. A dozen questions rushed to his lips, but right now the most important one was, "How long do you plan to remain in Cardiff?"

"Until the end of the month. Then I shall return to London."

Relief swept through him. He'd feared she'd say she planned to leave tomorrow. Three weeks...she would be close by for three weeks. His heart sped up to a ridiculous rate at the knowledge. Three weeks was certainly enough time to call on her again. For he knew with absolute certainty that he had to see her again. Learn about her. Get to know her better. See her smile. Hear her laugh. The mere thought filled him with a sense of anticipation and exhilaration he hadn't felt in a very long time. He'd invite her to dine with him—

"When my niece returns to London," Lady Lydia's voice broke into his runaway thoughts, "her father shall announce her betrothal."

CHAPTER FOUR

MAXWELL FELT as if all the air had been sucked from his lungs. An unpleasant sensation resembling a tight cramp seized his insides, and as quickly as his ridiculous hopes had been raised, they crashed back to earth. "Betrothal?" The word tasted like sawdust upon his tongue.

Lady Amanda's cheeks flamed bright red. "Yes."

With that single word it seemed as if a kindling flame had been irrevocably snuffed out. Keeping his features and voice coolly impassive, he said, "Please accept my best wishes. Who is the lucky gentleman?"

She appeared very disconcerted. "Actually, I don't know."

He frowned, then nodded slowly as understanding dawned. "Ah, your father is arranging the match."

She shook her head. "No. He is allowing me to choose among my...suitors."

"Oh, you should have seen her this Season, my lord," Lady Lydia said. "Declared an 'Incomparable.' I don't believe she was permitted to sit out a single dance. *Four* gentlemen have approached her father regarding marriage. Such an important decision to make! 'Tis why I brought her here, so she could have time to reflect. So she can choose wisely. After all, there is no decision more important than whom one marries."

The knot clenching Maxwell's stomach cinched tighter. Bloody hell, she had not one but *four* men pursuing her. And he'd wager none of them was saddled with a tarnished reputation or a sobriquet containing the words "crazed killer."

That was more than enough to free him from the net of madness which had somehow ensnared him from the moment he'd laid eyes upon her, making him for an insane moment consider pursuing her. He had nothing to offer a proper young woman like her. He barely knew her. And in less than a month's time she would be promised to another man.

Bludgeoning back that disturbing thought, he rose. "I fear it's long past time for me to return home." He slipped his handkerchief from his pocket and carefully folded the snowy material over the edge of the opened box. "So it cannot close all the way," he murmured. After rewrapping it, he tucked the bundle under his arm then offered a formal bow. "My thanks for the tea and hospitality, Lady Lydia."

"'Twas a pleasure." She looked up at him with a direct stare. "I'm glad you've ventured from your estate, my lord. I hope you continue to do so. You are always welcome here."

"Thank you," he said, not fully prepared for the rush

of gratitude that washed through him. He turned to Lady Amanda and bowed. "And my thanks to you for opening the box."

"You're welcome." It appeared she wished to say something more, and he hesitated, his heart suddenly thumping with an erratic beat.

"Will you…?" She paused, and the answer "yes" rushed to his lips, as he couldn't imagine denying her anything. He forced himself to remain silent, however, and she continued, "Will you let me—us—know if you discover anything about the markings inside the box?"

"Of course." He didn't add that it would be better that he do so by letter than by personal visit.

Her mouth curved upward in a slow smile, drawing his attention once again to the rosy plumpness of her lips, an alluring sight that threatened to discourage him from taking his leave. Giving himself a severe mental shake, he murmured goodbye, then walked across the flagstones toward the French windows—swiftly, lest whatever spell Lady Amanda had cast upon him lured him to remain. Yet he couldn't squelch the unsettling knowledge that she was lost to him forever—ridiculous as she'd never belonged to him in the first place.

Amanda watched Lord Dorsey disappear through the French windows. Even after his form was no longer visible, she continued to stare at the spot, filled with the conflicting sensations of relief and disappointment at his departure. Relief because the man's presence had the oddest, most unsettling effect on her. Disappointment because…well, she wasn't quite certain, but there was no denying she felt it.

"Oh, my. I don't think I've ever seen anything quite like that." Aunt Lydia's words filtered through the fog that seemed to have engulfed her, and she pulled herself from her reverie.

Determined not to show her discomfiture, Amanda lifted her teacup and offered a noncommittal nod. "Yes, 'tis very strange that only I could open the box."

"Hmm? Oh, yes, well, that was remarkable as well."

"As well? Is that not what you referred to?"

"Heavens, no. I was referring to Lord Dorsey. To the way he looked at you." Aunt Lydia blew out a long breath that could only be described as a gushy sigh. "It gave *me* tingles, and I was sitting on the opposite side of the table. I can only imagine how it affected you."

"I don't know what you're talking about—"

"My dear child," Aunt Lydia said, fixing her with a steely stare, "do not even attempt to convince me that you didn't notice the earl couldn't take his eyes off of you. Or that you didn't feel the weight of his intent regard. For if you do try to say as much, I shall be forced to summon the undertaker because you would have to be *dead* to have missed it."

Warmth crept up Amanda's neck. "Of course I noticed he looked at me while we conversed, but he looked at you as well."

"Darling, there was nothing even remotely similar

in the way he gazed upon you and the way he looked at me. He regarded me with polite interest. He beheld you much the way I imagine a man dying of thirst would contemplate an oasis."

An unprecedented heated thrill zoomed through Amanda. "And," Aunt Lydia continued, "his eyes were drawn to you even when you weren't conversing. As were yours to him."

An instantaneous denial sprang to Amanda's lips, but knowing her aunt was right, at least as far as Amanda's wandering gaze was concerned, she merely said, "I can't deny I found his visit interesting, although it only leaves me more irritated than ever that I wasn't able to purchase that box."

"Irritated? Is that how his visit left you?"

"Well, yes." *Among other things.* "Surely the fact that only I can open it means the box should have belonged to me."

"Well, my dear, perhaps some day you *shall* own it."

"I don't see how that's possible. Lord Dorsey clearly has no intention of selling it."

"Hmm, yes, I would say you are correct in that." Aunt Lydia set her cup in its matching china saucer. "I must say I was happy to see him looking so well. Indeed, I believe he's even more attractive than when I saw him last. So tall and broad-shouldered. And the combination of that dark hair and those startling blue eyes… very striking, don't you think?"

An image of him flashed in Amanda's mind, and her

pulse jumped. Yes, striking was an excellent word to describe Lord Dorsey. Before she could speak, however, Aunt Lydia waved off her own words with a dismissing flutter of her hands.

"Oh, but you probably didn't even make note of his appearance. Why would you, what with a gentleman of Lord Abbott's superior looks vying for your hand? Now *he* is a man a woman would be hard pressed to erase from her mind. Or Lords Branton, Remington and Oxmoor either, for that matter."

"Yes," Amanda agreed. "In fact, this is an excellent time to begin thinking about and evaluating my suitors."

"An excellent idea. Three weeks is not very much time you know."

Yes—a fact that Amanda would have very much liked to forget.

"Although…"

"Although what?" Amanda found herself asking in spite of not being convinced she really wanted to know.

"If any of your four suitors *truly* engaged your heart, you'd know it in, well, a heartbeat."

"And so I shall," Amanda said with far more confidence than she felt. "As soon as I fully apply myself to the task. Would you care to join me for a turn in the garden?"

"Thank you, but no, dear. I'm still enjoying my tea. Besides, one needs solitude and quiet when reflecting, especially on matters of the heart."

Amanda rose, kissed her aunt's soft cheek, then headed for the gardens, resolved to think of her suitors.

And no one else.

Two hours later, she plopped onto a curved stone bench situated in the lower garden beneath the shade of a copse of towering elms, and blew out a frustrated, defeated, disgusted sigh. She'd tried mightily to concentrate on her four suitors, to examine her feelings toward them, but her musings had been constantly interrupted by thoughts of Lord Dorsey.

Why couldn't she erase the man from her mind? How was it that he'd affected her so profoundly after such a short acquaintance, in ways that the suitors she'd spent months socializing with had not? What was it about him that had captured her so?

Since she obviously wouldn't be able to banish him from her thoughts until she gave the matter her full attention, she decided she might as well do so now and get it over with. Then she'd be able to devote her thoughts to the gentlemen she *should* be thinking about. Yes, that was an excellent plan.

So what was it about Lord Dorsey that had him so firmly embedded in her mind? Certainly it wasn't his looks. Why, all four of her London suitors were far more handsome. A frown pulled down her brows. Still, there was something compelling about Lord Dorsey's features, something that grabbed the attention and wouldn't allow one to look away. Made one long for another glance.

Perhaps it was his eyes. Their vivid blue color. Their sharp intelligence. The unexpected flickers of mischief and humor. At first glance she'd thought his eyes cold, but upon reconsideration decided that they instead were…wary. Guarded. Shadows of suffering were evident in his eyes, understandable given his circumstances. Did he realize that those shadows lurked in their depths? Most likely not.

Then there was the way he'd looked at her. With an intensity that had prickled awareness and warmth under her skin. And he'd listened with unwavering interest when she'd spoken, as if he hadn't wanted to miss a word of what she'd said. Although all her suitors were attentive, listening to her wasn't a trait she could assign to any of them. No, they were great ones for fetching her punch, or talking *to* her, but she couldn't recall any of them ever soliciting her opinion on anything other than the weather or fashion.

Or perhaps it was Lord Dorsey's smile. Her heart skipped recalling his quick grin, how it had transformed his stern features, making him look almost…rakish. It was the sort of smile that made her want to cast about in her mind for something clever to say just so she could see it again. Of her London suitors, Lords Branton and Remington had ready smiles that one did not need to expend any effort to see. Lord Oxmoor's smile was attractive, yet filled with an air of insouciance, and while Lord Abbott's smile showed off perfect teeth, it somehow did not ever reach his eyes.

Or perhaps it was the air of solitude and loneliness surrounding Lord Dorsey that intrigued her. Both were no doubt results of The Incident, but after today's meeting, Amanda agreed with Aunt Lydia's assessment of his innocence as she simply could not envision him as a killer. The fact that the gossip and rumors had clearly hurt Lord Dorsey, not to mention damaged his standing in the community, pulled on Amanda's heartstrings in a way that they'd never been tugged upon before. While her London suitors all had dozens of friends and enjoyed great popularity, Lord Dorsey seemed very much alone in the world, which again yanked at her heart. She couldn't imagine being so alone.

And suddenly it dawned on her precisely why she hadn't been able to erase him from her mind. It was because he was *different*. He stood out when she'd reflected upon the other gentlemen simply because he was so different from them. And now that she'd determined what had been niggling at her, she could cease thinking about him.

A wave of relief flooded her. Excellent. *Now* she could get back to solving her dilemma of which suitor she wished to marry. And that's exactly what she intended to do.

CHAPTER FIVE

ONE WEEK AFTER his visit with Lady Lydia and Lady Amanda, Maxwell sat in his private study, slumped in his maroon leather chair, tapping out a frustrated staccato on his desk while he stared at the enigma he'd purchased at Gibson's shop.

Bloody hell, an entire week spent studying and examining the box from every angle, utilizing his strongest magnifying glass to painstakingly scrutinize the carved swirls and star patterns, comparing them to his maps of the constellations and research books, but so far he had been unable to find a match. Still, he refused to give up. He simply could not shake the feeling that the carvings contained some sort of message. 'Twas good that he loved a puzzle as this one was proving extremely elusive.

Speaking of puzzles... Maxwell turned the open box so he could look at the woman gracing the glossy top. How many hours in the past week had he spent looking at her shiny image, wondering about her? Too many to count. Had she been real, or merely the figment of the craftsman's imagination? Surely real, and someone the craftsman had known well, even intimately, for how else could he have captured so much feeling, so much emotion in a mere silhouette? She was simultaneously sad and seductive, mysterious and alluring. And achingly, hauntingly familiar.

Reaching out, he brushed his fingertip over the glossy surface of her, and shook his head in bemusement at the tingle that rushed up his arm. "Surely you must be Aphrodite, the goddess of desire, to affect me so," he said softly.

With a groan, he cradled his head in his hands and closed his tired, gritty eyes. The woman on the box instantly materialized behind his eyelids, a dark-haired temptress who beckoned him with a crook of her finger and a low, throaty whisper, *Come with me....*

He followed, powerless to stop himself. When he finally caught up with her, he drew her into his arms and claimed the kiss he could no longer wait for. And when he lifted his head, he looked into her lovely face, into the golden brown eyes that had haunted his every waking and sleeping hour since he'd first seen them. The eyes and face of a woman who'd somehow bewitched him and who would never, could never, be his.

A knock sounded at the door and Maxwell lifted his head, dragging his hands down his face. "Come in."

Sutton entered, bearing a tea tray.

"Did I ring for tea?" Maxwell asked.

Sutton blinked. "No, my lord. But you're served tea at this same time every day."

Maxwell's gaze swiveled to the mantel clock and he shook his head. Where had the day gone? Damn it, he felt as if he were engulfed in a fog. Leaning back in his chair, he crossed his arms over his chest and watched Sutton set the silver tray on the cherrywood end table then arrange a variety of biscuits on a china plate.

"Sutton, when you first met Mrs. Sutton, did you feel as if…a lightning bolt had struck you?"

"Actually, 'twas more like a potted plant falling on my head," he said, filling a teacup.

"Oh. That sounds…painful." Not at all like the tingling jolt Maxwell had experienced.

"Indeed it was, falling from the second-story window as it did."

"I beg your pardon?"

"The potted plant. Geranium it was. Bright red. Fell right on my head." Sutton reached up and rubbed his head, wincing as if his skull still hurt. "When I came 'round, I thought for certain I was dead for surely I was looking at an angel. She had the most beautiful brown eyes I'd ever seen."

Maxwell nodded. He knew precisely what Sutton meant.

A faraway look entered Sutton's eyes, and a smile played around his mouth. "She asked me if I was all right. I told her yes, but I knew I'd never be the same again. In here." He tapped his hand to his chest. "I got a bump on my head and lost my heart in one fell swoop.

But that's often the way of it, my lord. Doesn't take the heart but a single beat to know what it wants."

Sutton crossed the cream and maroon Axminster rug. After setting Maxwell's teacup and plate of biscuits on the desk, the butler clasped his hands behind his back. "Does your curiosity about me and Mrs. Sutton have anything to do with what's troubled you this past week, my lord?"

Maxwell didn't bother to deny he was troubled, not to a man who knew him better than anyone. A man who had shared the pains and disappointments as well as the joys when Maxwell was growing up. Certainly more than Maxwell's father ever had. A humorless laugh escaped him and he raked his hands through his hair. "I'm not certain, Sutton. I can't put my finger on precisely what's wrong."

"I'm surprised to hear that, my lord, as you're such an intelligent man and it's very obvious."

"Indeed? Then enlighten me. Please."

Sutton's gaze flicked to the open box on the desk. "'Tis a certain lady that has you tied up in knots."

Maxwell nodded slowly, then reached out to brush the pad of his thumb over the glossy silhouette. "Yes. I wish I could decipher the carvings in this box."

"I'm not talking about the lady *on* the box, my lord. I meant the lady who *opened* the box. Lady Amanda."

Maxwell's head snapped up and he stared at Sutton whose eyes were serious with unmistakable concern. "You've been…different ever since you met her," the butler continued. "'Tis obvious she's made a profound impression on you."

Bloody hell. "When did I become as transparent as a pane of glass? Or have you developed some form of clairvoyance?"

"A bit of both I suspect, my lord." Sutton paused for several seconds, then said, "You can't stop thinking about her."

As there was no point in denying it to a bloody clairvoyant, Maxwell nodded. "It's as if she's embedded in my brain."

"Then why haven't you pursued her?"

"To what end?" he asked, his voice rough with frustration. "I have nothing to offer her."

Sutton's eyes widened. "Nothing to offer? You call a title, estates, wealth, a life of ease and luxury and yourself *nothing* to offer?"

"I can't imagine any woman relishing the title 'Lady Crazed Killer of Cardiff.'"

A muscle jerked in Sutton's jaw and anger flashed in his eyes. "You didn't kill anyone."

"*I* know that. But unfortunately not everyone else does."

"Does Lady Amanda believe that vile gossip?"

Maxwell hesitated. "She didn't seem to. I know she's heard the rumors, but she told me she preferred to form her own opinions."

"Sounds like an intelligent woman."

"Yes. But if you'll recall, Lady Roberta claimed to

believe me innocent, then one week later cried off from our engagement."

"Lady Roberta was spoiled and selfish and not worthy of you," Sutton said, raising his nose in the air as though he'd caught a whiff of something foul.

Maxwell blew out a long breath. Yes, Roberta had turned out to be spoiled and selfish, but she'd also been vivacious and beautiful. And for a brief time he'd believed himself in love with her. When she'd broken their engagement, the blow had cut deep. Yet he now realized that he'd been fully prepared to marry a woman who had never, at any point during their lengthy acquaintance, fascinated him as much or elicited such strong reactions in him as Lady Amanda had in a matter of minutes.

He shook his head. "Even if I were the most eligible man in the kingdom, it wouldn't matter. As I told you when we discussed my visit to Lady Lydia's estate, Lady Amanda leaves Cardiff to return to London in a fortnight's time to choose a fiancé."

"Perhaps she wouldn't if she had a reason to stay."

"Have you forgotten that *four* gentlemen have approached her father with offers of marriage?"

"No. But it seems to me that *you* have forgotten three very important things."

"Which are?"

"One—that any lady who can handle four suitors can certainly handle five. Two—while it's true that she's leaving in a fortnight, you clearly haven't considered that also means she shall be *here* for a fortnight. And three—she is not promised to anyone…yet." He regarded Maxwell steadily for a moment. "I'm a firm believer in Fate, my lord. If I hadn't been walking beneath that window at the exact instant my Sarah's elbow knocked over that geranium, I might never have met her."

"Are you suggesting that Lady Amanda cosh me with a potted plant?"

"No, my lord. I'm saying you own a box that only Lady Amanda can open. If she hadn't entered Gibson's shop to buy that very same box, at the very same time you were there, you wouldn't have met. You also wouldn't have known the box opened, or that only her touch could lift the lid. I'm saying Fate played a hand in that. And Hope as well. You ventured into the village hoping to find…something. Seems to me you found it."

Maxwell leaned back in his chair and considered. The facts Sutton presented were true. But did Maxwell want to risk himself, his heart, to another rejection? Was his meeting Lady Amanda really Fate or simply coincidence? While his scientific nature did not place much credence in Fate, neither did he place any faith in coincidence.

Perhaps he'd built up his encounter with Lady Amanda in his mind into something it simply hadn't been. If he saw her again, perhaps he might feel… nothing.

There was only one way to find out. And he absolutely had to know.

He pulled a sheet of vellum from his desk drawer, then reached for his pen. After writing a hasty note, he sealed the missive with wax, then handed it to Sutton. "Please see that is delivered to Tufton Manor at once, and have the footman wait for a reply."

"Yes, my lord." Sutton turned smartly on his heel and departed, and Maxwell spent the next hour pacing in front of the fireplace, his heart pounding, trying without success to tamp down the impatience and anticipation nipping at him. When Sutton finally returned bearing a response on a silver salver, Maxwell quickly broke the wax seal and scanned the contents.

"Did you receive the reply you'd hoped for, my lord?"

Maxwell looked up from the note and smiled. "Yes, Sutton. It appears we're having a dinner party this evening."

AMANDA ENJOYED another bite of delicious blueberry pie and allowed her gaze to drift around Lord Dorsey's spacious dining room. The aesthetically pleasing proportions of the room, its high ceiling decorated with a stunning al fresco, appealed to her greatly. Indeed everything she'd seen of his home since she and Aunt Lydia had arrived pleased her, much to her surprise as the forbidding exterior had suggested an equally forbidding interior.

When the carriage had pulled into the curved drive,

she'd looked at the massive house in dismay. With shadows of twilight darkening the facade and casting eerie stains upon the aged stone, while fingers of misty fog reached upward, Dorsey Manor looked like an inky specter rising from a ghostly vision.

Based on that initial impression, Amanda was caught completely off guard when she entered the black-and-white-tiled marble foyer. There was nothing forbidding about the huge sparkling crystal chandelier lit with dozens of candles. The entryway glowed with golden, welcoming warmth, and prisms of light reflected off cream silk-covered walls decorated with gilt-edged mirrors and framed landscapes. The pleasing fragrance of beeswax scented the air, mixed with the heady perfume from a stunning arrangement of white roses and deep purple lilacs set in a silver urn on a round mahogany table. Everywhere she looked, surfaces gleamed with loving care, and she'd been filled with an overwhelming curiosity to know if the rest of the house was as delightful as this first glimpse indicated. Certainly this lovely dining room, and the perfectly prepared and served meal, had exceeded her expectations. Even Mother, who was extremely particular in matters of meal preparation and service would have been hard pressed to find fault.

Her gaze shifted back to the head of the table where it had wandered more times than she cared to admit. Lord Dorsey was listening intently to Aunt Lydia describe the details of a musicale she'd attended in London. While many gentlemen, her own father included, would have politely feigned interest in the long-winded tale until they could interject a change of subject, Lord Dorsey's attention was clearly genuine. Indeed, he asked a number of probing questions, proving he was listening carefully. Aunt Lydia was only too happy to provide him with additional details.

Amanda couldn't count the number of times the man had intruded upon her thoughts the past week. Yet it was not just that she was thinking about him that un-settled her—it was the direction of those thoughts that disconcerted her.

Was his skin warm? Was his hair as thick and soft as it looked? How would it feel to be held in his arms? What would his kiss taste like? She'd continually cursed her curious nature and had almost succeeded in convincing herself that she didn't really want to know the answers, when his invitation to dinner had arrived, infusing her with anticipation and utterly dissolving her resolve to stop thinking of him.

Now, the soft, amber glow from the candelabra cast him in an intriguing contrast of light and shadows that Amanda simply could not resist watching. His Devon-shire brown jacket accentuated his broad shoulders, while his silver brocade waistcoat and snowy linen shirt offered a stark contradiction to his dark hair. Several errant locks marked his forehead lending an un-expected boyish air to a countenance that was otherwise supremely masculine. His quick smile flashed at something her aunt said, and she found herself staring at his mouth, hoping for a repeat performance, wondering once again what those lovely soft yet firm-looking lips would feel like pressed against hers.

"You mentioned a love of history earlier, Lady Amanda. Have you had the chance to visit the nearby ruins of Llandaff cathedral?"

Lord Dorsey's deep voice yanked her from her perusal and she jerked her gaze upward. Their eyes met, and a wave of embarrassment swept through her at being caught staring. And at his mouth, no less. Thank heavens he could not read minds.

"We visited the ruins earlier today," Amanda said, inwardly cringing at how breathless she sounded. "I found them fascinating."

"Fascinating, yes, but quite exhausting," Aunt Lydia declared with a laugh. "I don't believe I've met anyone who likes to walk as much as my niece. The instant we arrived home I retired to my bedchamber for a much needed nap."

"And did you retire to your bedchamber for a nap as well, Lady Amanda?"

An image instantly flashed in her mind…of her lying in bed…and him leaning over her, his lips only a hairsbreadth from hers. Heat flashed through her, and she knew crimson stained her cheeks. Good heavens, what was wrong with her? Why couldn't she stop these unsettling, uncharacteristic and completely improper thoughts about him?

She blinked away the image and cleared her throat. "No nap. I spent the afternoon walking along the beach, collecting shells."

Pleased surprise filled his gaze. "One of my favorite activities. I did not realize you were a fellow conchologist."

She smiled. "My knowledge of shell collecting is not nearly vast enough to qualify me with such an impressive, scientific title."

"Nonsense. One need only have a love of shell collecting. Did you find any interesting specimens?"

"I confess I gathered so many, I was forced to remove my bonnet and use it as a basket, lest I drop any of my treasures."

He nodded, as if he understood completely the unacceptability of losing a found treasure. "My favorite time to walk the beach is immediately after a storm," he said. "Nature, and the waves, deposit a veritable trove of new delights."

"I would love to see your collection."

"It's in my observatory. Since we'd already planned to visit there to view the stars through my telescope, that works out perfectly." He glanced at the empty dessert plates. "Would you like to go now, or shall we first retire to the drawing room?"

Amanda looked to her aunt who nodded encouragingly. "Now would be fine," Amanda said.

Five minutes later the three of them strolled down the flagstone steps leading from the spacious, moonlit terrace toward the gardens. "There is a path at the rear of the garden which leads to the observatory," Lord Dorsey said.

As they walked, Amanda breathed deeply, delighting in the scent of earth and roses combined with a whiff of the sea. "I love the smell of this place," she said, drawing in another breath. "After spending so many months in London, I'd forgotten how wonderful clean air could smell."

Lord Dorsey pointed off to the right. "That path leads down to the sea. Other than my observatory, it is my favorite place on the estate. You walk along and can hear the sea, and smell it, but only catch glimpses of blue through the trees and foliage, until you round the final curve, then…there it is. I've walked the route countless times, yet it's somehow always a wondrous surprise."

Amanda smiled. "My family's county home is in Kent, and while we do have a small lake and I've always loved it there, I must admit that I find the sea most alluring."

"Alluring," Lord Dorsey said slowly, looking at her. "Yes, that describes it very well."

Warmth spread through Amanda, and she scolded herself for entertaining the notion that there was more behind his words than a simple agreement with her. They rounded a curve and Lord Dorsey said, "This is where we leave the gardens. It's only about a ten-minute walk and no need to fear a turned ankle as there's a dirt path."

Amanda saw the observatory in the distance, atop a gentle rise, and anticipation filled her. But Aunt Lydia made a "tsking" noise. "Oh, dear. I didn't realize it was quite so far, and after all the trekking about I did today, I fear I'm not up to such a lengthy walk."

"My apologies, Lady Lydia," Lord Dorsey said, his voice contrite. "We shall return to the house at once."

"Nonsense," said Aunt Lydia. "I wouldn't dream of depriving Amanda the opportunity of viewing the stars or seeing your shells. There's a lovely seat right here." She walked to the stone bench and sat, then folded her hands in her lap. "I shall await you here and enjoy the lovely garden and this delightful night air. I truly need a rest before venturing back to the house anyway."

"If you're certain—" Lord Dorsey began.

"I'm positive. Of course, as my niece will be without her chaperone, I am entrusting her to your care, Lord Dorsey."

"You have my word that no harm will come to her."

"Excellent." Aunt Lydia made shooing motions with her hands. "Now off with you. I'll be right here when you return."

Lord Dorsey extended his elbow. "Lady Amanda?"

Firmly telling herself that the rapid pounding of her heart was due to the exertion of their walk thus far, Amanda settled her hand on his sleeve and they moved down the narrow, moonlit pathway. She was painfully aware of his solid, muscular arm, and she fought the urge to flex her fingers to test its strength, just as she fought the urge to breathe in sharply every time their shoulders bumped.

"I regret I've been unable to decipher the markings on the box," he said as they walked along. "But I'm not ready to admit defeat."

"You don't give up easily."

"No. A trait I imagine we have in common."

"Why do you say that?"

"You do not strike me as a woman who would quit if you truly wanted something."

Hoping some levity might relieve the tension gripping her, she cast him a sidelong glance. "Hmm. Are you calling me stubborn, Lord Dorsey?"

His lips twitched. "I think determined is a better word."

"Which is simply another way of saying stubborn."

"Perhaps." He looked at her and smiled. "But as I consider determination an admirable trait, I meant it in the nicest way."

"Thank you." A short laugh huffed between her lips. "I believe that is the most *unusual* compliment I've ever received."

"I fear I'm woefully inept with words."

Amanda considered his statement, then slowly shook her head. "I disagree. You speak simply, with a sincerity most gentlemen of my acquaintance do not possess. Just because you do not spout flowery sonnets does not mean you are inept."

There was no mistaking his surprise or pleasure at

her words. "Thank you. Although I take it that your suitors would have immortalized you with something called Ode to Lady Amanda."

His assessment was so accurate, Amanda laughed. "No doubt. A poetic waxing about my hair or the cut of my gown. Certainly not about my determination." She cut him a quick glance. "Do you really think I'm determined?"

"Yes. You entered Gibson's shop determined to purchase the wooden box."

"For all the good it did me. Nothing to show for my determination, even though I offered you a hideous amount of money for it."

"That was merely a case of me being more stubborn—and quicker—than you. Some might call it fate." She felt the weight of his regard. "Do you not see yourself as determined?"

"I…don't know. Sometimes I feel very…adrift, like a boat bobbing on the waves at the mercy of the currents. As if I'm constantly being told what to do, what to think, how to feel."

"Told by whom?"

"Mostly my mother. I know she has my best interests at heart, but we do not always agree on what is best for me. And she likes very much to be in charge."

"Do you listen to her?"

Amanda considered, then frowned. "Mostly, yes, I suppose I do. But not always."

"When don't you?"

"When something is especially important to me."

"Such as?"

"Well, most recently, coming to Cardiff. Mother was very much against me making the trip. She wanted me to decide right away which of my suitors to marry. But I simply couldn't. I insisted upon coming, and my father supported me."

"How fortunate you are that your father would stand behind you. I confess it is something I never experienced with my father."

Her fingers involuntarily squeezed his arm. "I'm sorry."

"As am I. How did you convince your father?"

"I told him that choosing whom I married was the single most important decision I would make in my entire life and I wanted time to myself to examine my heart to insure I made the right decision. He agreed, and here I am."

"Yes…here you are."

Something in those softly spoken words had her swiftly turning her head to look at him. But he was looking at the ground. "Watch your step here, Lady Amanda. There's a bit of an upward slope."

Amanda fell silent and concentrated on the path, and they arrived at the observatory several minutes later. At his instruction, she waited just inside the doorway while he lit several oil lamps. As a soft, hazy glow illuminated the room, she noticed the neat arrangement of shelves lined with books, glass beakers and what she surmised was other scientific paraphernalia. When he returned to her, he held a lantern in one hand and extended his other hand to her.

"Come. Allow me to show you the wonders of the night sky."

Amanda slipped her hand into his. His fingers instantly clasped hers in a warm, firm grip that shot pleasurable tingles up her arm. With his palm pressed against hers, she discerned the roughness of calluses, and she instantly wondered how a gentleman had come by them.

They passed under an archway into a second room, and Amanda gasped. The upper half of the left and back walls as well as a portion of the high ceiling were constructed entirely of glass panels. The full moon was visible, a brilliant white orb against black velvet, casting the room with a shimmer of pale, silvery light. In the corner, on a circular platform, stood a tremendous telescope.

Lord Dorsey led her to the platform, then helped her to climb up. "This is the largest telescope I've ever seen," Amanda said, utterly amazed.

"Have you seen many?"

She laughed. "Actually no. Only one other, and it was quite small. How does it work?"

He touched the eyepiece then a small knob beneath it. "Just look through here, fine-tune the focus there, and enjoy the magic."

Amanda leaned forward to look through the eyepiece then gasped in delight. "The stars look close enough to touch! As if someone tossed handfuls of diamonds against a swatch of black satin."

"You're looking at a grouping called the Big Dipper. Do you see it?"

Amanda studied the brilliant twinkles, then said, "Yes! It looks like a ladle." Her imagination took flight, and after gazing at the twinkling wonders a bit longer, she asked, "When you're looking through your telescope, have you ever wondered if perhaps there are people living on those distant stars looking back at you?"

"As a matter of fact, I have."

"Do you think they would be like us? Look like us?"

"I don't know. But I like to think that they would possess all of our good qualities and none of the unkindness and evil found in our world."

Any reply Amanda might have made died in her throat when he stepped close behind her. Heat suddenly surrounded her. Senses prickling with awareness, she drew in a quick breath. Her head instantly filled with the clean, masculine scent of sandalwood.

"Wait until you see this." He settled one hand on her shoulder, then reached around her with his other hand to slowly pivot the telescope. Her breath caught when his body brushed against hers, shooting tingles down her spine, and it required all her strength not to press back against him to experience the delightful sensation again.

The jewel-encrusted heavens shifted before her eyes, and when the telescope stopped moving, she found herself staring at a magnificent, fiery red ball. "Oh, my. What is that?"

"Mars." The word brushed softly against her ear, eliciting a barrage of quivers. "Commonly referred to as the red planet."

She gave a shaky laugh. "Given its hue, I certainly cannot see anyone calling it the green planet."

His deep chuckle whispered warmly across her skin. "The distinct red color has been observed by stargazers throughout history. Mars was named by the Romans in honor of their god of war."

Amanda studied the distant planet for nearly a minute. During that time she desperately tried to convince herself it was this astronomical wonder that caused her heart to flutter, but she was spectacularly unsuccessful. No, it was entirely the fault of the man standing behind her. Which meant she needed to put some distance between them. Now.

And that was her intention, truly, when she turned around. But suddenly she stood facing him. And his large hand, which had slid across her back when she turned, now lightly grasped her upper arm. And he was close…so very close. And he smelled so good. And he was looking at her in a way that cut off her breath and dissolved her knees.

She stood in an agony of still silence, her mind demanding that she retreat, while her heart commanded her to remain. To see what, if anything, he would say. What, if anything, he would do.

Maxwell stood perfectly still, his frozen stance at complete odds with the inferno roaring through him. She was so tantalizingly close. And God, she smelled so good. And she was looking at him in a way that nearly brought him to his knees. A tremor rippled beneath his hand and he flexed his fingers on her arm. Her eyes widened slightly. Unable to stop himself, he raised his free hand and brushed a fingertip across her cheek, then moved downward, to touch that single pale freckle near her mouth. Her skin felt like warm satin, and that whisper of a touch made him ache for more.

"You've been in the sun," he whispered, tracing his fingertip again over that beguiling golden dot.

"I…removed my bonnet to carry my shells. I suppose I shouldn't have as I tend to freckle."

"But you should have. The freckles suit you. They are unexpected. Disarming. Alluring. And utterly enchanting. Just like you."

She studied him through very serious eyes, a tiny frown forming between her brows. "You are not at all like what I'd initially thought."

"Oh? And what had you initially thought?"

A sheepish expression washed over her features. "I thought you irritating, rude and that you possessed frightfully inconvenient timing. To be perfectly honest, I wanted to cosh you and abscond with the wooden box."

Maxwell laughed. "Well, I can hardly quibble since I asked, and I appreciate your candor as opposed to some polite drivel. But I take it that your initial feelings have changed—and for the better, I hope."

"They couldn't have gotten much worse, I assure you," she said in a dust-dry tone. Her expression then turned contrite. "It was very unfair of me to form such an opinion based on such a short acquaintance. I don't know how to apologize."

"Just say 'I'm sorry.'"

"Very well. I'm sorry."

"And then kiss me."

She went perfectly still, except for her eyes which widened. "I should say 'kiss me'?"

"Well, I meant for you to actually kiss me, but either way is fine."

"I didn't know that a kiss was part of an apology."

"A terrible lapse in your education as it is the most important part. And very necessary to make the apology official."

She raised a clearly skeptical brow, but rose up on her toes, leaned in and briefly touched her lips to his cheek.

Maxwell shook his head sadly. "That was the sorriest kiss I've ever received."

"Is that not the point?"

"In the literal sense, I suppose so. But I had something more like this in mind...." He lowered his head and brushed his lips lightly over hers. A tiny, breathless sound escaped her and he touched his mouth to hers again, trying to capture the bewitching note. His hand stole around her waist, drawing her closer. She settled her hands on his chest, right above the spot where his heart pounded, and leaned into him. And every thought except her drained from his head.

He ran his tongue over her full bottom lip, and she opened for him, an invitation he instantly accepted. She tasted warm. Sweet. Delicious. Gathering her more tightly against him, he explored all the velvety softness of her mouth, his senses soaking up the lush feel of her pressed against him. The delectable taste of her in his mouth. The silky texture of her hair sifting through his fingers. The sensual friction of her tongue mating with his.

He'd wanted to absorb her slowly, drink her in with small sips rather than one huge gulp, but his control was rapidly sinking below the surface. He surely would have had a better chance at keeping his head above water if she hadn't been so incredibly responsive. She mimicked his every move, straining closer to him, sifting her fingers through his hair, skimming her hands down his back, until he knew he had to end this *now* if he had any hope at all of stopping.

He slowly lifted his head. A low groan rumbled in his throat at the sight of her, eyes still closed, her kiss-swollen lips moist and parted. He brushed a dark curl from her cheek, then, unable to stop himself, dipped his head to touch his lips to the soft skin of her neck.

"You smell like sunshine, even in the moonlight," he whispered, touching his tongue to the delicate pulse at the base of her throat. He raised his head, then tilted up her chin with his fingers until she looked into his eyes. The languorous heat simmering in those golden-brown depths left him in no doubt that she was as affected as he.

"I wish I was clever with words," he said softly, cradling her soft cheek in his palm, "but I'm not. I can only say that I've wanted to kiss you since the first time I saw you." *And I knew it would be like this, feel like this, when I did.*

She reached up and traced her fingertips over his face, as if trying to memorize his features. "I cannot deny that I'd imagined you doing so, my lord, although never in my wildest dreams had I imagined anything quite so marvelous as *that*."

And with those words she put to rest a question he'd tried his damnedest not to think about. Clearly, even if she'd been kissed by one of her London suitors, none had shared the heat and intimacy with her that he just had.

"Maxwell," he said. "I believe we're on a first name-basis…Amanda." God, he liked the sound of her name on his tongue. Indeed, it was a relief to say it out loud after hearing it echo in his mind for the past week. And because he wanted nothing more than to yank her against him and taste her again, he forced himself to release her and step back to put several feet between them—before he was unable to do so. "I'm afraid we must rejoin your aunt in the garden now."

She nodded slowly, then with more conviction, as if only slowly recalling their surroundings.

Something in her eyes spread unease through him and he sensed her subtle withdrawal. "Are you sorry?" The words pushed past his lips before he could stop them. Damn it, he didn't want her to regret their kiss.

She looked troubled, but her gaze did not reflect sorrow. "No, Maxwell. I'm not sorry. But you're right—we must return."

He clasped her hand. "Spend tomorrow with me, Amanda. We can collect shells along the beach, ride the horses, enjoy the gardens…anything you like."

She clearly wrestled with the decision of whether or not to accept his offer, and he took the fact that she hadn't instantly refused as a hopeful sign. Finally she said, "I would like very much to spend the day with you, Maxwell."

A warm feeling suffused him, and he basked in her response as he would a ray of sunshine. And for the first time in two years, he truly looked forward to the following day.

CHAPTER SIX

TEN DAYS AFTER sharing her kiss with Maxwell, Amanda sat on her aunt's terrace, sipping tea and staring at the sky's last fading embers of orange and gold visible through the trees. Tonight, for the first time in those ten days, she and Aunt Lydia had dined without Maxwell, who'd had some urgent estate affairs to see to.

As much as she'd tried to deny it, she simply couldn't any longer. She'd missed him. And his absence now forced her to face the question that had plagued her these past ten days with increasing urgency as the date of her departure from Cardiff grew closer—how was she going to face leaving here? Leaving him?

The days had passed so quickly, it seemed to Amanda that she'd barely blinked and they were memories. Memories which were among the happiest she'd ever known. She'd spent each day with Maxwell—properly chaperoned by Aunt Lydia, of course—and she'd enjoyed every minute of their time together. They'd walked his path to the sea, strolled through the gardens, ridden horses, examined his extensive shell collection, toured his observatory, played whist and even shared a picnic on the beach. With each new day she'd learned more about him, and she'd yet to discover anything she did not like or admire.

She'd discovered a shared love of animals and rare books, a fondness for oranges and apple cobbler. His interest had never flagged while listening to her massacre songs on his pianoforte, nor had his patience waned while explaining the finer points of billiards. He'd applauded her skill when she'd trounced him at backgammon, then kindly offered to explain the strategies of chess, a game at which she was quite hopeless. He'd known the scientific name of every plant and flower she'd pointed out, and introduced her to the culinary delights of the local shellfish.

Had she truly once thought him cold? Unfeeling? Yes, she had, and she could only shake her head at her own foolishness. He was…lovely. Delightful. Kind. Patient. Generous. Amusing. Not in any bombastic ways, but quietly. In ways that made her want to stay very, very close to him so she wouldn't miss a word he said. Wouldn't be deprived of even one of his smiles.

She couldn't help but notice and be gratified that the more time they spent together, the fewer lonely shadows she saw in his eyes. She could almost see him emerging from the shell he'd built around himself after his brother's death.

But perhaps the thing she liked most was that he would speak to her about anything and everything.

Books, poetry, science, art, philosophy. He never once made her feel like a bluestocking if she was well versed on the topic, or foolish if she was not. They spoke about their lives, their childhoods, their finest and worst hours. When she'd learned he'd spent much of his childhood alone, his nose buried in books, and that his butler, Sutton, had been his greatest ally, especially after his mother's death when Maxwell was twelve, her heart had broken for him. She could easily imagine him as the studious, shy, lonely child he'd described, over-looked because he wasn't the heir, and considered odd because of his scientific interests.

Maxwell was not only a nobleman, he was a *noble man.* A man without artifice, a man who, unlike her other suitors, did not hide behind a mask of polite dis-interest or wear a cloak of ennui and insouciance.

And then, of course, there was the way he made her feel. That heart-racing thrill every time he looked at her, every time she looked at him. He was tall, muscular and masculine, and so darkly attractive he positively stole her breath.

But while the past ten days had been filled with hap-piness, she'd also found them confusing and exces-sively frustrating. Confusing because none of her four prospective husbands elicited a fraction of the feelings Maxwell inspired. And frustrating because he had not kissed her again.

Oh, he bestowed proper, gentlemanly pecks to her fingertips in greeting and when they parted company, but in spite of her best efforts to get him alone so they could endulge in another heart-stopping kiss like the one they'd shared in the observatory, she found herself repeatedly thwarted.

Aunt Lydia had suddenly proved the most strident and intrepid of chaperones, never tiring, always ready for another outing, always the first one to suggest another activity. Gone was the woman so fond of napping on garden benches, and Amanda dearly wished for her return. For she desperately wanted, needed, to experience those wondrous, sensual sensations Maxwell had awakened in her. Sensations that should have appalled her, but instead had kept her awake long into the nights.

Despite that they were never alone, there were times when Amanda would feel Maxwell's gaze upon her. And when she looked at him, it was as if the world fell away, leaving only the two of them. Every touch of their hands, every brush of their shoulders, every look, was increasingly fraught with sensual undercurrents that kept Amanda in a constant state of awareness and yearning. He filled every crevice of her mind, and she constantly wondered if he was experiencing these same unsettling feelings.

The tension had grown in her until she thought she would burst with wanting to touch him, wanting him to touch her. She wouldn't have the opportunity to see him tonight, and time was running out. Only three more days until she returned to London. Only three days until, as she'd promised, she had to choose a man to marry. A man who wasn't Maxwell…

The sound of footfalls on the flagstones roused her from her thoughts, and Amanda turned to see Mortimer walking swiftly toward her bearing a silver salver. Aunt Lydia hurried after him, her shawl flapping behind her in her haste.

"A note for you, Lady Amanda," Mortimer intoned, presenting the salver.

"It's from Lord Dorsey, my dear," Aunt Lydia said, her bosom heaving from her exertions as she plopped into the chair opposite Amanda. "His footman indicated it was of an urgent nature. Pray, what does he write?"

Amanda broke the seal, then quickly scanned the few lines. "He believes he's deciphered the pattern of stars carved into the lid of the box. He's sent his carriage and asks that we come right away." She jumped to her feet. "Isn't this exciting? Come, let us go."

Aunt Lydia pressed the back of her hand to her forehead and slumped limply in her chair. "I'm afraid I'm not up to the adventure, my dear. I simply cannot walk another step today."

Amanda hoped she did look as disappointed as she felt. "I understand. I shall inform Lord Dorsey's footman we cannot join him."

Aunt Lydia straightened up as if a catapult were affixed between her shoulder blades. "Nonsense. Just because *I* am exhausted doesn't mean *you* shouldn't go and learn about this momentous discovery. Indeed, I insist you go and then report back to me so I do not expire from curiosity. You'll be properly escorted by Lord Dorsey's footman and driver, and his home is filled with servants. I've no doubt that Lord Dorsey will act...as he should."

Amanda's heart leaped. "If you're sure—"

"I'm positive. After all, you're leaving Cardiff in only a few days." Aunt Lydia grasped Amanda's hands and looked at her steadily. "This may well be your only opportunity."

Amanda nodded slowly. *Your only opportunity...*

She didn't intend to waste it.

MAXWELL'S ELEGANT black lacquer carriage drove her directly to the observatory where Maxwell awaited her.

"Lady Lydia is not with you?" he asked, glancing beyond her into the carriage's interior as he helped her to alight.

"She did not feel up to joining me, but insisted I come without her." His eyes seemed to darken at her words, quickening her breath. She didn't add that Aunt Lydia most likely would have thought twice about such encouragement if she'd known Amanda would be joining Maxwell at the secluded observatory rather than the main house.

"Your aunt is not ill, I hope?"

"No, just fatigued."

"I'm sorry she couldn't join us, but I'm very glad

you came. I cannot wait to show you what I've discovered." He dismissed the carriage, then tucked Amanda's hand in the crook of his arm and walked into the observatory. He led her directly to the room that housed the telescope, to a long table covered with a collection of large maps. In the center of the table rested the wooden box.

"After much studying and eye strain, I finally found what looks to be a match between the carving on the inside lid of the box and one of my celestial maps." He pointed to one of the carved dots. "This is what finally gave me the clue. With the help of my strongest magnifying glass, it suddenly struck me that this particular dot looked different than the others."

"Different how?"

"It was round rather than star-shaped. I wondered if perhaps it wasn't a star but a planet. And after much searching, I found a match. Compare the markings on the inside of the box with this map." He circled his finger in the area where he wanted her to look. Amanda studied both, then nodded with excitement. "They look identical. Which planet and stars are they?"

"Mars. The stars are those that make up groupings known as Pegasus, Dolphin, Arrow, Fox and Hercules."

"What do you think it means? Why would someone carve a portion of the sky inside a box?"

"I have no idea."

Continuing to ponder the map, Amanda said, "I think it must have something to do with the woman on the lid. Perhaps the box was a gift from a man who loved her, a token to commemorate what they'd seen in the sky the night they met."

"Or perhaps it was a gift from the lady to her gentleman, so he would forget neither her nor the night they met. But whatever the reason, I believe this box has something to do with *you*."

Amanda abandoned her perusal of the map and turned toward him. He stood no more than an arm's length away, and her breathing hitched at his nearness. "How could it have something to do with me? I'd never seen it before the day I spied it in Gibson's shop window."

"I don't know how. But for some reason, only you can open it. And you look like the woman on the box… something about the way she's standing, the curve of her cheek. She reminds me of you."

Amanda nodded slowly. "I must admit she somehow reminded me of myself. Do you think the box belonged to my ancestors?"

"I feel that's a strong possibility."

"Then how did it end up in a trunk in Mr. Gibson's attic?"

"Obviously it was sold, lost, traded or perhaps even stolen in the past. Has anyone in your family ever studied astronomy?"

"Not that I've ever heard." She touched her fingers to the stack of maps. "With all the time you've been spending with me and Aunt Lydia, when did you have the opportunity to study all these maps?"

"At night." He paused, then added, "When I could not sleep."

Amanda's heart skipped at his words…spoken in that deep, quiet voice. "Why couldn't you sleep?"

He reached out and whispered a single fingertip down her cheek, stilling her. "Do you really want to know, Amanda?"

God, yes. Please, yes. "Yes," she whispered.

"I could not sleep because my mind was too full…with thoughts of you."

She could barely breathe. "What sort of thoughts?"

"Thoughts of touching you. Holding you. Kissing you."

The words sounded torn from his throat and seemed to reverberate in the air gone thick with tension, mingling with the other words echoing through her mind: *This may well be your only opportunity.*

"Then your thoughts were identical to my own."

His eyes flared in the same way they had before he'd kissed her ten days ago, and she trembled with anticipation. But he remained still, a muscle jerking in his jaw, and she could stand the suspense no longer. Summoning her courage, she asked, "Why do you not touch me? Kiss me?"

"I don't want to."

Amanda shook her head. "I don't believe you."

"Believe it. And do you know why I don't want to?" Without waiting for a reply, he continued in a tight voice, "Because I'm afraid. Afraid I won't be able to stop at a mere kiss, a single touch. Afraid that I'll lose the battle with my control and I'll do something that you—we—will regret."

Drawing a deep breath, Amanda took a single step forward. Her gown brushed his boots and she could feel the heat emanating from him, smell the heady warmth of sandalwood. The need to touch him overwhelmed her, dissolving in mere seconds a lifetime of propriety. She laid her hands against his chest, absorbing the rapid beat of his heart through his clothing and his quick intake of breath. A purely feminine thrill coursed through her, emboldening her further. "A kiss, Maxwell. Just a simple kiss. Surely you wouldn't deny me such a simple request."

He briefly squeezed his eyes shut, and when he looked at her again, his eyes burned like twin braziers. But still he did not touch her. "All the years I've spent here alone, all the pent-up wants you inspire, all my self-control, you're shattering them. With a single look." He glanced down at her hands on his chest. "A single touch."

"You say that as if I should be afraid."

"You should be. God knows I am."

She shook her head. "I'm not afraid of you, Maxwell. My only fear is that you'll refuse my request and I'll never again feel the wonder of your kiss." She erased the last few inches between them. "A kiss, Maxwell… just one kiss…"

A shudder ran through Maxwell, and in a heartbeat

he lost the war he'd waged against his fierce desire for her. His arms went around her, crushing her to him. He slanted his mouth over hers, desperate to taste her. Her lips parted beneath his, and he instantly took advantage, deepening their kiss. Their tongues, their breaths, mated, melded, danced. Her scent seemed to skim beneath his skin, igniting him until every pore ached with need.

His honor demanded he stop, but honor was drowned out by the needs screaming through his system. Just as he'd damn well known, there was nothing simple about this, and just one kiss could not, would not, satisfy the raging hunger she'd awakened. More. He had to have more.

Anchoring her against him with one arm, his free hand roamed, scattering hairpins as he skimmed his fingers through her silky curls. He continued to explore, memorizing the gentle curve of her soft cheek. The delicate shell of her ear. The exquisite length of her neck. The slender perfection of her collarbone. Then lower, to palm the lush fullness of her breast. Beneath the soft muslin, her nipple beaded.

Her head tipped back, breaking off their passionate kiss, and a soft gasp emitted from between her moist, parted lips. Maxwell dragged his open mouth along the exposed ivory column of fragrant skin, touching his tongue to the spot where her pulse beat rapidly, tasting the delicious, delicate warmth.

He raised his head. With her eyes closed, cheeks

flushed and kiss-swollen lips wet and parted, she looked aroused and utterly, achingly beautiful. Her eyelids fluttered open and he looked into slumberous golden-brown depths, hazed with the same passion and need he knew was reflected in his own eyes.

"I've never felt anything like this before," she whispered. "This fierce, desperate…wanting. I don't know what to call it."

"Desire. It's called desire."

She studied him for several seconds, then said in a small voice, "So you've felt this way before then."

"No." The word rushed out, a harsh, swift denial. "I've experienced desire, but never like this." He reverently brushed a stray dark curl from her face. "I've never felt anything even remotely resembling this."

She reached up and feathered her fingertips over his lips. "Kiss me again. Please…"

God knows she hadn't needed to say please. Lowering his head, he kissed her deeply, his tongue exploring the warm silk of her mouth while his hands skimmed with increasing urgency over her luscious curves. His common sense tried to interject objections, but he shoved it roughly aside. Common sense was no longer in charge. Everything he felt, the culmination of all she inspired, boiled down to a single word that pulsed through him like the throbbing pain of a raw wound: want. He wanted her. He ached with wanting her. The dam had burst and he was beyond propriety, beyond subtlety, filled only with this consuming, devouring fire to make her his.

His fingers slipped below her bodice and brushed over her aroused nipples. Her low moan of pleasure, the way she squirmed against him, stripped away another layer of his nearly nonexistent control. Sliding his fingers beneath the short, capped sleeves of her gown, he slowly dragged the material downward. His lips followed the trail of fragrant, bared skin, tracing over the shallow hollow at the base of her throat where the pale skin quivered from her rapid pulse. With her chest rising and falling with her ragged breathing, he gave the material a final tug, then raised his head.

Full breasts topped with rosy nipples thrust upward as if begging for his touch. "Exquisite," he said, his voice a harsh rasp he barely recognized. He cupped her breasts, brushing his thumbs over her plump, velvety nipples. With a moan, she clutched his shoulders and her head dropped back limply. Leaning down, he lavished kisses across her chest, then laved her breast with his tongue. When he slowly drew the tightened crest into his mouth, she sifted her fingers through his hair and arched closer, urging him to take more, a request he immediately granted.

Mindless with need, his hands skimmed down her back, drinking in her tremors and low moans. He lightly kneaded the soft curve of her buttocks, then grasped a fistful of her muslin skirt and dragged it upward. A long, low moan invaded the silence. His? Hers? He was beyond knowing.

Her grip on his shoulders tightened. "Maxwell…"

Hearing his name in that passionate, breathless whisper dragged him back from the edge enough to lift his head. What he saw utterly bewitched and enchanted him. Amanda, her eyes closed, skin flushed, lips parted, hair mussed from his hands, rosy nipples damp and erect from his mouth. A more seductive temptress his imagination could not ever have conjured.

She was so beautiful. And desirable. And so achingly vulnerable in her blushing arousal, his chest constricted. He wanted her more than he wanted to draw his next breath. But not like this. Bloody hell, what had he been thinking? He *hadn't* been thinking—that was the problem. But from the moment he'd met her, she'd robbed him of his wits. With an effort that cost him, he released her skirt, slid her bodice back into place, then rested his forehead against hers and fought to catch his breath. When he could speak, he said, "You see now what I meant about kissing you."

Her head jerked in a nod, bumping their foreheads together.

"I'm sorry, Amanda. It was not my intention to allow things to go so far. You deserve far better than a heated grope while standing in my observatory."

She leaned back and he looked down into her serious golden-brown eyes. "Yes, I suppose I do. Although I was quite oblivious to that fact only moments ago. But now that you've brought it to my attention…"

"You have my sincerest apologies."

"I see." She studied him for several seconds in deafening silence while he cursed his lack of control. And then she smiled. A slow smile that bloomed across her features and filled him with a warmth unlike anything he'd ever known. "Of course you realize your apology is not official unless you kiss me."

A quick laugh that held more than a little relief escaped him and he hugged her to his chest. And in the blink of an eye, all the things he'd believed beyond his reach suddenly seemed so…reachable.

"Only you could bring laughter to a moment like this." He dipped his head and brushed his mouth gently over hers. "Only you. My beautiful, unexpected Amanda."

He tucked a dark curl behind her ear then cupped her face in his hand. She turned and pressed a warm kiss against his palm, and his heart swelled at the simple gesture.

"Amanda…" he said softly, the depth of all he was feeling voiced in that single word.

"Maxwell," she whispered back.

"Marry me."

She went utterly still. Her eyes widened. He couldn't tell if her expression was surprised or horrified. Heart pounding, he said in a rush, "I know your family expects you to marry one of your four suitors, but I'll speak to your father—"

"All right."

"—I realize that the rumors surrounding me won't endear me to either of your parents," he rushed on, ignoring the panic nipping at him, determined to get out all the words necessary to convince her, "but if you'll allow me to explain—"

"There's no need."

"Of course, I realize that the stigma of those rumors would attach itself to you and—"

"I don't care."

"I just simply cannot bear the thought of you being another man's wife, of you sharing your life with someone else—"

She touched her fingertips to his lips, ending his stream of words. "Neither can I."

He blinked. "I beg your pardon?" he asked, the words muffled beneath her fingers.

"For a man who is normally so attentive, you've not heard a word I've said." She cleared her throat, then said very slowly, very distinctly, "I agreed you should speak to my father. I assured you no explanation regarding those ridiculous rumors is necessary. No one who knows you could possibly place any credence in such ludicrous nonsense. And my darling Maxwell, after these past few moments, I know you *very* well. Not as well as I'd like to, but since you are a man of honor—not to mention great fortitude and willpower— I shall endeavor to wait until we're properly wed before allowing you any further liberties with my person. And before taking any of my own liberties with yours."

He could only stare. Was he hearing what he thought he was hearing? And did she just *wink* at him?

Before he could speak, she continued, "I'm not concerned about foolish rumors uttered by foolish people casting a shadow upon me. I can assure you it would be a very stupid person indeed who would dare to repeat such stories to me about my…husband."

"Your husband?"

"Yes, my husband," she said, her voice tinged with both amusement and impatience. "Unless you've changed your mind in the past two minutes?"

"You'll marry me?"

She cocked a brow. "I'd planned to, but perhaps I'd best give it some more thought as it seems the intelligent man I fell in love with has been replaced with a slack-jawed individual who does not understand plain English—"

Whatever else she might have said was lost as his mouth covered hers. He wrapped his arms around her, holding her tightly against him, unable to believe that she was going to be his wife. His.

"Say it again," he whispered against her lips.

"Which part?"

"All of it. No, that will take too long. I can make do with just the 'fell in love' and 'my husband' parts."

Her puff of laughter warmed his lips. Framing his face with her hands, she looked directly into his eyes. "I love you, Maxwell. With all my heart. You make me happy. I want you to be my husband."

He rested his forehead against hers and squeezed his eyes shut, welcoming the joy, basking in her words.

Then he leaned back until he could see her eyes. "I've loved you since the moment I saw you in Gibson's shop. I'm a man of science, yet there was nothing remotely scientific about my reaction to you. The way you made—make—me feel. As if I'd been wandering aimlessly for years and had finally come home. I'd lost my hopes, abandoned by dreams, until you came along and reawakened them." He drew a deep breath, then said quietly, "I want to explain about my brother."

She feathered her fingers through his hair and shook her head. "It is not necessary, Maxwell. I know you did not harm him."

"And I cannot express how much your belief in me means. But I want to tell you. I *need* to tell you."

"Very well, I'm listening."

Maxwell pulled in a slow breath to prepare to tell her what he'd never told anyone. "I never refuted the rumors surrounding my brother's death because I preferred to have people think the worst of me rather than tarnish Roland's honor and reputation."

"What do you mean?"

"The night of the accident, Roland and I had a terrible row. He was deep in his cups, as he always was, a situation that was growing steadily worse. Roland wasn't a belligerent drunk, or one who kept a slovenly appearance or staggered about and fell down. He'd developed such a high tolerance for alcohol over the years that unless someone knew him well, they wouldn't realize how much he'd been drinking. That night, however, he was in a rage. He'd just found out that his wife was expecting their first child."

"Surely that would be joyous news."

"Normally, yes. But Roland was convinced that the child wasn't his. In truth, knowing Marianne, I wasn't entirely convinced he was wrong in his suspicions."

"How awful."

"Yes, it was. I tried to reason with him, calm him, but he only grew increasingly agitated—and violent. When I attempted to subdue him, he ordered me to leave Dorsey Manor and never return. In the midst of our argument, through the window we noted Roland's phaeton being brought 'round. Realizing Marianne was attempting to leave the estate, his fury erupted. He stormed from the room, and I ran after him. Marianne was just climbing onto the phaeton. Harsh words were exchanged. A scuffle ensued during which Roland hit me with the riding crop he'd wrested from Marianne." He held up his hand and her gaze shifted to the scar on his finger. She gently touched the puckered skin.

"I wondered how you'd gotten that."

"Roland whipped the horses, and took off as if pursued by the devil. I ran to the stables then gave chase with our fastest horse, but I was too late. The phaeton went over a cliff." The image of the accident site, seared forever in his memory, flared in his mind and he squeezed his eyes shut to banish the horrible mental picture. "Servants had overheard our argument. Seen the tension between us. Heard Roland order me from the estate, then witnessed me chasing them. The rumors of murder started immediately, fueled by the fact that I secluded myself here at the estate."

"I'm so very sorry for all you've suffered. The pain and the loneliness." She drew his hand to her lips and pressed a kiss to the scar bisecting his finger. "But that's in the past. The future is filled with love. And hope. You aren't alone any more."

And with that simple gesture, those simple words, she eased his burden and lifted the dark curtain he'd lived behind for the past two years. "I love you, Amanda."

"I love you, too." Mischief gleamed in her eyes. "Although I think I've forgotten how much. Would you care to refresh my memory?"

"My darling Amanda. Nothing would give me more pleasure."

CHAPTER SEVEN

THE NEXT MORNING, Amanda could barely keep from skipping to the breakfast room in her happiness. After Maxwell had returned her home last evening, she'd thought surely the bright blush she knew stained her cheeks would alert Aunt Lydia before they could impart their happy news. Aunt Lydia had been delighted, and they'd all talked late into the night, making arrangements to travel back to London together so Maxwell could formally request her hand from her father.

When she arrived in the foyer, she greeted Mortimer with a smile. "Good morning, Mortimer. Has my aunt come down to breakfast yet?"

"Yes, Lady Amanda. She is in the drawing room with Lord and Lady Fenport."

Amanda blinked in confusion. "My parents are *here?*"

"Yes. They arrived a few minutes ago."

"Th-thank you." Her giddy joy replaced with concern, Amanda hurried into the corridor. What on earth would have induced her parents to travel all the way to Cardiff? She rushed through the first door, which led to the drawing room.

Her mother was seated on the brocade settee, her skirts artfully arranged, her dark hair swept back from her face in a complicated coiffure. Her father stood with his elbow braced on the marble mantel. Aunt Lydia sat on the other settee. She appeared pale and offered Amanda a weak smile.

"Mother, Father," Amanda said, greeting each of them with a kiss. "I am so surprised you're here. Is something wrong?"

"Heavens, no, darling," Mother said, shifting over a bit then patting the cushion next to her in invitation. "Everything is fine. In fact, everything is wonderful."

Relieved, but still confused, Amanda sat. Her mother leaned closer to her, then abruptly sat back, making the tsking noise that signaled her disapproval. "You're *freckled*. Very poorly done of you, Amanda. Such blights upon your complexion never completely fade away."

"I'll endeavor to remember that." She cast a quick smile at her father. "What brings you to Cardiff?"

"Why, you of course," Mother said with a laugh. "Your father and I have the most fabulous news to impart, and we couldn't wait another instant to tell you. Oh, I never should have agreed to let you be away for so long, not when such important matrimonial matters loomed on the horizon."

Amanda didn't bother to remind her mother that the matrimonial matters looming on the horizon were exactly the reason she'd needed to get away. "Please, do not keep me in suspense. What is this news?"

Mother reached out and clasped her hands. "You're engaged, darling!"

Amanda stared at her mother in stunned silence. She well knew Mother was a formidable force when it came to ferreting out information, but how on earth had she learned about Maxwell? Surely Aunt Lydia would not have told her before Amanda could do so herself. She cast a brief glance at Aunt Lydia who confirmed Amanda's assessment with a nod. "How…how do you know?"

Mother's brows nearly disappeared into her hairline. "How do I know? Why, because your father arranged it. After everything was settled, Lord Abbott stayed for tea, and we spent the most delightful afternoon."

"Lord Abbott?" Amanda's gaze bounced between her parents. "What does he have to do with my being engaged?"

Mother's trill of laughter filled the air. "As he is your fiancé, I'd say he has everything to do with it."

It took Amanda a full ten seconds to find her voice. When she finally spoke, her voice shook with angry disbelief. "You arranged a betrothal between me and Lord Abbott behind my back? Without my permission?"

"I'll thank you not to speak to me in such a tone, Amanda," Mother said sharply. "As for this being behind your back, you're simply indulging in dramatics. Of the four suitors, it was obvious that Lord Abbott was the best choice, and he was growing extremely impatient. During your ill-conceived absence from Society, Lords Branton, Remington and Oxmoor all lavished their attentions on other young ladies, as I'd warned you they would. Your father and I were convinced that if we did not act immediately on your behalf, Lord Abbott's interest would wander as well."

"I see. Well, as much as I appreciate your efforts on my behalf, I'm afraid you shall have to undo them."

"I beg your pardon?" Mother asked, frowning.

"Whatever arrangements you made with Lord Abbott need to be unarranged. You granted me permission to come to Cardiff to decide upon a fiancé. I have done so, and the gentleman is not Lord Abbott."

Twin flags of color rose on Mother's cheeks. "As I said, Amanda, I don't believe Lords Branton, Remington, or Oxmoor are still interested—"

"Nor did I decide upon any of them."

"What nonsense is this?" Mother asked.

"It is not nonsense at all, Mother. You took it upon yourself to betroth me and it's quite impossible as I am already betrothed. I met a gentleman here in Cardiff and I intend to marry him."

A combination of shock, horror and anger contorted

her mother's features. "Without consulting your father and I? Impossible. Who is this man?"

"Maxwell Wolford, the Earl of Dorsey."

Amanda could almost see the wheels turning in her mother's mind as she sifted through the mental files she kept on members of the peerage. Amanda didn't doubt for a moment that her mother would have heard of Maxwell. When a horrified gasp escaped her mother, Amanda knew what was coming next.

"Dear, God. He's that reclusive man they call the Crazed Killer of Cardiff! The man who killed his brother in order to gain the title." She arrowed an icy, accusing glare at Aunt Lydia. "How could you allow this to happen? How did she even come into contact with such a man?"

"I met him in an antique shop in the village," Amanda answered. "That dreadful name is nothing more than vicious gossip. Lord Dorsey has never hurt anyone."

Mother folded her hands in her lap. "Well, I don't care, and it is completely immaterial as you shall have nothing further to do with the man."

"That will be quite difficult as I'm going to marry him."

"You shall do nothing of the sort. You will marry Lord Abbott, as your father and I have arranged."

"No. I am going to marry Lord Dorsey." She lifted her chin. "I love him."

"*Love?*" her mother repeated in an incredulous

voice. "Good heavens, Amanda, have I taught you nothing? Love has nothing to do with marriage. Lord Abbott is handsome, charming, titled and wealthy."

"Lord Dorsey is all those things *plus* he loves me."

"You barely know each other."

"We know each other very well, I assure you."

Her mother narrowed her eyes at Aunt Lydia. "How is it that they know each other very well?"

Aunt Lydia hoisted her chin. "Lord Dorsey has spent every day with us. He is a delightful, thoughtful man who has been done a great disservice by the ugly and unsubstantiated rumors surrounding his brother's death. He is a fine gentleman and he adores your daughter, as she adores him."

"So you encouraged this?" Mother asked frigidly.

"I did nothing more than chaperone. Amanda is an intelligent woman, fully capable of deciding who she should marry." Aunt Lydia smiled at her. "I'm very happy for you, my dear."

"Thank you, Aunt Lydia."

"There is nothing to be happy about," Mother decreed, her voice seething with anger. She turned to her husband. "Reginald, you've not said a word through this entire debacle. *Do* something."

Amanda's father cleared his throat. "I fear I must agree with your mother on this, Amanda. You've known this man less than a month. And given his sobriquet, I admit I'm concerned. Lord Abbott is a very good match for you."

Triumph flashed in her mother's eyes, and Amanda felt as if she'd been kicked in the stomach. Her father, who normally always took her side in these altercations, had chosen a very poor time not to do so.

She drew a deep, bracing breath, then said, very calmly, "I agree Lord Abbot is a good match, but for someone else. I am going to marry Lord Dorsey. Nothing shall deter me."

Her mother's face turned a shade of crimson Amanda had never before seen. "If you do, you will bring shame and scandal upon this family."

"I don't see how marrying a nobleman can do that. Our union will certainly bring no shame or scandal to *me*."

"Very well, Amanda" said Mother, "I don't want to have to do this, but your willfulness leaves us with no other choice. If you marry him, you shall be disowned."

A shocked, heavy silence filled the air. Amanda slowly rose then walked toward her father who appeared frozen at the mantel. "You told me you wanted me to be happy, Father," she said softly. "You gave me your word you would allow me to choose my own husband. I have, and I promise you on my life he is the finest of men." She searched his pale face. "For this you would disown me?"

Her father studied her for a long moment then shook his head. "No, my dear." He clasped Amanda's hand and turned toward his wife. "I most emphatically do *not* agree with you on this, madam. Our daughter, who will not be disowned under any circumstances, shall be permitted to marry this man she claims to love—provided that I am convinced of his worth and sincerity once I meet with him."

Amanda flung her arms around her father's neck and hugged him tight. "Thank you, Father. You'll be convinced, I swear it."

"I do not see what difference his worth or sincerity makes," Mother said icily. "She has already been promised to Lord Abbott."

"An arrangement that can be gotten out of given the proper amount of compensation," Father said with some steel in his voice. "Compensation which shall come directly from your jewelry allowance, madam."

Mother gasped, then fumbled vainly in her reticule for her handkerchief. Father slipped a square of linen from his pocket, then looked at Amanda and heaved a resigned sigh. "For all the dramatic crises in your mother's life, you would think she'd take care to have a handkerchief at the ready." He patted Amanda on the shoulder and smiled. "Now go and make arrangements for your young man to call so I may meet him and interrogate him in my fiercest manner."

After bestowing another kiss on his cheek, she blew a kiss to Aunt Lydia who returned the gesture, then hurried from the room, intending to write a note to Maxwell asking him to come as quickly as possible. When she saw Mortimer in the foyer, however, and saw the object he held, her footsteps faltered.

"Where did you get that?" she asked, staring at the familiar glossy wooden box.

"Lord Dorsey left it with me. He told me to give it to you."

She accepted the box from him. "When did he leave it here?"

"Just a few minutes ago, Lady Amanda."

"Lord Dorsey is *here?*"

"Not now. He left." Mortimer cleared his throat. "I, um, believe he was distressed by the argu— I mean, conversation in the drawing room."

Amanda felt the blood drain from her face. "What exactly did he hear?"

Mortimer shuffled his feet. "No one was trying to overhear, Lady Amanda. 'Tis just that the door was open, and well, no one was exactly whispering."

"I understand. Now what did he hear?"

"That you were engaged to a Lord Abbott. And that you would be disowned if you didn't marry him."

"Dear God. Did you see which way he went?"

"Struck off across the lawns in the direction of Dorsey Manor. He walked here, Lady Amanda," he called as she dashed for the door, "and only left a few minutes ago. You should be able to catch him."

Clutching the box to her chest, Amanda sprinted down the flagstone steps. There, in the distance, just disappearing into the copse of elms, she saw him. Tossing propriety to the winds, she hiked up her skirts and ran as if rabid dogs nipped at her heels. Several minutes later, chest heaving, heart pounding, lungs burning, she arrived at the copse of elms. Onward she ran, until after what felt like an eternity she finally saw him up ahead.

"Maxwell!"

He turned, and when he saw her, he walked back toward her. She didn't stop running until she skidded to a halt in front of him. She sucked several breaths into her screaming lungs then managed to gasp out, "You left."

"Yes."

"I know what you overheard, but—"

"Then surely you know why I had to leave."

"No, no, you don't understand. My father is going to sever the arrangement with Lord Abbott—"

"Yes, I know."

"And I will not be disowned—"

"Yes, I know."

"Father will give his blessing—"

"Provided I am able to convince him of my worth and sincerity. Yes, I know. I heard."

She simply stared, utterly at sea. "Then why on earth did you leave?"

He shook his head. "It seems the intelligent woman I fell in love with has been replaced with a slack-jawed individual who does not understand plain English." He reached out and grasped her shoulders. "I left to fetch the Dorsey diamond ring. At eight carats it's dreadfully ostentatious, but I suspect your mother will be duly impressed. There's also a matching choker, bracelet and ear bobs. Been in the family for generations. I'll bring them along as well, just for good measure."

"Good measure for what?"

"My dearest Amanda, I am going to make my claim official. When I go see your father, it will be with a proper engagement ring and all the trappings. I intend to fight for what I want, and I've no intention of going into battle unprepared."

Understanding dawned and Amanda drew her first easy breath since she'd entered the foyer. "You left in order to fetch me an engagement ring?"

"Correct."

"And you were going to come back?"

"Most definitely. Bearing scads of gaudy diamonds in order to impress my future in-laws."

Amanda threw her free arm around his neck and pressed as close to him as the box between them would allow. "Have I told you today how much I love you?"

"You have not," he replied in a very put-upon tone. "And I must tell you I'm feeling very neglected."

"I love you."

"Ah. Much better. I love you, too." He kissed her in that magical, toe-curling way of his, draining all the strength from her knees.

"And now, let's continue to Dorsey Manor to fetch your engagement ring," he said, tucking her hand into the crook of his elbow, then urging her along at a brisk pace.

"Are you always in this much of a hurry?" Amanda teased, "or do I just bring it out in you?"

He stopped, pulled her into his arms, and gently kissed her. "My darling Amanda, it will take me a lifetime to show you and tell you all that you bring out in me."

Amanda hugged to her chest the box that had brought them together and filled them with hope for the future. "My darling Maxwell, how very fortunate we are that we'll have that lifetime together."

TODAY'S SECRETS

Julie Kenner

CHAPTER ONE

IT IS MY GREAT PLEASURE to introduce a man who needs no introduction—my son, Ryan Kinsey, the new president of Kinsey Applied Sciences.

Ryan let the words echo through his head, the pleasure from his new position marred only by the words his father had whispered on his way to the microphone: *Don't disappoint me, boy.*

Ryan grimaced. He wasn't about to disappoint. He knew better than anyone the extent of his father's wrath. More than that, he knew how much was riding on his leadership of the company. Kinsey Applied Sciences had made a name for itself in the transportation and communications industries under his father's direction, and it had just about killed Albert Kinsey to retire. But Doc Boorman's orders had been strict, and Albert might be a lot of things, but he wasn't fool enough to risk his life simply to stay at the helm of the company.

Now, at the postannouncement party, Albert was circulating, sharing old stories with new friends, and letting old friends know of his plans to head off to the south of France the following morning for some doctor-prescribed sun and relaxation. Not to mention undertaking certain treatments that weren't yet approved by the FDA.

"A true-blue miracle, huh?" Edward asked, grabbing the chair opposite Ryan, twisting it around and straddling it. Ryan winced. He'd sat like that a few times during his teenage years, but he'd stopped after his father had threatened to ground him for a decade. The eldest Kinsey son did not sit like a sailor. It simply wasn't done.

Apparently, though, the old man's wrath hadn't reached the younger Kinsey kids. The baby, Edward, got away with murder.

Ryan squinted at his brother, trying to focus on his words. "A miracle," he repeated. "What's that?"

"That Pop's actually going to leave you in charge. It's unthinkable. Unprecedented. Absolutely unbelievable."

Ryan shook his head, grinning. "Yeah, well, don't go overboard there with the vote of confidence little brother."

Edward had been taking a sip of his beer, but now he snorted, holding out a hand as he tried not to choke. "Give me some credit, Ryan. You're not the part I'm amazed at. I mean, hell, your qualifications are awesome. Chemical and aeronautical engineering, physics, biotech. Is there any area of science you *don't* have some expertise in?"

"Botany," Ryan replied dryly. "And I'm not much up on paleontology, either. At least, not more than I've learned from reading to Gizmo over the years," he added, referring to his older sister Margaret's five-year-old son Gerald who, for reasons no one could recall, got nicknamed Gizmo one summer. And it had stuck.

"My point," said Edward, not missing a beat, "is that you're more than qualified to run the company. I just can't believe that dad is actually going to let you."

"Well, that remains to be seen." Ryan took a sip of his own beer, swallowing the drink along with the hard truth. "He's still CEO and the board is in his pocket. He can countermand my decisions. You know it as well as I do."

Edward just stared at him like Ryan had grown two heads.

"What?"

"When did you turn dense, big brother? He's heading to France. He's taking treatments. Have you talked to Boorman? Dad's going to be too zonked to pay attention to what's going on here. This place is yours for the next two months. Longer, if dad's treatments need to be repeated." He tilted his head up slightly, his eyes focused on something above Ryan's head. "Don't you agree, Meg?"

"Absolutely," Margaret said, pulling out the last chair and sitting down. Ryan noticed the way she primly crossed her ankles, and he stifled a smile. Margaret was the oldest girl, and they'd shared a lot of the same "lessons" at their father's hand.

"You have free rein," she said. "You can institute new policies. Make new and exciting advances in science. Leap tall buildings in a single bound."

Ryan snorted, his sister's sense of humor amusing him as always.

"Of course," Meg continued, "if anything isn't totally perfect when Dad returns, you can pretty much kiss your ass goodbye."

"Thanks," Ryan said. "Love you, too, babe."

She laughed. "You know it's true."

He did know it, actually. Ryan had studied science because he loved the way things worked. He wanted to invent things, to foster change, to make the world a better more exciting place. Instead, he was holding down his father's fort, forbidden to do anything to rock the boat and possibly upset the little empire Albert Kinsey had built. A total crock, but it was the life Ryan chose. *Don't disappoint me.* Sure, Dad. Wouldn't dream of it.

He shook off the melancholy and smiled up at his sister. Margaret wasn't being mean-spirited. She was just announcing the facts, like someone might announce the weather.

"By all rights," he said, "it should be you. You're just as qualified as I am."

"Not entirely," she said. "I'm missing one very important component." She gazed pointedly at his crotch.

"He's an idiot," Ryan said. "We all know it."

"Maybe," she said. "But I consider myself lucky. I can go work for someone else without causing a major family crisis. You boys are stuck with the man."

"The lady has a point," Edward said.

"Anyway, I didn't come to talk about your fabulous new position. I came to see if you guys wanted to come with me and Jerry to The Bedroom."

Edward's brows lifted. "Excuse me?"

"Ha, ha," Margaret said. "It's a dance club. We've got a sitter tonight, and we want to go out. And it would be a fun way to celebrate Ryan's promotion."

"Sure," Edward said. "I'm in."

"Great. Ryan?"

"I don't think so," he said. He'd never been big on the club scene, and the idea of going now, with his brother and sister, really lacked appeal. "We corporate presidents don't do the club-hopping thing."

Meg rolled her eyes. "Oh, come on, Ryan. It'll be fun. Maybe you'll even meet someone."

"Oh, that's a rich enticement."

"I'm serious. You need to get out more."

"Maybe," Ryan conceded. "But I seriously doubt that the love of my life is waiting for me on a dance floor."

"Why not? I met Jerry at a club."

Ryan considered a snappy retort, but the truth was he thought Jerry was a great guy. "I don't need to find her now, anyway. I need to concentrate on running the company."

Meg put on her puppy dog face. "Come on, Ryan. Come out with us. I promise you won't meet the love of your life."

"You just said I'd meet a woman."

"Sure," she said, waving a dismissive hand. "But not a relationship girl. Just a fling girl. You could use a fling. You're too tense. You need some female interaction."

Ryan just shook his head, not quite able to keep the smile off his face.

"What?" she demanded.

"I should be taping this. Because I'll bet millions that this isn't the kind of advice I'll ever hear you giving Gizmo."

"Absolutely not," she said, her eyes dancing. "I'm not about to morally corrupt my child. But my brother…" She waved a dismissive hand. "I figure your morals are shot to hell already anyway."

Ryan met Edward's eyes and they both laughed.

"She's got your number," Edward said.

"Come on," Meg urged. She closed her hand over his wrist. "Tonight's a celebration. Live a little."

Ryan could think of better ways to celebrate his new position than going to a dance club with drunken yuppies and a bass so loud you couldn't hear yourself think. But he couldn't think of anything better than celebrating with his brother and sister.

And the funny thing was, as they stood up and headed out the door together, Ryan realized that he was actually looking forward to the evening. He hadn't been clubbing in forever. Why not have some fun? Burn off some stress?

And if he met a woman who wanted to move from the dance floor to his bed…well, that wouldn't be bad either.

MADAM ROMANA leaned forward, Marty's hand clasped in her own. The tent was dim, the only light coming from the glowing orb on the small round table. The greenish glow cast eerie shadows on Madam's face, making her jowls seem longer and her kohl-rimmed eyes huge and spooky.

Madam traced her fingertip over Marty's palm, then closed her eyes and muttered unintelligibly to herself. Marty fought the urge to yank her hand back, shooting a withering look in her cousin's direction. Ben just flashed a sheepish grin and shrugged.

Marty sighed and let her hand stay put. Ben's wife, Allison, had arranged this shindig for Ben's thirty-fifth birthday, including the psychic "entertainment." So Marty supposed that the least she could do was be entertained.

"The future," the psychic murmured, "mysticism… fate…yes, fate." Those wide, earnest eyes met Marty's scornful ones. "I see great things in you. Great things." She yanked Marty's hand forward, pulling Marty half onto the table as she pressed Marty's hand against her breast. "Yes," she whispered. And then, "*Yes!* I see it clearly. You will make a difference in the world. Your mark. Something…" She swayed a bit, her gaze drifting to the corners of the darkened room. "It is unclear. The signs are not there. But while I cannot say what, I can tell you with certainty that you *will*. My dear, *you will have an impact*."

Marty gasped as a cold chill seemed to trill up her spine. She jerked her hand away, casting her gaze down to hide the tears that had welled in her eyes, brought on by the wave of potent memories of her mother.

"My dear?"

"That's quite enough," she whispered, keeping a tight rein on her emotions. When she was certain she could look up without revealing too much, she did, focusing her sharp gaze on Ben.

"I'm so sorry to have disturbed you, my dear." The paint on the charlatan's face seemed to crack as she frowned. "Sometimes our destiny is difficult to accept."

Marty couldn't answer. She was too rattled by the woman's words. She pushed back her chair and stumbled out of the tent, blinking against the fading sunlight as she looked around, trying to find some quiet corner to sit down and think.

She found a place behind the tent, a small plastic stool that Allison had probably left after gardening. Marty sank gratefully onto it, her fingers automatically plucking at the soft petals of the perky daisies blooming nearby. Footsteps sounded behind her, and she turned to find Ben, his expression one of deep repentance.

"I'm sorry, Marty. I wouldn't have dragged you into the tent if I'd known you'd hate it so much. Allison just hired the woman on a lark. I figured you'd think it was a hoot."

She wanted to yell and scream and say that conjuring memories of her mom wasn't a "hoot." But Ben would never, ever do anything to hurt her, and so she held her tongue. She even managed a wan smile. "It's okay. It's just—I mean, she just caught me off guard."

He blinked at that. "Marty, she's a hack fortune-teller. You don't believe in that crap, do you?"

"Not *her*. What she said. *You will make an impact.* That's exactly what my mom used to say to me. Every night. For my whole life. It was like our little bedtime ritual. Only for her, it wasn't a ritual. She meant it. She always had absolute confidence in me."

"Oh, Marty." Ben's voice held a wealth of sadness. "God, I had no idea. I mean—"

She held up a hand. "No, no, Ben. It's not your fault. I'm just too sensitive, I guess."

"You're allowed. It's only been three months."

Marty blinked back fresh tears, remembering that day when her mother had quit fighting and simply let the cancer take her. "Do you know my father didn't even go to her funeral? 'Business commitments,' he said. 'Couldn't get away.' What a crock."

"Your father's a strange bird," Ben said, which was, to Marty, one of the bigger understatements of all time.

"He's a complete ass," Marty said. "But he's a brilliant one." She plucked the daisy, then methodically started tugging the petals off. *He loves me, he loves me not. He loves me, he loves me not. He loves me.* She plucked the last petal, then held it up for Ben to see. "He loves me not."

Ben's features hardened. "Like you said, he's an ass. But your mom adored you." He leaned down and pressed a kiss to her forehead. "And rightly so."

She offered him a watery smile. "I'm sorry. I don't mean to be all melancholy on your birthday. It's just—"

"What the psychic said. Sure. It would've thrown me for a loop, too."

"I'm sure it was just a coincidence. I mean, that's what you tell people who go see psychics, right? That they're going to have some huge impact on the world."

"I guess so."

"My mom really believed it, though."

Ben studied her. "But you don't?"

Marty shrugged. She'd loved her mother absolutely, but sometimes Angela Chamberlain's optimism had been even more than Marty could take. "That's my dad's department." Harold Chamberlain was a former NASA scientist, now head of his own company that focused exclusively on space travel and the technology related to it. When she was younger—back when Marty's grades in math and science had still been decent—Harold had waxed poetic about how his daughter would one day join him at the helm of the company, Allied International Technology. Together, he said, they would change the world.

When Marty's left-brain grades sank to just above passing, he'd backed off of that dream. But it wasn't until she'd decided to be a journalist like her mother that her father had turned nasty. "Do you know he actually told me that I'd never amount to something. Never make a difference in the world. That all I was destined to do was be a fly on the wall and write about other people doing interesting things?"

Ben snorted. "More evidence your father's an idiot. You *do* make a difference. Everyone makes a difference."

"A butterfly flaps its wings in China and you get a hurricane in Florida? You buy that stuff?"

"Maybe. But I was thinking more along the lines of Jimmy Stewart and old man Potter," he said.

"*It's a Wonderful Life?* Great movie. But somehow, I don't really think it's relevant to my life."

"Who said anything about relevance? I just think Donna Reed is hot."

Marty couldn't help it. She burst out laughing. "Okay. You win. Help me up."

She held out a hand, and when she was on her feet, Ben cocked his head in the general direction of the house. "You know, Allison arranged for a baby-sitter. We're going out dancing after this party winds down. Why don't you come?"

"I don't know. With my mom and the whole fiasco with Eli, the idea of spending a night on the town has lost a lot of its appeal."

Ben nodded, his face a perfect mask of calm. Marty knew the mask was for her benefit. Ben had been the one to introduce her to Eli. And her cousin had taken it very personally when the boyfriend of eight months had suddenly up and left one morning five months ago, citing no more of a reason than "he needed to find a different groove."

In retrospect, Marty had decided he was no great loss. *A new groove?* What kind of a freak talks like that, unless he's the lead llama in a Disney movie? Even so, she hadn't exactly been up for tripping the light fantastic for some time now.

"Come on, Marty. Maybe you'll meet someone. Push Eli that much farther out of your life."

"Not interested," she said. "I decided after Mom died that I needed to take a widow's year."

"A what?"

"A widow's year. You know. No big life changes. Status quo. Just to get my bearings again. No moving to a new house, no getting a dog. And absolutely, positively, no getting a boyfriend."

"In that case, just come because I'm your cousin and you love me and I'm inviting you and it's my birthday."

Great. The guilt card.

"Come on, kiddo. The night is young."

"Some people have to work tomorrow."

"But not you."

"Maybe I'm on the trail of a hot story."

"Are you?"

She frowned. "Sadly, no."

"Marty…no birthday cake for you unless you agree. And it's yellow cake with chocolate icing.…"

"Now you're just playing dirty."

Ben smiled. "I like to win."

Marty summoned a self-sacrificing sigh, even while trying to hide her grin. "Fine. It's your birthday. I'll go if only to humor you."

"Great. I'm thrilled. Allison will be thrilled. She's

been worried about you, you know. Ever since Eli left. And then with your mom... Well, she worries."

Ben's wife had become one of Marty's closest friends. Since the breakup, though, Marty hadn't confided much in her friend, and she wasn't surprised Allison was worried. But there really wasn't much of anything to confide. By Marty's own design, her life vis-à-vis the opposite sex was dry as a bone, and she intended to let it stay that way for a full twelve months. Which meant she still had nine Y chromosome-free months to go.

"Marty?"

She looked up with a start, realizing she'd gotten too lost in her thoughts to answer. "I'm fine. I'm fine. Really."

"Allison thinks you need to start dating again."

"Except I'm not interested in dating," she said, probably a bit too sharply.

He held up his hands in a defensive gesture. "Hey, hey, don't take it out on me. *I'm* not trying to force you to date."

"Good. Great. I'm glad to hear it."

He turned to her just long enough to flash a wicked grin. "Personally, I think your no-relationship plan is right on. But that doesn't mean you shouldn't go out and get laid."

CHAPTER TWO

GO OUT AND GET LAID. BEN'S EARLIER WORDS seemed to
float in the air. They hovered over the bar, drifting across
the wide selection of scotches, tequilas, gins and bour-
bons. They danced on top of the hunky bartender and
bounced from cute guy to cute guy as Marty stood there,
her mind in a muddle.

What on earth was she doing? She gave herself a little mental slap and once again shook her head, determined to ignore not only Ben's words but the images
they provoked. She was *not* interested in "getting laid."

She took a long sip of her Cosmopolitan and mentally corrected herself. Actually, getting laid sounded
pretty appealing. But she had no interest in the whole
meeting-dating-small talk ritual that necessarily preceded the going-to-bed thing.

She took another sip and pondered the conundrum.
Her widow's year plan required that she remain relationship free, and she intended to stick firm. After all, it was
a smart move. Wasn't a full year off what all those
shrinks and investment advisors and grief counselors ad-
vised widows and lottery winners?

But just getting laid… That wasn't the same as a relationship. A fling wouldn't break her self-imposed rule.

However, the truth was that the question was entirely moot. Recently, she hadn't met anyone she wanted to have coffee with, much less sleep with. Her overall attitude to the world had changed and, with it, the way she looked at men.

The realization was both startling and a little bit sad. When her intellect had imposed the widow's rule, apparently her libido had decided to take a breather, too.

Wasn't that something?

She twisted around on her barstool and started to scan the male faces in the room, wondering idly if one would inspire her to jump his bones.

Nope.

She wasn't certain if she should be relieved or disappointed, and she finished off her Cosmopolitan as she pondered *that* question.

Allison came up just as Marty slid the empty glass away. She held up a finger to the bartender. "Another, please," she said, then smiled at Marty. "Having fun?"

"Oh, sure."

Allison's smile was knowing. "Liar."

Marty laughed. Her friend knew her too well. "Well, it wouldn't be my first choice, but I'm glad to be here for Ben."

"This is *so* not his scene anymore. But we actually met at this club, so he thought it was fitting." She laughed again, then shrugged. "Well, it was that and the fact that it's his thirty-fifth birthday and he already has a three-year-old. I think he's trying to recapture his youth."

"I'm only twenty-six," Marty said. "But it's not my scene anymore, either."

Allison's smile was soft. "Do you think it will be again?"

Marty cocked her head, considering. "No," she finally said. "I really don't." Even after her status quo year was up, she didn't intend to go back to the bars and clubs, searching for men in smoke-filled corners. Events had changed her, and only time would tell if it was for the better or for the worse.

Allison squeezed her hand. "In that case, I'm extra glad you came tonight."

"I wouldn't have missed it," Marty said with a grin.

"Liar," Allison said again, then laughed.

"Actually, now that I'm here, I am glad. I just wish I'd known I'd end up at a dance bar before I got dressed for the party." Ruefully, she lifted her foot, revealing a red Stuart Weitzman stiletto. "First time to wear them, and they're killing me."

"Blister?"

"At least one."

Allison—toddler mother that she was—started rummaging in her purse. When she came up for air she had a little package of Band-Aids. She passed them to Marty. "Go fix your feet."

"Thanks." Marty took the package, hopping off the stool with a wince. "I'll be back in a bit."

As it turns out, the little package wasn't quite enough. It had two bandages. But when she pulled off her shoes, three blisters stared back at her. *Great.*

She was sitting there frowning—wondering if she should pop them and bandage the worse ones—when the light in the narrow hallway seemed to dim. She looked up, startled, and saw the cause—six foot something of positively gorgeous male anatomy stood sideways at the mouth of the passageway, his regal profile effectively blocking most of the light from the dance floor.

Marty shivered. She wasn't entirely sure *why* she shivered. In fact, at the moment the only thing she was sure of was that she couldn't take her eyes off the man…and would love to have her hands all over him.

Stop it! Stop it, Marty!

She shook her head and concentrated on her blisters. She wasn't going to look at the gorgeous man. She wasn't going to look at the gorgeous man. She wasn't going to look at…

Oh, *heck.*

She looked up. Why not? She hadn't been attracted to a guy since Eli. Before, really, since Eli's looks had grown on her. They hadn't knocked her off her feet like this man had.

And now—

Uh-oh. He turned and looked in her direction. She

jerked her foot back up onto the bench and started inspecting the blisters in earnest.

"Really," he said, tossing the words over his shoulder. "I just need to make a quick phone call."

As Marty focused on her feet, he came over and picked up the handset for the pay phone. It crossed Marty's mind that he was probably the last man on the planet not to have a cell phone surgically attached to his belt, but when he picked up the handset and pretended to dial, she figured she understood.

She waited a second, debating whether she should say something, then decided what the hell. "Skipping out?"

He turned to face her directly and stared, his eyes penetrating and dark and utterly sexy. "Pardon me?"

"The phone call," she said. "It's just an excuse, right? To get away from someone in the club."

For a moment, she thought the man wouldn't answer her. Or, worse, that he *would* answer her and tell her to mind her own business. But no, instead he smiled, and when he did, Marty felt a trill that started in her toes and sent fire all the way up to her nipples, now hard under the lace bra she wore beneath her sleeveless black T-shirt.

"Shall I assume you have some experience in these things?"

"A bit," she admitted.

"This kind of place not your style?"

She shrugged. "It's not that as much as this." She ruefully held up a shoe. "They looked great in the Galleria, but they hurt like hell. And I sure can't dance in them."

He took it from her and held it up to the dim light. "Hmm. I'm not sure I could do much better."

A burst of laughter bubbled through her. His easy familiarity surprised and delighted her, and the fact that she couldn't seem to stop looking at him was certainly a plus in the overall appeal department.

She cocked her head a bit and smiled back at him. "They look fabulous on me. But looks aren't everything."

"No, they're not." He looked her up and down, his slow heated gaze starting at her bare toes and moving all the way up to her face. By the time their eyes met, she was sure she was blushing. She swallowed, stifling the urge to press her hands against her cheeks. "Looks may not be everything," he went on. "But I'm sure you've never had a problem in the looks department—or ever will."

"I...thank you."

He inclined his head just slightly. "You know, I *was* planning on sneaking out that door back there—"

"Oh. I'm sorry." A wave of embarrassment crashed over her. She'd presumed too much. She pulled her feet up and turned sideways on her bench, widening the space for him to pass.

He didn't move, but his smile broadened just a bit and his eyes seemed to dance in amusement. "Ah, what I meant was that I'd been planning to leave. Now I'm thinking that I might want to stay a bit longer. Maybe do a bit of dancing." His eyes flashed with mischief. "I'm Ryan Kinsey, by the way."

"Martina Chamberlain. Marty."

"Well, Marty. Care to take a spin around the floor with me?"

She lifted an eyebrow and dangled the shoe by its strap from her forefinger. "I still have my little problem of sore feet. Remember the impractical shoes?"

"Then leave them here." He held out his hand, and without thinking, she reached out and took it, letting the shoe on her forefinger tumble to the ground. Before she knew it, she was in his arms, and they were on the dance floor and she was in her bare feet. He was holding her close and they were slow dancing despite the fast beat of the music and the rhythmic thrum of the bass.

Marty pressed close against him, hypnotized by the very beat of his heart. But before her thoughts lost their purchase and drifted away on the music, she caught one coherent idea: *This* was why she'd come tonight. She hadn't realized it at the time, but now it was so obvious. This man. This moment. This night.

Surprising and abrupt and probably a little bit crazy. And, so help her, she didn't want it to end.

RYAN HELD THE WOMAN in his arms, her body firm against him as they swayed to their own rhythm despite the soul-pounding rock beat that filled the large club. They'd slow danced to six songs now, and not one had actually been a slow song. People were beginning to stare, and Ryan really didn't give a damn.

From the moment he'd first seen her, his body—actually, one particular part of his body—had been running the show. He couldn't remember ever having been so affected by any woman before her. One look and he'd simply wanted her. Not forever, but for now…oh, how he wanted her now.

Maybe Meg and Edward's ribbing had gotten to him. Maybe he'd just been too long in an empty bed. Whatever the reason, his body was primed, and this woman had started his senses humming. He wanted more. And he wanted it now.

As his hands stroked her back, he leaned in close, his lips almost touching her ear. "Any interest in getting out of here?"

The look in her eyes as she whispered "yes," shot straight to his crotch, firing his blood and fueling an already red-hot desire.

He took her hand and urged her toward the exit door. They crossed the parking lot, making a beeline for his Mustang. "I hate to sound cliché," he said, as he opened the passenger door for her, "but your place or mine?"

"Well, normally, I'd say mine since I'm just around the corner, but this car is awesome. Maybe we should drive far, far away." She stroked the upholstery, then leaned forward and stroked the dash. Ryan made a concerted effort not to think about how those hands would feel stroking his chest, his thighs, his back, his—

"Did you restore her yourself?"

Her question pulled him back to his senses. "Yeah. Hobby of mine."

"I'm impressed," she said, her voice filled with flirtation. "And I do like a man who's good with his hands."

"Yeah? And I like a woman who lives just around the corner."

"Looks like we're going to get along just fine," she said. Her smile lit a fire in her honey-colored eyes. Her light brown hair seemed almost golden, lit as she was by the overhead glow of halogen. The overall effect was both sensual and innocent…and damned appealing.

She pointed toward one of the three exits, and once he'd turned onto Westheimer, she directed him the rest of the way to her apartment, a tidy little second-story flat with a big yellow cat guarding the front door.

"That's Killer," she said, giving the cat a nudge with her toe. The cat mumbled something that was probably a kitty obscenity, but didn't move. "He's my attack cat."

"I can see that he keeps you very safe," he said, stepping gingerly over the yellow pile of fur.

"Oh, yes. I wouldn't feel comfortable living alone without Killer."

They moved through the darkened living room, the only light coming from the full moon shining through the sliding glass door.

She sat on the couch, but when he sat next to her, she bounced back up again, like some rubber toy. He took her hand. "Are you okay?"

She nodded, her smile wry. "Sorry. I just don't usually… I mean, it's just that you…"

He nodded. "I know. Me too."

"I'm usually very sensible. I'm a journalist. So watch yourself or you'll be all over the front page." She flashed a self-deprecating grin. "Well, the front page of the Life and Arts section, anyway."

"I'll be good," he promised, then looked her up and down. "You don't look like Woodward or Bernstein."

"I'll take that as a compliment."

"Good. That's how I meant it." He studied her, wondering what made her tick. "Do you like your job?"

She looked at him, clearly unsure whether he really cared. It was a fair reaction. After all, they'd come to her apartment with one purpose in mind. The gentlemanly thing to do would be to talk up the woman before ravishing her in bed. In Marty's case, though, he realized he was truly interested. "I'm serious," he said. "I'd like to know."

For a moment, he thought she was going to argue. He might want to know her better, but for all he knew, she wanted to jump straight to the bedroom portion of tonight's program. Surprisingly, the possibility depressed him.

After a moment, though, she nodded. "All right. If we're going to share life stories, then we at least need wine. Would you like some?"

He followed her to the kitchen, nodding approval when she opened a bottle of merlot.

"So, do I like my job?" she said, as she passed him his glass. "I love it."

"I sense a 'but.'"

"You're perceptive."

"So?"

She took a sip of wine, possibly to enjoy it, possibly to stall for time. "So, it's the age-old story. My dad doesn't approve."

"Ah, yes. Approval of the father figure. You're right. I have heard this story."

"Then you know how it ends. The earnest daughter can never quite make the old man happy. She tries, but she just doesn't have the interest—or the skills, for that matter."

"Skills?"

"Math, science, that kind of stuff. He wanted me to follow in his footsteps, but the first time I got an F in algebra, it became pretty apparent that wouldn't be happening."

"What's he do?"

"Invents stuff. From his perspective, though, he changes the world. And he thinks it's beneath me just to write stories as if I was in a train watching the world go by through the window." She held up her glass as if in a toast. "Those are his words, not mine."

"Do you believe that? That you're just an observer, I mean?"

An amused expression flashed across her face, and she shook her head slightly. Not in denial, but as if she was trying to shake a thought loose. "This is the second time I've had this conversation today. Are the planets aligned weird tonight or something?"

"I'm pretty sure that the universe is expanding as usual."

"Hmm."

"Does that mean you're not answering my question?" he asked.

"I haven't decided," she said.

"To answer? Or whether or not your job has an impact on the world?"

"Both, actually."

"What's your mom's take on all of this?"

"That's the hard part," she said after a pause. "She always said that I would change the world. And even though I don't really care about doing a damn thing for my dad, for my mom, I'd pretty much move mountains. And now that she's gone, I feel like I want to act on that legacy. Does that sound crazy?"

Her eyes were wide, innocent and brighter than the alcohol could account for. He realized with a start that the sheen in her gaze was tears, and he knew then that her loss was recent. An invisible band around his chest seemed to tighten, and he wanted to pull her close and comfort her. Instead, he took her hand. "I don't think it sounds crazy at all. In fact, it seems to me that reporting the news has some impact. And even a small change can shift the course of history."

"So I've heard."

"Trust me. I know."

"Yeah?" The fire was back in her eyes, and he was glad to see the melancholy had faded. "And what do you do, Mr. Kinsey?"

"I change the world, too. I'm a scientist." Like a neon sign being turned on, a thought suddenly buzzed in his head. "Wait a minute. Your name is Chamberlain? As in Harold Chamberlain? Allied International?"

"Guilty. So you know my dad?"

"Never met the man. His company's got a good rep, though. Very well-respected. Very innovative."

"That's what you get when you're out changing the world," she said dryly. "Innovation."

Well, hell. He'd managed to put his foot in it, and there was no graceful way out. "Sorry. But I stand by what I said earlier. Not everyone can be a scientist. The world can only use so many staid and boring people."

"So are *you* staid and boring?" she asked, taking the opportunity to back out of the conversational minefield.

"Absolutely. Terribly dull. The convertible is just my clever disguise."

"Really?" Her voice was pitched low, and she moved a bit closer to him, leaving her wineglass stranded on the kitchen counter. "So if you're so boring, how come you're here? A bit out of character, wouldn't you say?"

"Absolutely. Must be the alcohol."

"Damn," she said, her eyes glittering with mirth. "And here I thought it was my effervescent personality."

"That too," he said.

"Uh-huh." She moved closer, breaking through that invisible barrier people keep around them, encroaching on his personal space. But with Marty, it wasn't an invasion, it was a full-frontal assault. His heart picked up tempo, and he stifled the urge to pull her close, and kiss her senseless.

With massive effort, he kept his cool, his fingers finding her soft hair, then gliding down to stroke her cheek, her lips. He wanted to touch her, to pull her to him. But part of him held back. Something about Marty called to him, and the air between them seemed to crackle with electricity. He hadn't come out tonight looking for anything real. He hadn't wanted to find substance, hadn't wanted to find a woman he could connect with.

And yet here she was, and he was actually afraid to kiss her. An absurd fear—he hadn't been afraid of a woman since tenth grade—but there it was.

"Ryan?" His name slipped off her lips, soft and breathy, and the timbre of her voice shot straight through him. Blood pounded in his ears and his entire body seemed to be on fire.

Screw expectations. Screw responsibility. And screw fear.

He wanted her. He'd have her. And in the morning, they could figure out the rest of it.

"Come here," he said. And to his absolute delight, she moved into his arms without hesitation or argument.

He pulled her closer, delighting in her little gasp of surprised pleasure. He'd barely touched her since the dance floor, and the brush of his fingers against her now sent jolts of pleasure through his body. He *had* been working too hard. He deserved this. Deserved *her*.

Her mouth was hot against his, and the temperature between them was rising, creating a fever that seemed to burn all other thoughts from his mind. Her hands stroked his back, each movement inching his shirt up until he gasped in pleasure at the delicious sensation of her palm against his bare skin.

His hands had found their own paradise, and while he held her close with one hand firm on her hip, the other had found her sweet breast. The shirt she wore was thin, the bra flimsy, and he slid his palm over the hard pebble of her nipple, his own body getting harder when she broke their kiss to toss her head back and moan.

It was a sound that cut right through him, fueling the hot mass of need that he had become. He slid his hand down, lower and lower, until he cupped her crotch. She whimpered slightly, and he whispered just one word: "Now."

She nodded, her eyes closed, lips parted, and he brushed a quick kiss over those waiting lips. She led him to the bedroom, pausing in front of a plain oak dresser.

He glanced down, realizing that it wasn't the dresser she was concerned with but a glossy box about the size of a loaf of bread. It had a curved lid inlaid with the image of a woman and, though he didn't know much about antiques, he thought it must be incredibly old.

"I'm playing a hunch here," she said, not quite meeting his eyes. "But you're a scientist, and I think you might think this is cool."

"A jewelry box?"

The corner of her mouth quirked up. "Sort of. My mom called it my hope chest."

"I thought a hope chest was a big hulking cedar thing."

Her delighted smile pleased him a lot more than it should. "Well, see? I can even teach something to a scientist."

He let his gaze drift to the bed. "Oh, I bet you can teach me a lot of things…."

"You're bad."

He kept the teasing tone in his voice. "No way. I promise I'm very, very good."

"I bet you are." She smiled, then, and took his hand. Slowly, she traced his finger down the image of the woman, then paused and applied a bit more pressure. The box felt warm and smooth under his finger, but otherwise, nothing happened.

"Is my scientific curiosity supposed to be piqued yet? Or did you just think I'd rather fondle a woman's engraving than the real woman standing in front of me."

"Behave," she said. "Or I won't show you."

He had absolutely no idea what he was waiting for, but there was such a sense of wonder in her voice that he canned the sarcasm and simply nodded. "Show me."

With much bravado, she removed his hand from the chest, then held up her own finger. "Watch." She mimicked his movements exactly, but this time, the result was different. This time, the lid popped open about an inch. She turned back to him, her face lit up and her entire body quivering with the delight of someone who knows she's just one-upped the world.

He didn't bother to temper his fascination. He hadn't seen a mechanism, and certainly his touch hadn't opened the box. Was there an indention that made the box pop? "Spring latch?"

"Not exactly." She stepped back and he took that as an invitation to examine the box more closely. He opened the lid, revealing packets of letters, tied with string, the top one addressed "to my darling daughter." Souvenirs of her mother, undoubtedly.

He ran his finger along the edge of the box, then inside as well, but she was right. No spring latch. Nothing, in fact, that appeared like any sort of a mechanism that would open. How fascinating. How odd. How very—

"The lock only works for my family," she said, stepping in closer behind him.

Her breath tickled the back of his neck, and he wanted to pull her close and run his hands over her. At the same time, though, this box was absolutely fascinating.... "What do you mean, only your family?"

"Just what I said. It opens for me, my mom, my grandmother, my great-grandmother. You get the drift. I think it's tuned to our DNA, but I've never entirely figured it out."

"What does your dad say?"

Her laugh held a hint of bitterness. "He was fascinated, of course. But he wanted to take the box apart, figure it out. My mom put her foot down. She wouldn't even let him look at it in any detail. She was afraid he'd break his promise and start disassembling the thing." She cocked her head. "What do you think? DNA? Magic? Tiny little elves who live inside the chest?"

"I'm going with the elf theory." He spoke the words lightly, but there was nothing indifferent about his fascination, and his gaze stayed fixed on the box. Completely and utterly fascinating....

He shook his head in pure, scientific wonderment. The inside was covered with an intricate design, and as she moved back in front of him, some of the markings caught his attention. Something familiar. *Mathematical formulas?*

He squinted, trying to see the faded markings more clearly. What on earth would equations be doing on the inside of a hope chest?

He started to reach for it, wanting just a bit of a closer look, but her hand closed over his.

"Sorry," he said, feeling sheepish. "You were right to think I'd be intrigued." He stepped back, contemplating the chest from a distance. "So it's been passed down in your family," he said. "Do you know who built it? Is there a maker's mark?"

"Nothing. I'm pretty sure my mom told me that it was found one day in a little shop and my great-great-great- et cetera grandmother bought it. But why the lock would work just for her—just for our family—is a total mystery."

"So you don't know any of the chest's history."

"Well, I don't know much. The truth is, I think I might know a little bit more than anyone else."

He frowned. "What do you mean?"

"I found a journal in it a few months ago, after my mom died. A slim little book that was hidden up here. See?" She pointed to the inside of the lid which was made of the same enamel-like material and covered with a celestial pattern.

"So what did the journal say?"

She frowned. "Unfortunately, the journal was something of a mess. I think it got damaged when my grandmother's house flooded. She managed to dry the box and its contents out, but since she didn't realize there was a hidden compartment, the journal got water damaged. Pages mildewed and ink ran and faded. But I could read enough of it."

"What did it say?" Ryan asked. He leaned forward, completely fascinated, not so much with the idea of finding a hidden journal, but with the way her face had lit up. With a start, he realized that she could be telling him *any* story, and he'd want to hear it. Almost as much as he wanted to take her in his arms and lose himself in her.

She brushed the question away with a wave of her hand. "Nothing much."

"Oh, come on. Now that you've got me interested, you have to follow through."

She licked her lips, and the heat that flooded her eyes was unmistakable. "Oh, really. Is that the way it works?"

"Absolutely," he said, his gaze never wavering.

Color flooded her cheeks, and she looked away, but a smile tugged at the corner of her mouth. "Well, if those are the rules, I certainly won't break them. The journal was all about colonization. I couldn't read enough to get the details, but it talked about how hard they were working and how difficult the conditions were and how their efforts were going to pay off soon. I assume she was talking about their having come to America. It's amazing, really. Holding that bit of history in my hand." She shrugged, the gesture almost apologetic. "Anyway, it did make me start thinking again about what my mom said—that I'd make an impact. Because my ancestor certainly did. She may have written about it in her journal, but she was also out there *doing* it. I want to as well." She pressed her lips together and looked away, fighting an expression of amusement. "Plus, I want to show up my dad."

He laughed. "Another sentiment I wholly identify with. Don't worry. You will."

She moved closer, head tilted back to look up at him. "Yeah? How would you know? Writing features isn't exactly a springboard to the Nobel Prize. Besides, you hardly know me."

"Maybe I see a lot." He pressed the tip of his finger to her lips, then trailed it down to the neckline of her blouse.

"Really?" The tease in her voice completely turned him on, erasing any remaining hesitations and taking his mind entirely off their conversation and her enigmatic hope chest.

"Oh yes," he said. "And right now, I'd like to see a lot more."

She slid into his arms and brushed his lips with a kiss, then stepped back, her hands lifting toward the buttons of her blouse. "As a matter of fact," she said, "I think that can be arranged."

CHAPTER THREE

MARTY WOKE UP limp, her body completely sated and her stamina pushed to the brink. He'd been *amazing*. No, beyond amazing. Something she didn't even have a word for, and so she did the only thing she could do— she snuggled against him, delighted when he shifted in sleep to close his arm around her.

She sighed, happy to know his subconscious was as attracted to her as his conscious mind was. And she assumed that his conscious mind was *very* attracted. He'd done some amazing things with the heated Kama Sutra massage oil. And when he'd found the whipped cream at the back of her refrigerator…well, that had taken her all the way to heaven and beyond.

She wanted to go back to sleep, to lose herself in his embrace once again. But it was already past eight o'clock. And even though they'd only drifted off a little after three, Marty was certain she'd never felt so refreshed. *Who needs sleep when you've had great sex?*

Trouble was, now she was awake alone when she wanted to be awake and with him.

She was contemplating the problem—specifically,

wondering if she was gutsy enough to wake him up by sliding down the bed and urging him awake with a few selectively placed, highly erotic kisses—when his soft voice tickled her ear.

"Good morning."

"Good morning yourself," she said, smiling. "I was just trying to decide how best to wake you up."

"Were you?" His eyes were still heavy and dreamy, but the quirk of his mouth suggested that he had already picked up on the subtle hint in her voice. That pleased her more than it should, and she told herself that she didn't have to be planning on a long-term relationship with the guy simply to be glad that they communicated so well. Good communication was just as important with a no-strings-attached, picked-up-at-a-bar lover.

A tiny part of her mind chimed in that this man could be so much more than that, but she firmly quashed the errant thought. She'd made a promise to herself not to do anything rash in her life financially, romantically, or any other-ly. So she was *not* going to get her hopes up about the possibilities of a future with a man she'd known for less than a day. If things grew and developed between them over time, then great. In nine months maybe they could start something. But she wasn't leaping to conclusions—or relationships.

He shifted up onto one elbow, the sheet falling away to reveal even more of his tanned and taut chest. "So, now I'm curious. How were you going to wake me? Cold bucket of water?"

"I thought I might be a tad more subtle. And hopefully more enjoyable."

"Is that right? Maybe I should go back to sleep. This doesn't sound like the kind of thing I want to miss out on."

"Oh, it's not," she said. "Definitely not."

"Mmm." He closed his eyes and leaned back into his pillow, flat on his back with his fingers twined behind his head. "Enlighten me."

She wasn't usually this bold with a man in bed, but something about Ryan erased her inhibitions. She moved over him, her knees on either side of his waist, then bent forward until her lips brushed his chest. He shivered slightly under her touch, and her mouth curved into a self-satisfied smile. *I am woman.* Oh, yes. This man made her feel *all* woman.

Slowly, she trailed her lips down his chest, then followed the thin line of hair that marked the path to his belly button. He tasted delicious, all warm and male, a hint of salt lingering on his skin from the sweat they'd worked up the night before.

Beneath her hands and mouth, she could feel his body harden. Lava flowed through her veins, a raw, heated desire fueled by the power of being female. Of turning this man on.

With her hands, she stroked his flat stomach, tracing her fingertip around his navel. He reached down, burying his fingers in her short hair, and easing her up toward him. She relaxed, pressing her body against his, almost melting from the heat generated between them as she slid up his body to close her mouth over his.

Heaven.

Dear Lord, he tasted so good. Her lips parted, and his tongue found hers. Searching and tasting and generally driving her wild.

She moaned, just a little, as his hands slid down, stroking her back and bottom, then cupping her waist as he flipped her under him, then straddled her. His thighs pressed against her hips, and there was absolutely no mistaking how incredibly turned on he was.

He leaned forward, and the sensation of his mouth closing over her breast sent shockwaves of pleasure rushing though her body. She felt warm and weightless, and her pulse pounded through her, all the pressure culminating at the apex of her thighs. She was hot and wet and she wanted him. Heaven help her, she wanted him *now*.

She arched her back, silently urging him to give her more. And, just in case he missed it, she whispered the word, too. A soft, sensuous demand: "More."

Bless the man, he didn't even hesitate. He eased off her and gently urged her legs apart. With one hand, he cupped her sex, the pad of his thumb teasing and exploring. He stroked her smoothly and with a certainty that made her tremble. "Please," she whispered. "Please…"

Again, he didn't disappoint. With a surety that aroused her almost as much as his touch, he slipped on a condom, then thrust inside her. She gasped as her body took him in, closing around the hard length of him.

She pressed against him, wanting more, her body and consciousness dissolving into nothing more than need and desire as he filled her, thrusting slowly at first and then building to a frenzy.

Colors seemed to fill her head, dancing in her imagination, their hues becoming more and more vivid as her passion crescendoed. Suddenly, she was lost in sensations. His mouth on hers, his body slick against hers. Her fingers dug into his back and she had the vague thought that perhaps she was hurting him with her nails, but there was nothing she could do about it. He was thrusting harder, desperate to take her to the edge, and she was desperate to go with him. She'd passed the point of rational thought. She could only feel, and right then, all she wanted was to feel him.

Their bodies met, again and again, and she could feel every atom inside her building up pressure, waiting for an explosion that was close…so very, very close…

And then.

Oh, dear Lord, yes!

Tremors ripped through her, the pleasure so intense it was almost painful. She gasped, pulling him closer and closer until he was firm against her, his weight too much for her frame, but she wanted and needed the contact.

"That was fabulous," she whispered once words returned to her.

He nuzzled her ear in response. "*You're* fabulous."

"Mmm."

"And I'm probably squishing you." He rolled over, then pulled her into his embrace, a position that seemed almost more intimate than the wild sex they'd just shared.

"So," he murmured, his lips so close to her ear that his breath tickled her as he talked, "do you know what I'm thinking?"

"After that? I'm so limp, it's a wonder I can think all."

"Too bad," he said, then trailed his fingers up her bare arm. She felt the hairs rise one by one until her whole body seemed to tingle from a mild electrical shock. "I was just thinking that I know exactly what we need to do now."

"Yeah?" Her voice was low and lazy, but inside, her heart picked up tempo. Men always left. That was standard operating procedure. If they didn't leave the night before, they left in the morning, racing for the door with some lame excuse. Not only was this man *not* leaving, he was actually suggesting another activity. "Let me guess. It involves you and me, and clothing is so not necessary."

He laughed. "Actually, I think clothes might be a good idea. Not that I don't enjoy the view, mind you." He let his eyes drift over her, and from the heat she saw, she could tell that he did, in fact, enjoy the view very much. Her nipples peaked, and she longed for his hands to cup the soft flesh.

"What is it?" she whispered as she gave in and eased herself closer, pressing her breasts against his chest. Sweet contact. It tamped one fire, but completely stoked another now burning at the apex of her thighs. She pressed her legs tighter together and repeated her question. "What is it you want us to do?"

His hand stroked her back and he leaned in close to murmur, "Actually, I was thinking breakfast sounded good. Maybe we could go out somewhere and grab a bite, then come back here. I mean, if you're game."

A bubble of laughter rose in her throat, and she realized that right then she really did want food. Even more, something about the two of them sharing breakfast, in public no less, made their wild night seem a little less wild. Not that she was looking for permanence or anything, she reminded herself, but she wasn't the hedonistic type. Not usually.

She hooked her arm around his neck. "Yeah," she said, "I'm game. But if you don't mind, I think I'd like to work up more of an appetite."

And with that, she moved in closer, claiming his mouth with hers, and then claiming his entire body with touches and kisses.

Breakfast, it turned out, became lunch. But neither of them really seemed to mind.

MARTY CHAMBERLAIN.

It had been over two weeks and she was as fresh in Ryan's mind as the moment they'd met, and he still couldn't get enough of her.

They'd seen each other every day, talked on the phone more times than he could count. They'd made love, watched movies and eaten fabulous food at scary-looking local dives.

Everything about her turned him on. Her sense of humor. Her self-assurance, despite that it was tempered by her fear of never doing anything to change the world. He knew better though. She'd already changed his world.

Damned if the woman hadn't gotten under his skin. And the truth? He liked the way that felt. She'd become his lover, his late-night liaison. And, honestly, she'd become his friend. An unexpected benefit that he now cherished.

The sex was great, of course. But what Ryan had discovered was that he enjoyed simply hanging out with her just as much. Lately, in fact, they were as likely to share a bucket of popcorn and camp in front of the television as they were to share a bottle of wine and spend time between the sheets. They usually saw each other late in the evening because of work, but she didn't seem to mind his erratic schedule. Or when he fell asleep exhausted during *Letterman*.

They'd settled into a wonderful, delicious pattern, but the truth was, he wanted even more. He'd even subscribed to the *Houston Chronicle* just so that he could search the Lifestyle section for her byline. Lately, he'd been trying to think of a story for her. She occasionally covered the science and technology beat, and he knew she wanted something juicy. As a matter of fact, just that morning, she'd asked him if Kinsey Applied had anything in the pipe that was newsworthy, but at the moment, they really didn't. About the most he could offer her was a fluff piece on…what?

He couldn't think of a thing, which probably explained why he was the scientist and she was the journalist.

Still, he wanted to help. He felt full when he was around her, which was a completely unfamiliar feeling to him. But he wanted to give to her. His thoughts. His help. Anything and everything. Sappy romantic bullshit, probably, but true.

He wanted to try to forge something permanent between them, but so far, he'd gotten no indication from Marty that she wanted anything more substantial than their current arrangement. In fact, she'd hinted at exactly the opposite, telling him over breakfast one morning that after her bad breakup and then the death of her mother, she'd decided "not to make any major life changes" for a full year. By his count, that meant she had just shy of nine months to go.

He didn't want to wait that long. And he hoped to hell that Marty felt the same—and that she'd decide to break her promise to herself in order to be with him. Until then, though, he needed to keep the relationship on track and give her time. No problem. He was willing to freely give her his time, at least what little time he had after trying to keep the company on track.

At the moment, Ryan was at the office behind his desk. He was holding the phone in his hand and thinking about dialing. He'd seen some new releases advertised at the video store near Marty's house, and that was as good an excuse as any for an early dinner with her.

It was only five, but he deserved a break. He'd been working his tail off trying to bring three new projects in, at or below budget. He'd found solutions for two, but the third had him stymied, and the best answer he could come up with at the moment was to sleep on it. Or at least, to forget about it for a while and let his brain have a rest by watching some sort of action-packed spy thriller.

That was another thing he liked about Marty. She genuinely preferred action films over chick flicks. Not that he had anything against angst and love. He'd just rather see guns and fast cars. He was a guy. So sue him.

He was just starting to dial her cell phone when Edward burst into his office waving an envelope and shouting joyfully, "You're not going to believe this!"

Ryan looked up, reluctantly abandoning his plans to call Marty for his brother's unbridled enthusiasm.

"You are *so* not going to believe this."

"I'm getting the impression something exciting and unusual has happened," Ryan said drolly.

"Picked up on that, huh, big brother?" Edward slapped the envelope down on Ryan's desk, the NASA return address glowing like a beacon. "Read it."

Ryan realized his heart had started pounding double time as he reached for the envelope.

Edward snatched it away. "No, don't read it. I'll just tell you. We're in, brother! We. Are. In."

"You're kidding."

"I'm not," Edward said.

But the news was too big and Ryan wasn't about to rely on hearsay. He stood up, leaned over the desk and snagged the letter. He had it open in no time and was scanning the contents.

Oh shit, oh shit, oh shit! It was true! NASA had preliminarily accepted his proposal to bid on a new propulsion system. Kinsey Applied was one of three companies given the opportunity to submit specs for approval. The job was high-priority, recently funded, and specs were due in the ridiculously short time of two weeks.

"Didn't I tell you?" Edward said. "Can you believe it?"

Ryan shook his head, his legs suddenly weak. He *couldn't* believe it. An opportunity like this…it was unthinkable.

And, frankly, it was also completely unprofessional. Ryan should never have submitted the proposal in the first place. He'd done it under the table, without going through the proper channels, never expecting that NASA would accept a proposal from a company with no practical credits in the space travel arena, though Ryan himself had published numerous papers on various related topics. It had been hubris that had caused him to submit the proposal and hubris that had caused him to draft the proposal in such a way that NASA might reasonably think the proposed propulsion system was further along in development than it was (as in, a prototype rather than a gleam in Ryan's eye).

"Uh-oh," Edward said, finally calming down enough to sit in one of Ryan's chairs. "I know that look."

Ryan scowled. "We can't submit a bid."

Edward rolled his eyes, then leaned back and kicked his feet up on Ryan's desk. "The hell we can't."

"Come up with a workable, new propulsion system in just two weeks? It's insane. What was I thinking?"

"You were thinking that you've already got the makings in here," Edward said, tapping his temple. "You've been doing theoretical work on antimatter and plasma-based propulsion systems since you were in diapers."

"Not quite that long," Ryan said, but he couldn't help but smile at his brother's enthusiasm.

"My point is that you've already got the framework. We just need to fill in the gaps."

"Unfortunately, those gaps are wide. It's going to be a lot of work."

Edward spread his arms. "Oh, come on. You know we can do it. Dad may be a character, but he filled this place with the best minds."

"That he did." Ryan drummed his fingers on his desk. "And Dad's the other problem."

At first, Edward's expression was blank, then his eyes widened and he nodded slowly. "You didn't tell him about the proposal...."

"What's this *you* business? You were right there with me when I typed the thing up and shipped it off to NASA. We both avoided the Albert issue because neither one of us really expected the proposal to get selected." Ryan rubbed his hands over his face. "And that's the kicker, too. We *haven't* been selected. Not officially. Not yet. If we already had the project and the guaranteed income, I could go to Dad and flash my fabulous success. But this way…" He trailed off with a shake of his head.

"This way you might lose the bid, and you'll never hear the end of it from Dad."

"It's worse than that, little brother. If we're going to get the bid and full proposal in on time, I'm going to need to reorganize the workgroups and shift everyone's projects and priorities. Except for the most pressing deadlines, current work will get shoved aside, and we can't take on new projects."

Edward nodded slowly, finally seeing the big picture.

Ryan spelled it out, just in case. "If we put in the work, submit the bid and *don't* get the contract, then my ass is grass. Dad will never let me hear the end of it. I'll have damaged the company, and even though we'll recover, in Dad's eyes, it'll be a total failure."

"True. But you're in charge now, and the upside is substantial. If we do get the contract, then Kinsey Applied Sciences is thrust into the heart of the space program. Not only are you golden with Dad, but you're golden in the industry. Plus, you're working on a project you're passionate about." He held up a hand, forestalling Ryan's objection. "Don't even say it. I know the party line. You're passionate about every project, blah blah blah. But I'm your brother and I know the truth."

Ryan hid his smile. "You're very perceptive."

"So go for it."

"You understand what's involved, right? Long hours. Tons of overtime. It's going to be a financial drain on the company, but it's going to be a drain on us, too."

"I understand," Edward said. "Do you?"

Ryan didn't have to ask what Edward meant. *Marty.* Already, he was barely able to squeeze her into his life. Now, though, he'd need to work literally around the clock. To make it worse, the project was confidential, so he couldn't even tell her what he was up to. Just that he was "busy."

"You guys aren't engaged, you know. Tell the girl you've got work to do, see her when you can, and chalk it all up to kickstarting your career." Edward presented Ryan with a wry grin. "It's either that or forget the project altogether. Because if you can't give this thing your all, then it's not worth it. Not only will we lose the bid, but Dad will have your ass in stirrups faster than you can say 'corporate integrity.'"

"You're just a bundle of encouragement," Ryan said.

"There's more," his brother said. "It's not just a question of time, it's a question of talk."

Ryan shook his head, not following.

"Here," Edward said, passing him another sheet of paper. This one included the other bidders on the project. And there, at the top of the list, was Allied International. "She can't know," Edward said. "If she told her dad…"

"She wouldn't," Ryan said.

"Probably not. But even if she said something in passing. It could—"

"Ruin everything," Ryan finished. "Don't worry. I know the stakes." And he did. The situation was a career maker, and if this leaked, he'd be up a creek.

He trusted Marty to keep a secret—he did—but this was just too touchy. Not only was she a journalist and this a potentially hot story, but her father was his competition. And Ryan wouldn't put it past Harold Chamberlain to pump his daughter for even the tiniest bit of information.

No, he simply needed to back off and buckle down. He'd see her when he could, but he wouldn't talk about his work. She would understand; she had to, because Ryan didn't want to lose her. But he didn't want to lose this opportunity, either. For the first time, he was faced with a true make-it-or-break-it scenario.

Ryan, of course, intended to make it.

CHAPTER FOUR

"YOUR PROBLEM," Ben said, "is that you're stubborn."

Marty took a bite of hot dog and settled herself on a bench in front of the Children's Museum. She was doing a piece on the museum's anniversary celebration, and she'd invited Allison and Ben and, of course, Toby, to join her at the invitation-only celebration. At the moment, Allison and Toby were inside playing on the various kid-friendly exhibits. Marty had toured the center, interviewed the director and perused the press kit. Now her blood sugar had nose-dived, and she'd escaped outside to grab a bite. Ben had followed her, claiming starvation as well.

Now, though, Marty knew the truth: he simply wanted to harass her.

She swallowed, then took another bite, determined not to answer her cousin.

"Did you hear me?" he said.

"I heard you." She looked down her nose at him. "I'm not answering you. It's part of my stubborn trait."

He shook his head in frustration and took a bite of his own dog. "Seriously, Marty. This guy is perfect for you. Just drop the defenses and go for it."

She took a sip of her Diet Coke and turned away, fighting to keep her expression calm. Part of her really *did* want to go for it. She wanted to throw caution to the wind and tell Ryan that she'd fallen for him.

But somehow she just couldn't take that step.

Ryan had already moved to the top of the food chain of people she wanted to spend time with. And not just for sex, either, though the sex was utterly fabulous. There was just something comfortable about the man, and she enjoyed hanging out with him as much as she enjoyed more, well, *active* pursuits.

The truth was, Ryan had become the best thing in her life. Certainly better than her work. Lately, all she'd had was fluff pieces. Little nothing bits of writing that couldn't even be called journalism. She'd been searching for a hard news story, but so far she'd found nothing. Maybe she just didn't have a journalist's nose, and if that was the case, she could live with it. But if she wasn't covering hard news, then she'd like to write opinion pieces. So far, though, all her ideas for columns had been soundly shot down, and her op-eds had yet to make it into print.

At least with a column or an editorial she could tell herself that her mom was right—she was making a difference in the world. But Marty was pretty sure that her most recent stories—a restaurant review and an information piece on various types of food processors—weren't exactly sparking the kind of change that her mom had contemplated.

But while all her work woes might have bugged her a month ago, now with Ryan in the picture, her office problems lost some of their teeth. He'd gained importance in her life, and obsessing about her work had lost some of its appeal.

The problem was, she wasn't *entirely* sure that she was as important to him. She wanted to believe it—and on a good day, she did believe it—but she could never be certain. Not without asking, and she couldn't do *that*.

The brutal truth? She was falling in love with the man. And, frankly, that scared her to death.

"You know what I think?" Ben asked.

She scowled at him. "You think too much."

"I think you're using that widow's year crap as a crutch. I think you're scared to put it on the line, and so you're hiding behind your stupid rule."

She raised an eyebrow, trying not to show how much the words stung. "Are you sure you're a guy? Because I don't think guys talk like that. Allison, yes. You—"

"Give it a rest, Marty," Ben said. "I'm right, and attacking me isn't going to change that."

Well, hell. How was she supposed to answer that? Especially since he was absolutely, positively right. She sure didn't want to give her cousin the satisfaction of saying so though.

"Marty?"

She heaved her arm back and tossed the rest of her hot dog across the stone courtyard. A dozen pigeons swooped down to attack the feast.

"Not hungry after all?"

"Damn it, Ben. You're right, okay? There. I said it."

He looked at her, wide-eyed. "Wow. I can't quite believe you said that out loud. You want to repeat it so I can get it on tape?"

"Oooooh, you!" She beat ineffectually against his arm with her fists, then dissolved into a laugh that was punctuated by tears. "Look at me! I'm an absolute mess. I *hate* this. I don't know what to do or what to say or—"

"Just tell him how you feel."

"Yeah, right. He's given me no indication he wants to take this further."

Ben crossed his arms and stared her down. "You're kidding, right? The guy spends every spare moment with you. He puts up with your wacky family, namely me and my hyperdriven toddler. Not to mention the way he looks at you."

Marty curled her toes in her shoes, desperately wanting to believe everything Ben was saying, but terrified of setting herself up for disappointment. "What if you're wrong?"

"I'm not. But even if he hasn't thought about it, that doesn't mean you can't put the idea in his head. All you have to do is tell him what you want. And then fight for it."

"Fight for it?"

Ben shrugged. "Sometimes men are idiots. I thought you knew that."

This time, her laugh was genuine.

Marty thought about it, and decided that maybe Ben was right. What did she have to lose—other than her self-esteem, of course? After all, she put her heart and soul into her work every day, then splashed it across the *Chronicle* for millions to read. She was used to setting herself up for humiliation. Could this be any worse?

It could, of course, but she was going to risk it anyway. Ryan was worth the risk.

"All right," she finally said. "I will."

"There you go," Ben said. "I'll even help you. He's coming over tonight, right?"

She nodded, wary.

"After the museum, I'll send Allison and Toby home, and I'll head back to your place with you. I'll help you figure out a late-night dinner menu that'll knock the socks off Kurt Russell."

Marty made a face, but in truth she was a tiny bit amused. Ben's reference to *The Computer Wore Tennis Shoes* really did fit Ryan to a *T*. And Ryan was at least as cute as the famous actor. As for the dinner, Ben was an amazing cook, whereas Marty could barely boil water. If he was offering to help, then maybe she could offer Ryan something more appealing than Kraft mac and cheese....

IN THE END, they decided on homey elegance. Roast chicken, rosemary potatoes, fresh bread (well, from a bread machine), steamed broccoli and a very expensive bottle of wine. The appetizer was a bit more tony, and at the moment, Ben had just finished showing her how to wrap a brie in filo dough.

"That should do you," he said. He leaned forward and gave her a kiss on the cheek. "Just tell the man how you feel. Allison told me, and I pretty much melted on the spot. Trust me. It works."

"Maybe. But I'm thinking I'll just play it by ear. I'll back off my widow's year plan, and if something develops, then it develops. I don't think I should force anything though. I'll just go with the flow."

"In other words, you're afraid that if you tell him you want more, he'll balk and run."

She scowled. "Something like that."

Ben laughed. "All right, all right. I'll quit bugging you. Just give it time. Don't go getting all paranoid and weird. You're a helluva catch. Sooner or later, he's going to realize that *he* wants more."

"The way Eli did?"

A flash of anger crossed his face on her behalf, and she felt a flood of warmth and thankfulness that she had Ben on her side. "Eli was an asshole," he said. "And that's being polite."

She nodded; she certainly wasn't going to disagree.

"Ryan's not an ass, at least not what I've seen so far."

Again, she nodded. Ben truly liked Ryan, who'd brought his little nephew Gizmo over to play with Toby last Saturday on one of Ryan's rare days off. Despite the two-year difference in ages, the kids had got along great, and both Ben and Allison had pulled Marty aside and expressed their approval of her latest romantic conquest.

"Just tell him," Ben repeated.

"We'll see," she said, not willing to commit to such an extravagant plan.

He headed out the door and Marty set in to wait. The chicken needed another hour in the oven, which meant it would be ready around 9:30, which was the time Ryan usually appeared on her doorstep. She understood what he did at work about as well as she understood her dad's job—i.e., not at all—but there was no mistaking that he was passionate about it.

At nine, she changed into a little black dress.

At nine-fifteen she tossed the dress in the back of the closet and put on jeans and a casual top.

At nine-thirty, she raced back to the bedroom, pulled off the jeans and slipped on a flirty summer dress. Nothing fancy, but not too down-home, either.

At nine-forty-five, she was pacing the kitchen.

At ten, she was beginning to get worried. She took the chicken out of the oven so it wouldn't get hard and stringy, but she laid foil over it so it would still be hot when Ryan finally got there.

By ten-thirty, she was seriously considering calling the cops. Or the hospitals. "Don't panic," she told the toaster. She stabbed some of the potatoes with a fork and shoveled them into her mouth. "He's fine," she said after she swallowed. "Houston traffic. He's probably stuck behind some construction crew in a cell phone dead zone."

Pretty lame, really, but it was the best explanation she could come up with on short notice.

Flustered and out of sorts, she headed back to her bedroom to check the answering machine. She would have heard it ring, but you could never be too careful....

As it turned out, the power light on the all-in-one cordless phone and answering machine was blinking, a tell-tale sign that there'd been a power surge and the entire piece of crap system needed to be reset.

Usually, this irritated the hell out of her. Right then, though, she wanted to kiss the machine. *He'd tried to call!* Of course he had. He'd tried to call, and he couldn't get through. A simple, elegant explanation.

She sat on the edge of the bed, relief flooding through her. If he'd called her house and gotten nothing, the next thing he'd try would be—

She scrambled for her purse, hating the way her blood was pounding in her ears and feeling like a high school sophomore with a crush. But there wasn't a thing she could do about it. And when she found her purse under a pile of discarded outfits, she heaved a huge sigh of relief. She rummaged in the bottom, finally coming up with her cell phone and—*yes!*—a single voice mail.

She pressed the speed dial, listened to her own spiel, punched in her pass code, and then closed her eyes in silent thankfulness as Ryan's smooth voice filled her ear. "Marty, sweetheart, I'm tied up at work. It's a huge project, and it's going to be a big drain on my time, but it's a huge opportunity, too. I'm sorry. I'll try to swing by if I can, but don't wait up for me."

And then he clicked off. She'd held her breath at the end, hoping he'd end with a casual "I love you," but he hadn't. Which wasn't a surprise since neither of them had said those words to the other yet. But what *was* a surprise was how much she'd been secretly hoping to hear those words. Because, dammit, somewhere in the midst of all this, she had fallen in love with him.

And damned if the day she realized that was the day that he decided not to come over after all.

She thought of Eli and fought a little shiver. This wasn't bad. Ryan wasn't leaving her. This was just work. Just normal day-to-day stuff.

Heck, she couldn't even justifiably be angry with him. After all, dinner was a surprise. For all he knew, all he was missing was another late-night movie on AMC.

Just work. Not personal.

She repeated that to herself over and over.

If she said it enough, maybe she'd actually start to believe it.

HE NEVER CAME, of course, and four days later, Marty realized she'd been a fool for thinking he would. She'd clued in after he'd left her hanging for the second time, standing her up on even his simplest offer last night to "drop by and bring ice cream on the way home from work." They only lived ten miles from each other. He wasn't just standing her up; he was downright avoiding her. It was Eli all over again. But this time, it was hurt she felt more than anger. Dear Lord, it was like her insides were being ripped out every time he stood her up.

Of course, Ryan apologized profusely each time. "I've literally been sleeping at the office," he said. "It's insane here."

No, Marty thought. She was the insane one.

To his credit (Was she *really* letting the guy off the hook? Even a tiny bit?), he could tell she was upset. "I'm sorry," he'd said when he'd called her this morning. It was Saturday, and he'd called at seven, managing to wake her up. "Give me one more chance. I promise I'll come by this afternoon. I have to run some documents across town, and I'll pop in on my way. I'll only be able to stay a minute, but I really want to see you. I'll call you and let you know when, okay?"

Like a little puppy dog who'd been thrown a bone, she'd said yes. And now here she was, sitting not two feet from the phone. Her laptop was open on the desk, and she was supposed to be working on her profile of a local boy who'd just starred in his first major Hollywood movie. A nice interview piece that she could probably rework and sell to one of the celebrity magazines for another feather in her journalistic cap.

She should be all over the story. Instead, she was barely managing to drag out the words, too preoccupied with staring at the silent telephone. Already two-thirty and still no call.

A sick feeling started to settle in her stomach. She

wanted to kick herself. How stupid could she be? She'd told herself she wasn't going to fall for another man so quickly after Eli. And yet here she was, already in love with Ryan, and he was pulling the same crap Eli had. Only Eli had just up and left. Ryan was pulling slowly away, leaving her all alone to nurse a whole heartful of hurt.

Damn it all.

Enough. She wasn't going to think about it. She wasn't going to think about him. She wasn't even going to think about work. She was going to pamper herself and forget about everyone else.

Determined, she snapped her laptop shut, then moved to the living room. She popped in a DVD, poured herself a glass of peach-flavored wine, then settled on the couch. She didn't normally drink in the afternoon, but it was a beautiful summer Saturday. Besides, a nice glass of wine would take the edge off. And she desperately needed to relax.

Three glasses and two episodes of *Buffy the Vampire Slayer* later, her head was swimming, and Ryan was still right there at the top of her thoughts.

Dear Lord, she was a pathetic mess of mush.

Hugging herself, she eyed the phone, willing it to ring even as she imagined his smooth voice washing over her.

And then it rang!

She snatched it up, her entire body deflating when she recognized the voice at the other end of the line. "Oh," she said. "It's you."

Ben's laughter bounced across the phone line. "Sorry to disappoint."

Marty sighed. "Give me a break. I didn't mean it like that, and you know it."

"He hasn't called?"

"He's supposed to. Supposed to come over, too."

"And you're actually talking to me? I'm honored. What if he calls while I'm on the phone?"

"Not a problem," she said. "I have call waiting. Soon as it beeps, I'll drop you like a hot potato."

Ben laughed. "I was right. You do have it bad."

She took a deep breath and said, "Yeah. Yeah, I do."

"Wow," said Ben, obviously surprised that she'd admitted it. "So you forgave him for blowing you off last night?"

Forgave, no. Understood, maybe. "I—"

Beep.

"I've got to go." She stabbed the button without waiting for Ben to answer. "Hello? Ryan?"

His warm laughter bubbled over her, and she practically sagged in relief. "Hey there. It's great to hear your voice."

She leaned back, melting into her pillows as Ryan's voice filled her. "Hi. I've been looking forward to your call." Had she really said that? Gads, what a geek. "I'm looking forward even more to seeing you."

A pause, and Marty's fears started to fill the silence. She licked her lips. "Ryan?"

His words came on a heavy sigh. "Marty, you're going to kill me, but—"

"You're not coming." Her voice was flat, her eyes closed.

"I'm so sorry. Something's come up and I have to—"

"Just *don't*." She raised her hand in a "stop" gesture, as if the man could actually see her. "Just forget it, okay? It…it doesn't matter."

"Marty—"

She hung up. She didn't know what he was going to say, and she told herself she didn't care. A tear trickled down her cheek, and she brushed it away. This was for the best. She shouldn't have fallen for him.

After Eli, you'd really think that she'd have known better.

The tears flowed freely now, and she rubbed her hand under her nose, her tears making her all snotty and stuffed up. Damn the man. He was making her a total mess.

She got up and poured herself another glass of wine, determined to enjoy the evening without Ryan Kinsey. She didn't need him around to enjoy herself. She'd been doing perfectly fine before he'd weaseled his way into her life.

She channel surfed for a bit, surprised when she lifted the glass for another sip and found it empty.

She poured another glass and sipped again, pausing when the remote landed on the biography channel. Mel Gibson. That was worth a few minutes. And more wine.

By the time the credits rolled on Mel, she'd had another glass of wine and managed to work herself back up again. Ryan wasn't Eli. She'd never felt as close to someone as quickly as she had with Ryan. She'd fallen hard and fast, and until recently, she'd been certain he felt the same.

What was it Ben had said? That she'd have to fight for what she wanted?

Well, she wanted Ryan.

She poured the last dregs from her wine bottle into her glass, then took a long sip.

Yes, indeed. She wanted Ryan and, dammit, she wasn't going down without a fight.

CHAPTER FIVE

$$C_2H_5OH$$

RYAN STARED at the screensaver on his computer, the chemical symbols circling endlessly in a three-dimensional font. Ethanol. Not incredibly sexy as fuels go, but it was usable. And it was the first formula Ryan had ever memorized, all the way back at good old Mercy High School.

He'd picked the formula as his screensaver as much for nostalgia as for inspiration.

Today, he really needed some inspiration.

Unfortunately, lately he'd been sadly lacking in that ephemeral quality.

Edward slid through the doorway, his whole body vibrating with excitement. "They're here. Elise is making them comfortable in the conference room. You ready?"

"I better be," Ryan said. He wasn't, of course, but confidence was a good thing, and he intended to effuse it.

The "they" that Edward referred to were Alan Deary and Leo Martin, two of the NASA big shots—men who had some decision-making authority with regard to the contract Kinsey Applied was gunning for. They'd called a few hours earlier, saying that they wanted to come by and chat about the project. An "informal talk" they'd called it, but Ryan saw through the rhetoric. They wanted a sneak peek at what Kinsey was developing. And they wanted to see how the company—and Ryan—dealt with unexpected and possibly unwelcome surprises.

He intended to knock their socks off.

It was a plan, he thought, that would work much better if he'd found the elusive solution to his state-of-the-art antimatter-based propulsion system. Despite spending every waking hour, and getting very little sleep, there was still a piece of the puzzle missing. A containment factor that was absolutely necessary if he was going to submit a bid for the development of a feasible system to safely transport humans to the far reaches of the solar system.

"How's C group coming along?" Ryan asked, as he and Edward walked toward the conference room.

Edward sighed. "Kepler had the right idea, but none of our simulations are pulling together right."

Ryan nodded in understanding. In the 1600s, Johannes Kepler noticed the tail of a comet bending away from the sun and commented that sails should be fashioned to harness the heavenly breezes. The C Group—Edward's group—was working to do just that: create solar sails that would utilize the power of billions of photons zooming away from the sun. The project was coming along, but it was far from ready to be implemented on a broad scale.

No, the hope for the NASA contract lay with the two projects Ryan was overseeing: antimatter- and plasma-based propulsion.

For years, Ryan had been secretly toying with the theoretical ramifications of both methods. The very afternoon that Edward had brought in the letter from NASA, Ryan had halted all but the most essential work within the company and divided the research and development department into three teams, each with a directive to nail the various theories to the wall.

Ryan had assigned another scientist to lead up the plasma team, but he was personally heading up the antimatter project. And they'd almost—*almost*—nailed the containment problem. The answer was right there. So close he could almost touch it. And the really frustrating thing was that he was certain that he'd *had* the answer before. That he'd actually seen something that had triggered the synapses in his head. But whatever it was it was gone now.

That, however, was not information he wanted the NASA guys to be privy to.

No matter what, he had to make a good impression at this meeting. He had to get this contract. It was absolutely essential. Not only for his career, the company and his relationship with his dad, but also for his own satisfaction.

Day after day, he'd come into the office to sit at his cluttered gray metal desk in his small office, its walls covered not with pictures, but with chemical formulas and maps of the solar system. Why? Not for his dad. And not for the pleasure of winning a contract that some other company was bidding on.

No, it was so much more than that. It was the glory and wonder of space exploration! It had always held such huge fascination for him. And now this opportunity had dropped in his lap—the chance to be even a tiny part of something expansive enough to touch every life on the planet and the lives of those to come. To help implement something that might someday make it to the far reaches of the solar system, even the galaxy.

Maybe he'd watched too many *Star Trek* episodes as a kid, but to Ryan, space really was the final frontier. He wasn't naive enough to think that he'd ever go into space himself. But if he couldn't do that, he wanted to somehow be a part of it. A big part.

He wanted his name and his work remembered.

This contract was his ticket, and he fully intended to take the ride.

As they moved down the hallway, their assistant, Elise, ran up to greet them, looking a little befuddled.

Ryan frowned. "Everything okay? The guys settled in the conference room?"

"Oh, sure," she said. "They're fine. Nursing coffees, reading our brochure. It's just that—"

But she didn't need to finish, and Ryan held up a hand, silencing her. He knew what the trouble was. The trouble was standing right behind Elise.

Marty.

He must have said her name out loud, because she marched forward, her chin held high. She looked sexy and determined and mad as hell. And Ryan was struck by just how much he'd missed spending time with her.

He expected her to stop in front of him, but she didn't. Instead, she poked him in the chest with the tip of her finger. Hard.

"You and me, mister. We need to talk."

Beside him, Edward looked uncomfortable, and Elise faded gracefully back to the front office.

"This really isn't the time," Ryan said, wishing it was, but knowing he had his career, his staff's jobs and the company's financial security sitting in the front conference room.

"Make the time," she insisted.

He drew in a breath, wanting to kiss her hard and freeze this moment while he went off and dealt with the men in the conference room. That wasn't an option, though, so he sent Edward to go play host while he tried to wrap this up quickly. "Marty, look, I'm sorry I couldn't come. I've got this thing—"

"I know. This thing you can't talk about. Can't tell me. Can't share with me at all other than to say you have to work. Well, that's fine, Ryan, but there's something I want to say and you're just going to have to bear with me while I say it."

She'd moved even closer, and he could smell the fruity tinge of alcohol on her breath. He stifled a groan. He already knew that Marty was a total lightweight where alcohol was concerned. If she'd been sitting home stewing about him not showing up and drinking fruity wine…

"It's after five on a Saturday, Ryan," she went on, before he could think of anything to say. "Work is fine, but, what? You can't take a break? You can't take five stupid minutes to go visit your girlfriend or even one minute to drop by with a flower or something?" She sniffed, her eyes glassy with tears. His stomach twisted.

"God, Marty," he said, his voice pitched soft and calming. "Don't you think I want to?"

"Ryan—"

He pressed a finger over her mouth. He couldn't hear any more. Couldn't feel guilt about being an asshole. Not right then. Not now. "Look," he said. "If you want to wait for me in my office, do that. I'll be in right after I finish this up. But I have a meeting. It's important."

She flinched as sharply as if he'd slapped her. "Important," she repeated, then nodded slowly. "Right. Of course." She hooked her purse over her arm. "I'm sorry. I was stupid. I shouldn't have come."

And then she was gone, her heels clicking on the polished floor as he looked after her in shock, wondering what the hell he'd said. What he'd—

Shit. "Important," he'd said. As if she wasn't. And he'd said it right after she'd used the word "girlfriend." Shit, shit, shit.

Never once had she called herself his girlfriend. Never once had he really had an inkling of where she thought they were or where she thought they were going. She'd picked today to tell him how she felt, and then to tell him in a roundabout way at that.

He took a step in the direction she'd gone, then stopped himself. *No*.

He'd meant what he'd said. This meeting was important. He'd handle it, and then he'd head over to Marty's house and try to figure out some way to make it up to her.

But when he walked through the doors and saw those men in suits sitting there, something shifted inside him. *Important,* she'd said. And right then, he knew what was really important.

"Gentlemen," he said, "I hope you'll forgive me, but I have a personal emergency." He gestured toward his brother. "You're in good hands with Edward. In the meantime, though, let me assure you that Kinsey Applied is up to the task. If you want the project details, however, you're just going to have to wait for our actual proposal."

He turned then and walked out, the memory of the men's faces—surprised, intrigued and a little bit impressed—burned on his brain. He didn't have time to analyze though. Had he just made a huge career mistake? Or had he shown such unwavering confidence that the contract was surely locked in?

He didn't know, and at the moment he didn't care. All he could think about was Marty.

And the truth was, opening his mind back up to her felt pretty damn good.

THE SOFT TAP on the door woke Marty and she sat bolt upright, then immediately regretted the motion as her head spun and her stomach churned.

Oh, God...

She pressed her hand over her mouth, her nausea caused just as much by her absurdly bitchy and over-the-top behavior at Ryan's office (Had she really gone there? Had she really accosted him in front of his co-workers?) as it was by her foray into the joys of peach-flavored wine.

She'd rushed home, filled with mortification, Ryan's blank stare as she'd called herself his girlfriend swelling to monsterlike proportions and completely filling her brain. She'd so desperately wanted him to hold her, to tell her that he loved her and that she was special and that, of course, she was his girlfriend. Instead, he'd suggested that she wasn't even important. With those ill thoughts swirling in her head, she'd promptly fallen asleep on the couch.

More nausea. Dear Lord, she was in a bad way.

Another tap at the door, and she jumped, suddenly reminded of what had awakened her in the first place.

She caught a glimpse of herself in the mirror over the couch as she passed by on her way to the door. Her makeup was smudged and her hair was a mess. Just as well. She wasn't in the mood for visitors. If she scared them off, then all the better.

Her front door didn't have a peephole, so she called

out, "Who's there?" and paused, her hand on the door-knob as she waited for an answer.

When it came, she drew in a startled breath, her pulse picking up tempo, and when she closed her hand over the knob, she realized her palm was sweating. All from two little words: "It's Ryan."

Her first instinct was to run. Her second, to run a comb through her hair and put on some makeup. She ignored both. Why should she run? And why on earth did she care what she looked like? She was over him. *Over*. Or, if not, she should be.

With a deep breath for courage, she tugged open the door. And there he was. All six foot something of him, with those dark eyes and sandy brown hair. Perfectly groomed and perfectly gorgeous. He looked like the president of a fraternity, not a chemical engineer with a Master's degree in aeronautical engineering and astrophysics and a bunch of other stuff she'd neither understood nor could remember.

He cleared his throat, and she realized she'd been standing there staring at him. Damn. So much for cool sophistication.

"Can I come in?"

She stood back, holding the door open. "Suit yourself."

For a moment they stood awkwardly in the hallway. She wanted to reach out and touch him, to prove to herself that he was real, but that wasn't her place, and it really didn't matter. She didn't know why he'd come, and she wasn't about to get her hopes up. For all she knew, he just wanted to retrieve the toothpaste he'd left on her bathroom counter.

He swung a thumb toward the living room. "Um, do you mind?"

She shook her head and followed, perching on the edge of the uncomfortable wooden chair she kept meaning to paint. He settled on the couch, nervously pressing his hands against his legs, then clasping them together, then pressing them into the couch cushions.

"So," she said, after she couldn't take it any longer. Her own hands were pressed between her knees. "What brings you here?"

"I wanted to see you," he said. He met her eyes and his jaw tightened. "No. I *needed* to see you."

Her breath hitched, and she tried to keep her voice nonchalant when she answered. "Oh? Why's that? Leave something here you need for work? Your periodic table maybe?"

He flinched as if she'd slapped him, and she immediately regretted the words. They'd popped out before she could think, and she'd give anything to call them back. She didn't want to antagonize him. She wanted to make up. She wanted *him*. No matter how much she wished she could deny it, that was the simple truth.

"I'm sorry," she said, twisting a strand of hair around one finger. She caught herself and jerked her hand down, sliding it under her thigh. "I didn't mean to be bitchy. It's just—"

"I deserve it." His mouth turned up in *that* smile. The

one that had sucked her in at the club. The smile that had gotten him in her bed.

She returned it with a genuine grin, a sudden warmth flooding through her veins. "Yeah, you do," she said, but her tone was softer. She licked her lips and looked down at her hands. "But I should never have bugged you at the office."

He shook his head. "No. I'm glad you did. I obviously needed the wake-up call."

She swallowed. "It's just that I missed you." She held her breath, hoping she hadn't said something stupid, hoping she hadn't given away too much.

When the response came, "I missed you, too," she sagged with relief.

"Forgive me?" he asked. He'd gotten up from the couch, and now he stood in front of her, his hand outstretched for her to take.

She took the hand he offered, letting him pull her up into his arms. "There's nothing to forgive," she said. "Truly. I was … unfair. I shouldn't have put you on the spot."

"It was a slap in the face, all right," he said, but he was grinning. "But I needed to feel the sting. I was working on something incredibly important to me, and forgetting that there are other things in my life that are also important. Like you."

His brown eyes bore into hers, and she swallowed, her entire body flushing with a pleasure as warm and gooey as melted caramel. "Yeah?"

"Yeah," he said. Then he held out his arms, and she moved easily into them.

"What time is it?" she asked, snuggling closer, her head resting on his shoulder. Despite her nap, she still felt tired, and now a languid warmth had settled inside her. She wanted just to hold onto this man forever.

"About six-fifteen."

She pulled away, her sudden motion fueled by surprise. "That can't be right. I'm sure I slept for more than ten minutes!"

He grinned. "I have no idea how long you napped for, but I can tell you that I came straight from the office. Well, I stopped to buy you flowers."

She narrowed her eyes. "Where are they?"

"I thought you'd think they were a bribe, so I left them in the car."

"Roses?"

"Of course."

"A dozen?"

"Absolutely."

She nodded, fighting a smile. "Well, okay then." The smile turned into a frown as another thought occurred to her. "But your meeting. Isn't it incredibly important? Was it over that fast?"

"It was incredibly important, and I don't know how long it lasted because I left."

"But—"

He pressed a finger to her lips. "But you're important, too. And I wanted to make absolutely certain you realized that."

"I— Oh, Ryan…" His name came out on a single breath, and she closed her eyes, suddenly completely happy. "I'm so, so sorry. I shouldn't have bugged you. Your work *is* important, I'm sure of it, even if you can't tell me what you're doing."

"I shouldn't," he said, "for a lot of different reasons." And then right after that, he said, "We're pitching a NASA contract. Innovative propulsion methods. Very complex, very cutting edge, very newsworthy. And your dad's bidding, too."

"And you were afraid I'd either run a story or tell my dad." The words came out flat, and Marty realized she wasn't entirely sure how she felt about this latest bombshell.

"I'm sorry."

She nodded slowly, processing. "You didn't trust me," she said, a finger of hurt snaking up her back.

"No." He shook his head slowly. "*No*. I never believed you would run a story, but the bid was supposed to be confidential. And, yes, I was afraid if I told you anyway, you might slip up and say something to your father." He met her eyes. "*Him,* I don't trust."

"I hardly ever talk to the man. You know that."

Ryan shrugged. "He's still your dad. No matter how much distance, the relationship is still there."

"Spoken like a man who knows."

He nodded, but didn't say anything else.

She licked her lips. She wanted to believe him—oh, how she wanted to believe him. And what he said made sense. She may not have covered much hard news, but she'd protected her sources in the past, and she knew well the danger of a leak. That he might consider *her* a leak stung, but that didn't mean she didn't completely understand. She drew in a breath, released it, then faced him. "And now? Why are you telling me now?"

"Those men—the ones I was supposed to meet with—they're the guys who'll ultimately decide who gets the contract."

She was taking in everything he said, but finding it hard to process. Suddenly, though, it clicked, and she snapped fully to attention. "You came here instead of meeting with the NASA folks?" That couldn't possibly be right. She must have heard wrong.

"I needed to see you."

Oh, dear Lord. A tear snaked its way down her cheek, her emotions a mass of delight and horror. "But…but… but you need the contract. You can't just…I don't want you to…" She trailed off, her hands fluttering as she tried to pull thoughts from the air.

He kissed her forehead, amusement and love shining in his eyes. "Don't worry. I left them in good hands with Edward."

"But shouldn't you have been there?"

"Probably." He smiled. "Actually, this may work out even better. Our most promising method right now is the antimatter propulsion system—"

"Like *Star Trek?*"

He laughed. "Something like that, yeah."

"Wow." She knew her dad was working in propulsion techniques, but she didn't think he'd advanced as far as the realms of science fiction turned fact. Oh, he'd worked with antimatter before. *That* much she knew. But he'd certainly never managed to harness it or use it for propulsion. No wonder Ryan was worried about Harold Chamberlain latching on to the concept. "Antimatter," she repeated. "You've really managed to use antimatter for propulsion?"

"In theory, yes. And if we can get the details worked out, it's an excellent propulsion mechanism. As it stands, antimatter offers the greatest specific impulse of any currently available propellant. Lots of labs are working on antimatter, but the problem is storage. I'm close to figuring out a storage method that blows the lid off of anything out there. Totally revolutionary."

She shook her head, smiling. "I have absolutely no idea what you're talking about, but if I'm getting the gist of it, you've solved some huge scientific problem, and it'll help out NASA and space travel and the whole shebang. And if anyone else knew what you were working on—like, for example, my dad—it might trigger their own work in that direction, and they might find the answer before you do."

He laughed. "Pretty much. The problem is, I'm missing a piece. In the lab, on the computer, there's just something I can't get, and without that piece, we're not going to get the contract."

She'd never understand quite what he was doing, but she reached out and took his hand. "You'll get it. You're brilliant. I'm sure you'll figure it out."

"Thanks for the confidence. I appreciate that." His smile was quick and bright. "And the truth is, in a way you probably saved me. Antimatter is my project. So if I'm with you, I can't answer any questions the NASA guys might have. Edward can just tell them that all is on track, and everyone will be happy."

"And that will work?"

"For a few more days it will. If I don't have the answer by the proposal deadline, there will be no hiding the truth. And no way we'll get the contract."

"Oh." She wished she could help. Ryan's goal was exactly the kind of thing that her mom had dreamed for her and that her dad was sure she'd never accomplish. A chance to make a mark on humanity. Her brain didn't work like that, though, and all she could do was kiss his cheek and let him know she believed in him.

They stood there for a while, locked in a silent embrace. He stroked her arm with his forefingers, and her already heated blood started to boil. Her nipples tightened into hard nubs, and she pressed her legs together tight, both fighting and enhancing a growing pressure at the apex of her thighs.

She ought to tell him to go back to work, to solve his problem and come back when it was done. She should tell him she believed in him and then tell him to go.

But the words wouldn't come. She wanted this man.

Had been craving him for days, actually. And now he was here. Warm and willing and oh, so tempting.

It would be absurd to push him away. Absurd. Ridiculous. Utterly foolish.

Marty might be a lot of things, but she certainly wasn't a fool. And as she lifted her head to meet his lips, her mind cleared of all but one thought: if this was a mistake, being wrong had never felt so good.

Her fingernails dug into his shirt as he pulled her closer, his mouth taking hers passionately, almost violently. God, how she wanted this release.

He was right here, touching her in all the right places. His hands stroking her. His lips crushing against her. His body pressed tight against hers.

"Marty," he murmured, his breath hot against her ear. "Dear God, Marty, I've missed you."

Her heart fluttered with the words and she snuggled closer. "I'm glad you came." It was an understatement, but she hoped he understood how much she meant the words.

"I'm glad I came, too."

"Yeah?" She realized she was grinning and felt utterly goofy, but she couldn't help it. He'd come back and she was happy, and that's just the way it was.

She took his hand and gave a little tug. "Come on. There's no sense standing in the hallway. Do you want something to eat? Some wine? A beer?"

"All I want right now is you."

"Oh." A quick trill of delight shot up her spine. "Well, that's okay, too."

And then he was right there, his lips on hers, his hands stroking her. She closed her eyes and let her head fall back, lost in the pleasure of his touch. His hands slid down her body until his fingers found the hem of her T-shirt. And then his thumbs stroked her skin, his hands moving up. With his palms on her belly, his fingers teased the soft flesh of her breasts. She wasn't wearing a bra, and when his thumb stroked her nipple, she cried out with a pleasure that was dangerously close to pain.

"Ryan…"

"Hush." One hand was no longer in her shirt—she was having a hard time keeping track of his touches— and suddenly she felt the pressure between her legs, his hand stroking her through the thick material of her jeans. Oh, dear Lord, she was going to lose it right there.

She lifted her hips, the motion automatic as her body responded not to her thoughts but to his touch. She wriggled a little, wanted to feel the pressure of the denim seam *right there*. She wanted to close her hand over his, to show him exactly where to press, exactly where to stroke, but at the same time she wanted to draw the moment out. Wanted to lose herself in the slow build of excitement as he teased and tormented her.

And then his hand was gone and she gasped, a soft sound of frustration stifled only by his lips pressing against hers. He laid her back on the couch, and she realized that his hand hadn't traveled far. Now it was on the button of her jeans. Now it was on her zipper. And now—oh, sweet heaven—his fingers were sliding under the band of her skimpy satin panties.

He stroked her, his fingers gliding over her already damp curls and finding her spot, *that* spot. He stroked and caressed her at the same time his lips danced over the soft skin at her throat. She heard a tiny mewling noise and realized it came from her.

She was close, so close, and she didn't want his touches to stop. She wanted more. Wanted everything. Wanted to explode right there in his arms.

Almost desperately, she shifted her legs, opening them wider even as she lifted her hips. He groaned, then. A low growling noise that seemed to come from deep in his throat and that turned her on almost as much as his touch.

He continued to stroke her and she writhed against him. She was on the brink, and she closed her eyes, letting her mind and body float away, his touch the only thing real in the world. His touch. His hands.

Her Ryan.

And then he touched her just so, and suddenly she wasn't thinking anymore. Not in words, not in images, not in anything. Instead she was simply exploding, her entire body undone by the pleasure of his touch.

As wave after wave of orgasmic pleasure pummeled her body, he held her close, whispering softly in her ear, urging her to lose herself to his touch.

She didn't need the encouragement, and when the last tremors finally settled, she exhaled, long and loud, and laid back on the couch, boneless and sated.

"Did you like that?" His grin was playful.

She shrugged, her own grin matching his. "Not sure. I really can't remember it. Maybe we ought to try it again and find out."

He trailed a finger down between her breasts. "I think that could be arranged...."

But she caught his finger as it grazed her belly button. "No, no, no," she said. "As much as I'd like that, I think it's your turn."

He raised his eyebrows, looking at her in mock seriousness. "Oh really?"

She sat up, shifting herself on the couch until she was straddling him, her knees on the cushion on either side of him. "As a matter of fact, yes." She pressed a finger to her cheek and cocked her head, hoping she looked suitably minxish. "What to do…what to do?"

His eyes danced with amusement, and she poked him lightly in the chest.

"You have a suggestion? After all, I aim to please."

"I seem to recall a certain treasure trove," he said, his eyes darting toward the bedroom where she kept a shoebox filled with decadent and sensual things like the Kama Sutra oil they so often indulged in.

"Oh really?" She pitched her voice high, unable to disguise the hint of laughter. "Well, we'll just have to see what delights are in store for you, won't we?"

She made a production of sliding off his lap, her whole body overflowing with the delight of playing with him. She felt such an easiness with this man. None

of the shyness she'd often felt with other lovers. Even
Eli. She'd never quite been herself with him, a perverse
shyness always washing over her in bed despite dating
him for so long.

She led Ryan into the bedroom and then nodded toward the bed. "You. Up there. I'll see what delights I
can pull from my treasure chest of fun." She started to
head toward her dresser and the shoebox that still sat
next to her hope chest, but Ryan shook his head.

"Oh no. I get to help pick it out."

She laughed. "Just a bit of a control freak?"

"Guilty." He stood next to her, and as she opened the
shoe box, she realized that he was no longer watching her.
She turned, and saw that he was staring at the hope chest.

"Ryan?"

He blinked.

"Ryan," she repeated. "You still with me?"

"Sorry. There's just something…" He ran his hand
over the chest's curved top. "I don't know. I just can't
shake the feeling that I'm missing something important."

"Your meeting?"

"No." He shook his head, his face clearing. "Something about your hope chest. Maybe something I read
or something I saw…"

She perked up, instantly interested. "Did you research it for me? The mechanism, I mean."

"No, not yet." He moved his finger as if to open the
box. Nothing happened, of course. "One day I will,
though. It's just too damn fascinating."

She couldn't argue with that. And the mystery of what made the latch work was certainly ripe territory for a scientist.

Knowing Ryan would get a scientific thrill, she pushed his hand aside, then opened the box herself with one fluid motion. He just shook his head, totally bewildered.

"I just don't get it. I mean, this thing is an antique. The science behind this thing must be amazing. You're sure I can't—"

"Enough with the chest, already," she said with a laugh. "No taking it apart and analyzing it. No dissecting it. You can try to figure it out in theory if you want to, but *not right now*." She gave him a playful smack, and he backed away from the hope chest, his hands up in a show of surrender.

"That's better," she said. She crooked a finger. "Now come here. I have other plans for you."

CHAPTER SIX

HE'D KNOWN he wanted her, but it wasn't until she was in his arms that he realized how much he'd missed her touch. How much he craved the feel of her skin next to his. He couldn't explain it, didn't even want to analyze it. He was a scientist, after all, but this wasn't the time to think about chemicals and pheromones and animalistic mating rituals.

He didn't want to think about anything but Marty, in his arms, naked.

She stroked a finger down his chest, lower and lower until it was all he could do not to grab her, throw her back on the mattress and lose himself in her right then.

"Uh-uh," she said, apparently reading his mind. "I get to have my fun first." She eased him down so that he was lying on the bed. She straddled him, then reached over to pull a silk scarf off her bedside table.

She teased him with it, trailing it along his neck, over his shoulders. He closed his eyes, the soft, cool material refreshing against the heat of his body. He smiled to himself, wondering what other treasures they might explore from her secret stash. He pictured the shoe box filled with tiny bottles of massage oil right next to the hope—

The chest!

The realization ripped him from his languid reverie, and he sat up. He must have been a sight, his body tight and hard, desperate for Marty, and his eyes wide with surprise.

"Ryan?" Alarm colored her features. "Ryan, are you okay?"

"Your chest." He searched her face as if it held the answers he was searching for. "I need to see the inside of your hope chest."

Confusion flitted across her features. "What? Why?"

"Please," he said, taking her hand. "Please just let me see it."

MARTY'S CHEST tightened with an unexplainable fear as she stood in front of the box, her finger pressed against it. It opened, and she stepped back, letting Ryan have access.

A soft curse escaped his lips. "Dear God," he said, "this is it. This is really it."

She shook her head, baffled. "What? What is it?"

"I thought there was something familiar the first time I saw it, but I didn't get a close look, and later I didn't make the connection. I can't believe I didn't see…" He was talking to himself, and she moved in front of him, determined to grab his attention.

"Ryan! What?"

"These markings," he said. "The pattern in the inlay. It's an odd script, so I couldn't read it that clearly, just enough to know it was a mathematical formula. And this," he pointed to another area, "is a chemical equation. And damned if they both don't impact my research."

That made no sense whatsoever. "You've got to be kidding. This thing was made hundreds of years ago. How could there possibly be stuff in here that has to do with antimatter?"

"I don't know, but it's here." A quick frown. "Not all of it, though." He reached out. "Maybe there's more under the inlay, where you found the journal."

Without thinking, she smacked his hand away. A wave of anger and hurt had flared up, firing her blood and making her practically quiver with pent-up emotion. "*This* is why you came back. Dammit, I should have known! You ignore me and ignore me and ignore me, and then suddenly you realize the error of your ways? I don't think so!"

He flinched. "Marty, no! You came over, I realized I'd been an ass, and I—"

"Don't even," she said. Tears filled her eyes, and she mentally kicked herself for being so stupid. "Maybe seeing me reminded you. Kickstarted something in your brain, but dammit, Ryan, I was the last thing on your priority list and then suddenly I'm the first. And *then* you realize that, oh gee, maybe I have the answer to your prayers. I may not be as smart as you and my father, but I'm not stupid."

He stared at her, something dark and disturbing in his eyes. "You may not be stupid," he finally said, "but right now you're not being very smart either."

She clenched her fists, determined not to cry, then pointed toward the door. "Go."

"Marty, goddamn it. Didn't you tell me you wanted to make a difference? Wanted to prove your mom right and show your father that you can? *This* will make a difference. Space travel. Space exploration. I swear to you the answer is somewhere in those equations, in those symbols. You couldn't ask for a bigger contribution to history or mankind."

It was her turn to flinch against his words, and she shook her head slowly. "That's not me doing anything except handing over a box."

"But if you don't hand it over—"

"Then you or someone else will still figure it out. You told me yourself how close you are. How close the other labs are." She clenched her fists, steeling herself in anger. "But don't worry. I won't show my dad either."

He just shook his head, and she could almost see the frustration coloring his complexion. "Marty. Damn it, I love you!"

She let the words flow over her, wishing with every ounce of her being that he'd said them before he'd lunged for her hope chest. Because now was too late. Now, she just couldn't believe. Now, he was just saying it to get what he wanted. "Please," she whispered. "Please, just go."

This time, he went.

And as the front door closed behind him, Marty fell onto the bed, buried her face in her pillow, and wept.

SHE DIDN'T TRUST HIM. That one fact kept spinning through Ryan's mind as he sat in his office staring at his notes.

He'd tried to write down everything he remembered from the inscription inside the box, and the equations had sparked a plethora of additional thoughts and theories. But no answer. No matter how many different angles he tried, he still couldn't quite figure out how to approach the problem, much less how to solve it.

And it wasn't just the problem of how to solve the antimatter propulsion problem. Ryan was also struggling with the problem of Marty.

He'd told her he loved her, and she'd thrown his words back in his face. And the hard, sad truth? He really couldn't blame her. He'd never said the words before. Not until she'd kept the box from him. Then suddenly the words had flown off his tongue.

What an asshole he'd been. And he had no idea how to make it better. He did love her, but he'd blown it.

Now he didn't have Marty, he didn't have the hope chest and he didn't have the answer. Any hope he'd had of winning the contract was spiraling down the drain and even though he was going to work his tail off until the proposal was due, Ryan already knew he wouldn't find the answer. The equations from the box were complex, pulling in formulas and theories that Ryan had never seen before, had never even contemplated. Extensions of his own theoretical calculations, but so much more sophisticated. If he had time…

But he didn't.

He couldn't give up, though. If there was even the slightest chance, he had to take it. And so he was going to buckle down and attack the formula.

And only when he'd solved the mystery or time had run out, he'd turn to the mystery of Marty. Somehow he'd get her back. Because Ryan may not know the key to the antimatter problem, but he did know that he didn't want to live without Marty in his life.

CHAPTER SEVEN

MARTY SIMPLY COULDN'T shake her funk. No matter what she did, her thoughts kept coming back to Ryan.

He'd used her. Tried to play off her need to hear those three little words. And that was what really made her stomach hurt.

She knew it was ridiculous to be so completely flummoxed by a relationship, but she was. She should never have gone home with him from the club that day. And she certainly should never have let him into her life. She should have stuck like glue to her widow's year.

Instead, she'd opened her heart. And Ryan had walked all over it.

For the past two days, she'd called in sick at work. It was near the truth; she was definitely heartsick. And she'd spent her time away from the office doing such highly productive things as vegging on the couch, watching really bad television and eating chips, ice cream and frozen cookie dough. She'd probably gained five pounds, and she now knew more about the folks on *General Hospital* than she really wanted to know.

The trouble was, she didn't feel any better. Ryan still

filled her head, and now the anger had dissipated, replaced by both a sadness and a longing so fierce it was almost physically painful.

He'd hurt her, yes. But still she wanted to see him again. Wanted it so badly should could almost taste it. Wanted it so badly, she was almost—almost—willing to take him the box.

But not quite.

She sat on the couch a bit longer, feeling at loose ends. Now, though, the box was on her mind, and so she got up and plucked it off the dresser, then perched on the edge of the couch.

The hope chest had been part of her life for as long as she could remember, and although she *knew* it was a bit magical, her heart had never really processed the fact. To her, it was simply her heritage. To Ryan, it was a scientific wonder. Now, Marty tried to see it through a scientist's eyes.

The mechanism *was* unusual. And if what Ryan said was true, the markings on the interior of the box had no business being present on something so old. The thing really was a mystery—and right then she wanted nothing more than to share the mystery with Ryan.

She shoved the thought away, along with the wave of sadness it provoked.

That thought was replaced by another: if the markings really could help Ryan, then maybe she should—

No. She didn't need to help him. She didn't owe him anything.

Frustrated, she tugged at the inset, revealing the hidden journal. Even though it was battered and hard to read, just holding it made her feel better. It was somehow comforting to touch a piece of history from someone in her family who really *had* made a difference, and had made it on her own terms.

Except this time, the journal felt different.

Squinting, she looked down. How odd. She couldn't put her finger on it, but the water-stained cover of the tiny notebook seemed slightly less mottled than before. She flipped it open, and then gasped in surprise.

It wasn't the same!

Not the words, not the ink, not anything.

What the hell was going on? How could the journal just change like that? Were there two? Had she somehow managed in all these years to never notice this one?

It was an absurd theory, and she didn't really believe it. Especially when she actually read the faded ink of the page open in her hand:

They've reduced our rations again, and of course we cannot complain. I recall reading about slave labor so many years ago on Earth. Never once did I believe that in this day and age such a thing could happen. But it has, and it is my life. I don't believe it was supposed to be like this. Something in my heart says this is wrong. And so I'm going to take a great risk and try to send a message....

The rest was too garbled to read.

Marty felt sick.

This couldn't be real; the journal couldn't have *changed!* And yet there seemed to be no other explanation. Ryan had been right: the equations and markings hadn't originated with one of her ancestors. They'd originated with one of her descendents. Somehow, someway, one of Marty's descendents had sent the hope chest back through time.

How was that possible?

She didn't know, and once again she craved Ryan's presence. If ever there was a question for a scientist…

She shook her head, trying to clear her thoughts. The chest was sent from the future to the past. She didn't know why, but she did know that for some reason, the future had changed. The optimistic message of colonization was now replaced by a message of despair and desolation.

Why?

It was a rhetorical question, because Marty knew the answer. *Her.* Marty Chamberlain. She'd chosen not to give the chest to Ryan. Without it, he never figured out the answer to his antimatter issue. As a result, he didn't win the NASA contract. Somehow another power won this new space race, and Marty's descendants were at their mercy.

That wasn't something that she could live with.

But what could she do? She'd already made her decision. History had already been changed.

Her entire life, she'd wanted to make a difference, and apparently she had. Oh, boy, had she ever. She'd not only had an impact on the world, she'd changed the future. And not for the better, at least not for her family. *Shit*.

Tears stung her eyes, and she could practically hear her father's voice, telling her that she'd screwed up once again.

No. But what could she do?

There isn't anything to do, a little voice inside her said.

But the little voice was wrong. It had to be. And Marty knew exactly what she had to do. She just wasn't sure she wanted to.

RYAN STARED at the phone on his desk, still not quite sure he'd properly processed Elise's words. "Come again?"

"I said that Marty Chamberlain is here to see you."

"Right. Thanks. Send her in."

He stood up, then swept a hand over his desk, knocking the collection of fast-food containers into the trash. He'd been living at the office for days now, trying to figure out what he was missing. The code in the chest took his own theories to the next logical, if highly innovative, extreme. But still, that one piece of the puzzle evaded him.

A piece that Marty could so easily share with him.

Was that why she was there?

He didn't have long to wonder because she walked through the doorway, a large totebag slung over one arm, and her eyes looking everywhere but at him.

"Hi," she said to the floor.

"Hi," he said, surprised by the flood of desire that hit him. Not a sexual desire. Just a desire to have her in his life again. Forget the equations, forget the chest.

All he wanted to think about was Marty. "What can I do for you?"

He indicated a chair, and she sat down, the tote bag perched securely on her lap.

"I need to tell you a story," she said. "And I need you to believe me."

As a conversational opener, that one got his attention. "All right," he said. "Tell me."

And she did. A fantastical story of changes in the very fabric of time. When she was done, he just stared at her, not quite willing to believe he'd heard what she was saying. More than that, not quite willing to believe the story.

"You don't believe me," she said.

He shook his head automatically. "No," he said. "When you tell me something, I believe it." Her eyes widened, and he realized with a start what he'd said. "I'm sorry," he said. "I shouldn't have said that."

She just sat there looking miserable. "It's okay. I deserved it. You told me that you didn't come for the chest, and I didn't believe you. I thought you'd pulled this whole sneaky routine and—"

"And now you know I was telling the truth?"

She nodded.

"Why?"

Her eyes went wide with surprise. "Isn't it obvious? We weren't supposed to have had that fight. You were supposed to have gotten the chest and figured it out and the world was supposed to turn out differently." She licked her lips. "It's like we're fated to be together, and I did something stupid and screwed up the natural order of things."

After all of that, there was no way that he could admit that he really was a little dubious of her whole story. Who wouldn't be? Rips in the fabric of time? Theoretically possible, yes, but…

He shook his head. "Let me see the journal," he demanded.

She complied, pulling it from the tote, and passing it to him. He took in the words, compared them to his memory of her earlier description, then swore softly under his breath.

"We can't let that happen," Marty said. She got up and put the totebag down on his desk. "Use it," she said. "Solve this thing, get the contract and make this right."

He looked in the tote, saw the hope chest sitting there in the dark recesses. She'd already opened that miraculous latch, and now the chest was propped open by a folded magazine, ensuring that he'd be able to get to the interior even if she wasn't there with him.

The thought didn't sit well, and he drew a breath, finally asking the one question that he'd wanted to voice since she'd walked into the room. "So, are we okay then? I mean, you and me. If we're supposed to be together…"

But his voice faded into a whisper as she shook her head, her eyes sad. "I'm sorry, Ryan. I…I…need a little time."

"What for? I love you, Marty. I thought you loved me."

"I thought I did, too." She blinked. "No, that came out wrong. I *do*. I guess I'm just not sure if it's real."

"What's more real than love?"

He watched as her brow furrowed, etching a little vee into the space above her nose. "You know how I wanted to make a difference? Well, I did all right. I did something so stupid it messed up the universe. And then I did something else. I fixed it. Or, at least, I think I'm fixing it. I guess we'll know soon enough."

"There's no guarantee, you know. Even with the chest, that doesn't mean it will all go back to right again."

"Please don't say that. It has to be all right. You have to make it all right."

He nodded. "I'll try, sweetheart."

She smiled, then. "Well, see? We're both getting what we wanted. We're both making a difference, contributing to history, all that jazz. Except I don't feel like it's really us doing it. We're just doing what fate says we're going to do."

Her words cut through him like a knife.

"It's not fate," he said "It's not preordained."

"No? Even with the journal? How can you say that?"

He shrugged. "How can it be? If you're really leaving me, I mean, then how can our future together have been preordained?"

She didn't answer, but she did pause in the doorway. And when she looked at him, he thought he saw interest—and hope—shining in her eyes.

Right then, that was the most that he could ask for.

RYAN CAREFULLY maneuvered the thin piece of metal, gently prying back the inlay to reveal the secret compartment where Marty had found the journal.

Almost reverentially, he removed the thin piece of polished wood, wood that had been designed to fit so well inside the chest that centuries had passed before anyone had even known it was there. Once the piece was removed, he simply held it, not quite able to turn it over and look at the symbols he knew were inscribed there. Damn it all. He needed to look, needed to study the equations and make progress.

Marty's words, though, played in his head. Just fate. Not really making a difference. Just playing some preordained role in the universe. Not his intellect. Not his theories. Not his work.

Damn.

His eyes drifted to the journal and a lump settled in his stomach. No matter what, he had to finish the work. He had to use the secrets hidden in Marty's hope chest to make this work, because there was no way he was letting that future stand. Not without a fight.

Determined, he turned the inset over and started copying the equations onto a notepad. At first, he thought the answer was right there, spelled out with a simplicity that made him feel like an idiot for not seeing it himself.

And then there was nothing more.

What the—?

He turned the inset over, examined the sides, the edges. Nothing. He opened the hope chest, peering up at the lid, hoping the rest of the equations and formulas were there.

They weren't. The solution was incomplete.

His stomach twisted. And at the same time that a cold, gray fog of dread settled over him, a ray of hope shone through. He really was going to have to figure this out himself after all.

He just hoped that he could do it in time.

As IT TURNED OUT, he just managed to make it. The proposal was due Friday at five. Friday at noon, Ryan finally figured out the answer. And once he'd seen it—once he'd turned the formulas on their side and looked at them from a different angle—well, then the answer seemed so simple he was embarrassed that it had taken days to figure out.

He chalked it up to lack of sleep and dove back into work, determined to get the proposal in tip-top shape before he e-mailed it to NASA.

At four-fifteen, he hit Send on the e-mail, the file with the proposal included as an attachment. At four-twenty, he received an acknowledgement back, along with a note letting him know he'd hear about the results of the selection process "soon."

He didn't know if he could bear the waiting.

At least there was one thing he *didn't* have to wait on. The journal sat on his dresser at home. He could go there, open the pages and see if the text had changed.

If, somehow, Ryan and Marty had managed to make the world right again.

He damn sure hoped so, because at this point, it was out of his hands.

He hoped fate was on his side. He hoped the world had shifted back into place, and he hoped Kinsey Applied got the contract.

But that wasn't what he wanted most of all.

What he really wanted was Marty. And no matter what, he intended to get her back.

AT ALL OF three years old, Ben's son, Toby, was a wild child. The kid stood on top of his little plastic playscape and waved at Marty. "See me! See me! I'm a tiger, Aunt Marty! I'm a big tiger!"

Marty laughed. "You sure are! You're the biggest tiger there is!"

Beside her, Allison laughed. "Yesterday, he was an elephant, and the day before, he was a garbage truck. That was actually pretty cool, because he cleaned the entire living room floor. Too bad it didn't last."

Marty smiled and hugged herself. She'd been spending more and more time with Ben, Allison and Toby, and the truth was, she was really starting to doubt herself. Every time she looked into the backyard, she saw a little boy who looked like Ryan. And every time she passed a mirror in their house, she saw the shadow of Ryan's reflection behind her.

Had she made a huge mistake walking out?

She was beginning to think she had, especially since she may have—oh, well, just screwed up the fabric of time.

She gnawed on her lip. At least she'd tried to set it right. But even now, she didn't know if Ryan had managed to interpret the formula. And even if he had, how could she know for certain that was the road back to making everything all right in the universe? She hoped so, but…

With a sigh, she turned to Allison. "Do you ever feel like you're not going to make an impact on the world?"

Allison laughed, which wasn't really the response Marty expected. "No way." She pointed toward the playscape. "I've already made an impact."

Marty looked at the toddler dubiously, then opened her mouth to protest. She didn't say anything, though, because just as the words were about to come out, she realized how wrong her thinking was. Who's to say what will change the world? She'd had a fight with her lover, and the world had shifted. Maybe Toby would grow up and cure cancer. Maybe one of her articles would change someone's life. "Yeah," she said softly. "I guess you have."

Allison shot her a gentle smile, then crossed the lawn to gather up her little boy, leaving Marty to her own thoughts.

The truth was, she had no idea what had changed in the world since she'd joined the population. Sure, reviews of the Children's Museum might not be earth-shattering, but maybe some parent had seen her article and taken a child who otherwise wouldn't have ever visited the place. And maybe her article on literacy inspired someone to help an illiterate friend. Who knew? The point was that maybe Ben was right. Perhaps the world was more Capraesque than she'd thought, and maybe she really was Jimmy Stewart. Or at least Donna Reed.

Too bad she didn't have a guardian angel. She could really use a Clarence right now. Someone who could bring Ryan to her side so that she could tell him what an idiot she'd been and make everything right again.

And then she saw the figure moving across the lawn toward her. *Ryan.* Her heart skipped a beat. Maybe she didn't need that guardian angel after all. Or maybe he was at her shoulder right now, working overtime.

"I thought I'd find you here," he said, his mouth curving up into a smile.

"I'm glad you came. I wanted—"

"Wait. Me first."

"Okay."

He lifted the journal. "Do you want to see?"

She eyed it uneasily, then took it from his hand. She waited a beat, but didn't open it.

"Aren't you going to look?"

She shook her head. "Not just yet. There's something I want to tell you first." She drew a deep breath. "I'm sorry. You're probably incredibly mad at me and it doesn't make any difference what I say, but I wanted you to know that I'm sorry. I should never have accused you of using me to get the chest, or of telling me you love me just to get what you want."

She blinked, then realized she was crying. Good lord, she was a bundle of waterworks lately.

"Oh, sweetheart." He stroked her cheek, then pulled her into his arms. "I should never have waited. I should have told you that I love you the minute I knew." He pressed his hands gently on either side of her cheekbones, then tilted her face up toward his. His eyes held no doubt. "I do. I love you. And I want you. I don't care about fate, I don't care about predestiny. I don't care. I just want you, and I'll do whatever it takes to get you back."

She smiled, a bubble of laughter rising in her chest. "Okay."

He squinted at her. "Okay?"

She nodded, happier than she could remember being in a long time. "Okay." She shrugged. "You've got me back."

His forehead furrowed. "Oh."

She laughed. "You sound disappointed."

"Not at all. I'm just readjusting. I was all prepared to fight dragons and scale mountains."

She leaned forward and kissed him. "No need to fight. You already have me."

He held her tight and she leaned against his chest with a sigh. Across the yard, Allison and Ben were grinning like fiends. Good. She snuggled closer, feeling completely loved and utterly happy.

"Aren't you going to look now?"

"Oh!" She'd actually forgotten the journal she still held tight in her hand. With a little nod, she stepped back from him, giving herself room to open the book, look and—

Thank goodness!

She smiled up at him. "You got the contract!"

He shook his head. "I don't know, actually. But I did figure out the formula. I guess that was enough."

"You'll get it," she said, then smiled. "I think it's predestined!"

He laughed. "Well, I hope so. But I honestly don't care. We did it. We made the world right again. All except for one thing."

She frowned, afraid something else had shown up in the journal. Some other piece of the future she'd managed to mess up. "What's not right?"

"Us," he said. "We won't be right until we're back together."

She stared at him, completely baffled. "But I just said so. You got me back, remember?"

"I mean completely. I love you, Marty. I want to be with you forever."

"Is that a proposal?"

She held her breath until he answered, and when he said, "Yes. Yes, it is," her entire body tingled with relief and love.

Before she could answer, he dropped to one knee, her hand in his. "Marty Chamberlain, will you marry me?"

Her mind screamed, *yes, yes, yes!* but she just smiled

coyly. "I guess I have to," she said. "From what I can tell, we're fated to be together."

"And that doesn't scare you?"

She shook her head, happier than she could ever remember being. "Not at all. I mean, really? Who am I to mess with fate? You just never know what might happen...."

TOMORROW'S PROMISE

Susan Kearney

CHAPTER ONE

Earth 2405

MARS WAS CALLING to Dr. Sara Tolliver in more ways than one. Feeling like a college student on her first day on campus, she anticipated her trip to Mars where she could put her degree in Martian archeology into practice. With lots of hard work and a little luck she could expand upon the discoveries Professor Dixon had already made on the planet's North Pole. She looked forward to reuniting with her former mentor, a man married to his archeology. However, she didn't intend to end up a salty old soul like Dixon, who might study the mating rituals of other peoples, but likely never experienced any sex firsthand. And since Mars was no longer considered a raw frontier, she planned to enjoy a social life along with her work, preferably with a man who didn't necessarily ask for more from her than great sex.

Studying relics was one of her passions, but she liked the old-fashioned physical kind of passion, too. In fact,

Sara impatiently contemplated being pursued—almost a guarantee due to the lack of available women on Mars. Although many women had ventured into space, the majority of the first Mars explorers had been male, and females remained a rarity among the planet's population. She liked the idea of having choices. There certainly hadn't been enough men in her life recently. Her colleagues believed she was too picky—that she shouldn't compare the Alpha men of history to the civilized men of today, but she disagreed. She just hoped the men on Mars might be more to her liking, individualistic, entrepreneurial, dynamic—not the I-want-to-get-in-your-head intellectual archaeologists that she tended to meet. Sara preferred a make-love-and-move-on kind of relationship to one that required…feelings. Feelings opened up too much risk of pain. And from the assortment of men around her right now, she suspected that she just might find a man to satisfy her needs—one who would overlook real intimacy for a good time and a willing partner.

One of only two women among twenty males in the boarding line for a rocketship, Sara appreciated the ratio in her favor, a reflection of the population of her soon-to-be home planet, Mars. Even in her baggy jumpsuit, she was drawing the attention of several hot-looking men.

Hmm. She could become accustomed to this kind of advantage. The men who surrounded her in the boarding line, tall men, short men, husky men, kept eyeing her as though she were a prize. One shot her a charming, knock-your-spacesuit-off smile, and she nodded back, but lost sight of him as her line advanced toward the ticket agent.

So far, Sara had no regrets about her imminent departure from Earth. The planet was overcrowded and even the oceans had few places left to discover. She craved the excitement of exploration, of seeing new sights and meeting new people, especially men who wouldn't be too demanding on her time. Sara was smart enough to comprehend that her fear of intimacy stemmed from the fact that everyone whom she'd ever loved had been taken from her. However, recognizing the source of her problem and eliminating it were two different things. While she couldn't change the way she felt, that didn't mean she had to be alone. She simply had to find a man who had a full life that kept him occupied when he wasn't sharing lusty companionship with her.

Filled with hope, eager to get to work, more than ready to leave her old life behind, Sara looked forward to her departure and her new life, which made the slowly moving line seem to creep.

"Next!"

Finally. Sara stepped forward, holding an heirloom that had been in her family for generations, a box that contained all her earthly possessions. With care she set the box on the scale, pleased when it weighed in at twenty-eight pounds, the maximum allowance for the Earth-to-Mars trip without paying a penalty.

Sara couldn't afford a penalty. She'd spent all her credit on the box's precious contents. Inside were computer chips that held her life's work, research and reference material, book and music chips, pen and paper and holographic scenery of Earth. She might not be able to take her favorite beach, Daytona, to Mars, but she'd carefully packed a vial of ocean water to help her remember the scent and a pinch of sand for the computer to replicate. She'd also brought thousands of e-books—romance, science fiction and fantasy—to keep her company in the Martian Outback. Among her luxury items were precious seeds to grow a variety of tropical flowers and plants as well as her ancestor's journal from the 1800s, several magazines that had sentimental value, her mother's dried wedding bouquet and her father's chronometer.

"Identichip, please."

Sara pressed her finger onto the access plate and the travel agent read her essentials. "Dr. Sara Tolliver. Martian archeologist. Age thirty-two. Single. No living relatives. No life insurance. Your will is in order. Residence on Mars?"

"Station 32."

"That area isn't open for colonization."

And Sara hoped the area would remain uninhabited for decades. Professor Dixon had told her the ancient ruins were extensive, and Sara's excitement rose every time she considered the alien art, exotic buildings and curious relics waiting to be uncovered, catalogued and studied. Sara had explored ancient pyramids in Egypt, the legendary Anasazi cliff dwellings in Mesa Verde and the mystery of Tiahuanaco, but Earth's greatest sites of antiquity couldn't compare to those built a millennium ago by an unknown race of beings that might not even have been humanoid. And after Dixon had sent her the mysterious visuals of his latest find, Sara was even more intrigued than ever.

Out of habit, she kept her excitement from her tone. "Station 32 is a designated research area. I'm an archeologist."

Sara had been lucky to be assigned the post. Most Martian archaeologists had to study the ancient ruins from Earth by examining holographic visuals, so her opportunity to examine them firsthand was rare, precious— worth a one-way ticket from Earth—and she had Professor Dixon to thank for the invitation. There was nothing like working on a dig, uncovering the remains of ancient civilizations with one's own two hands, and Sara longed to walk the site with one-third Earth's gravity, breathe the otherworldly air, and view the relics without even the Plexiglas visor of a spacesuit to mar the view.

Since scientists had terraformed Mars and released

oxygen from the water hidden in the planet's core, the atmosphere was thin—but fit to breathe. Exploration at even the poles of the planet was now possible. So far only the one site had been discovered but the concept that man was not the only intelligent race was still difficult for many people on Earth to accept. But not to Sara. With billions of stars in the galaxy, it seemed likely that other intelligent life had formed. That they'd visited their solar system and left behind artifacts that she could study left her breathless and filled with adrenaline—and more than ready to be on her way.

"Proceed to the medical station." The agent finally passed her through to the next line.

Mars had attracted Earth's first interplanetary astronauts, who had reached the solar system's fourth planet from the sun at the beginning of the twenty-first century. Thanks in part to one of her ancestors, Ryan Kinsey— a NASA scientist who'd discovered a fuel formula that had shaved years off interplanetary travel—engineers, agricultural and terraforming specialists could make the journey in a few weeks. Sara clutched her box tighter, pleased that part of Ryan's precious formula was inscribed inside the lid and that she would take it with her to Mars. The journey had become safe, if not routine. With new drugs to place the body in cold sleep, the weeks would pass like minutes, her body resting in deep hibernation for the trip's duration.

The medical line moved forward. Her chart must have come up automatically because the medic held up a hypodermic needle. "Ready for your vaccination?"

"Yes."

The medic swabbed her arm with alcohol. "You're aware that this injection may cause a fever?"

"Yes."

"That this will prevent pregnancy?"

"Yes."

"That you will be fuzzy-headed when you awaken?"

"Yes." Sara had been warned of the potent side effects, but apparently the technician's job required him to inform her again.

"For several days after you arrive, your inhibitions will be very low."

"I understand." And the men on Mars were known to take advantage. After the first women arrived, rumors of orgies had reached all the way to Earth. While she very much wanted to find a passion partner, she was particular. That's why she'd arranged for her pod to drop at the North Pole at a remote location where Professor Dixon would seal her into a chamber until Sara had fully recovered from the shot's effects.

The medic injected her arm and opened a sleeping pod. A good thing she wasn't claustrophobic. The pod was the size of a casket. She set the box in the baggage niche and yawned as she lay down, sanguine in the knowledge that the doctors would monitor her vitals during the journey. The drug flooded her system. Her eyelids grew heavy. She closed her eyes, confident that when she awakened, she'd be safely ensconced in a private chamber at the dig site of Mars. Meanwhile, she'd dream…erotic dreams.

Three hundred years later
Mars 2705

KENDAR STRODE THROUGH Station 32, imagining what the first people from Earth, whom offworlders now called Terrans, must have thought when they'd discovered the ancient alien ruins. The exotic machinery fashioned out of elements unknown on Earth must have puzzled the archaeologists and scientists alike, especially the woman, Dr. Sara Tolliver, who, according to his extensive historic research, had heroically spent every waking moment trying to understand the alien machines. No one knew who'd turned them on. Maybe Dr. Tolliver herself had accidentally triggered the machinery that caused Mars to blink in and out of time, disturbing the time continuum and causing the deaths of all women on Mars. Those who tried to flee died in space. Those who stayed died, too. Doomed by the lack of a Y chromosome, their DNA targeted by an unknown alien force that had been unleashed, women still avoided Mars, an automatic death sentence.

According to Kendar's research, Sara had worked on this very site three hundred years ago, frantically struggling to shut down the machines. Outside Station 32 was a statue erected in memory of her courage.

As a womanologist, Kendar spent his time studying women from rare books, holovisions and transmissions from Earth. Although he had male friends, he always felt something was missing from his life, hence his fascination with women. And one woman in particular intrigued him most, Dr. Tolliver, or Sara, as he fondly thought of her. She had become more like an imaginary friend than a historical figure. According to the records, she'd been beautiful, bright, young and enthusiastic and had come closer than anyone else to reading the alien language before death had prematurely ended her work. Unfortunately, most of her research had died with her. In retrospect, her feverish dedication, although admirable, had been in vain. In the three centuries since her death, no one had solved the ancient mystery or understood the principles behind the ancient machines abandoned by a race that only partially resembled humans.

The secrets apparently had died with the aliens who'd built the time machine. And unfortunately, no one had learned to turn off the machine or counter its ill effects on women. To Kendar's deep regret, due to the accident on Station 32 when the time machine was activated over three hundred years ago, he'd never met a woman.

However, men had remained behind to colonize the planet and mine the precious vidium needed by humanity for their computer chips. Forced to adapt, Martian men imported ova from Earth and raised babies, all males, in crèches. The vidium was sent back to Earth on unmanned pods—no human personnel or passengers allowed. And no woman from Earth ventured near his world.

Kendar yearned to meet a woman—however, the trip from Mars to Earth was not merely forbidden, but the route ferociously guarded. Any Martian ship attempting to enter Earth's atmosphere with human life aboard was summarily shot down—no questions asked. Terrans feared contamination and ruthlessly protected their women. Kendar didn't blame them. If he'd had a woman to love, he'd protect her, too.

Especially if she was as smart and determined as Sara had been. The records from that era had survived to reveal that Sara Tolliver had been a woman of uncommon resourcefulness, who had fought her fate to the last with a bravery and determination that inspired songs and legends. Cities and streets and spaceships were named in her honor. Yet, in the end, she'd failed.

Ducking into an underground passageway, Kendar tried to imagine Sara's feelings, thoughts and mental processes as she'd walked this very corridor. According to his research, women were supposed to be more sensitive and intuitive than their male counterparts. He wondered if she'd sensed that she would fail, if she'd wished she'd stayed on Earth. Had her last weeks of discovery been worth losing her life?

Had she spent that time alone? Or had she had friends or a lover to comfort her? Personal details of her life remained sketchy. Only one holopic of her remained, and to the amusement of his crèche brothers, Kendar had spent hours studying the strong face, the curious eyes, the full mouth.

Kendar supposed that upon her arrival, she must have been excited and fascinated, eager to explore and uncover the greatest relic in the solar system. In her boots, he would have been. And yet, women didn't react like men. Study upon study had concluded that men and women processed data and experiences differently. Terrans of the twenty-first century had attributed those differences to genetics and hormones. Scientists in the twenty-eighth century had discovered that those differences could be lethal on Mars, which blinked in and out of time, altering the time line by causing electromagnetic distortions that killed those without a Y chromosome but left men unharmed.

Kendar often regretted that Sara Tolliver hadn't passed on her genes before she'd died. Bold, beautiful and brave, she'd faced death as she'd embraced life—with curiosity and little regret. Kendar supposed that he'd built her up in his mind so much that no living

woman could compare to his Sara, but since his likeli-
hood of ever meeting a woman was highly improbable,
he allowed himself dreams of Sara, the fantasy of Sara,
carrying her image close to his heart.

One moment, Kendar was standing, peering at the
alien time machine and thinking of Sara, and the next,
he stood in the exact same spot, only the time machine
was covered with Martian dirt.

So what in stars had happened? Mars didn't have
quakes.

He frowned and surveyed the chamber more closely.
At this time of day, the lights should have been bright,
not dim. Moments ago this section had been huge, not the
size of his living quarters. And where were the guards and
the force fields to shield the alien machinery's delicate
mechanisms from tampering? Alarmed, Kendar turned
around, wondering if he'd wandered into a restricted area.

No, he hadn't taken a wrong turn. He recognized the
chamber—the alien pictographs on the exposed machinery remained exactly as he recalled—yet the chamber was smaller, darker, different. Instead of clean air,
he inhaled a whiff of disinfectant and stale dust, a
closed-in, old smell as if the air rebreathers were
clogged. He gawked at the alien machine encased in
sand, instead of fully excavated as it had been since
Sara's time. Had there been a cave-in? But where were

the monitors and security cameras? And who was the boy sleeping on the alien platform, his face to the wall?

Kendar approached the boy in hope of getting an explanation. But as he neared, the hair on the back of his neck prickled. Either someone had laced his breakfast with Martian dust or the exceptionally pretty and smooth-skinned creature with curves that tented the sheet wasn't a *he*...but a *she*.

Surely, this couldn't be a woman? He had to be hallucinating because her face resembled Sara's statue, just outside the main airlock.

Impossible.

Yet, undeniable.

"Wake up." Kendar strode forward and briskly pulled off the sheet, baring...curves that stole away his breath. Lamplight on the woman's face exposed lightly tanned skin. Voluptuous breasts. A narrowed waist. Abundant hips. Her chest rose and fell evenly with her breath.

A woman on Mars. The first living, breathing woman in almost three centuries.

Stunned, excited, Kendar felt like a kid on his first trip to the Martian caverns that sparkled with crystals of fantastic terra cotta, burnt sienna and meteorite gray. Unprepared for the way his pulse rose or his breath hitched in his chest, he was hit hard by the shock of realization that reading and studying from a distance simply couldn't convey the experience of looking at a woman in the flesh. No matter how much he'd studied, he couldn't have imagined that the mere sight of a real woman would make him feel like he was in free fall. He barely knew which delectable part of her he should focus on first.

She lay on her side, one arm stretched under her head beneath a pillow, her blond hair fanned around her face like Saturn's halo. Her long blond eyelashes hadn't so much as fluttered at his words. Words he couldn't repeat, not when wonder had sucked the saliva from his mouth, leaving it dry as the Martian desert.

Where had she come from? And why wasn't she affected by the instability in the time continuum that had killed every woman on the planet for the past three centuries? Was it possible the alien machinery had finally broken? Had someone turned it off?

Kendar didn't know.

He let his gaze feast on the smoothness of her complexion that reminded him of ripe melon, dewy fresh with morning condensation. With the delicate arch of her neck, her straight nose and the feminine crescent of her brows, delightful as sunrise, she was as unique and rare as a Martian ruby.

A woman. On Mars. Bless the stars! Who would have thought?

Leaning forward, he sniffed. Her scent reminded him of sweet cakes filled with ripe cherries, persimmons and pomegranate; a springtime banquet in bloom. So different from his hard body, her skin, sleek and smooth as violet petals, lush as a lily, called to him like sweet starlight. Like a kid unable to resist a treat, he traced one fingertip over her cheek, brushed back her hair and marveled at the sudden desire coursing through his veins. Despite three centuries of men without women on this planet, his body had still not been conditioned to forget that for millions of years women were meant to be men's partners.

Although she shouldn't be here, his body responded to her like a flower rising to the sun. His blood went straight to his groin, until he ached with a need to spend his seed. Shifting uncomfortably, he tried to remain calm. His mind must be playing tricks on him. Perhaps he was suffering from oxygen deprivation, because she looked so much like the woman in his fantasy that he had to question his sanity.

Had studying Sara, fantasizing about Sara, finally driven him over the edge?

Martian men satisfied their basic needs with holosex. The simulations were supposed to be realistic—but Kendar now knew that the hyped-up fabrications were simply a poor imitation of a living, breathing woman. No holovision had this woman's sleek, yet lush lines of deliciousness. No holovision could inspire the purpose and rightness that he felt just standing beside this woman.

And Kendar had enough knowledge of the past to realize that the holosex creations were meant to relieve men's basic urges in ways fast, mechanical and efficient, not necessarily the same way a real woman would receive a partner. According to his research, women needed priming to feel sexual desire. They required stroking, kissing, feelings of intimacy to turn on their passions.

His hands itched to touch. His tongue yearned to taste. His flesh ached to feel her against him.

Would this woman be receptive to his touch?

She hadn't moved when he'd trailed his fingertip over her cheek. She hadn't awakened when he'd spoken to her. He'd read that women liked to sleep nestled against the warmth of a man. Should he join her on the platform?

Every trembling electromagnetic pulse in his body told him this was the opportunity of a lifetime. He didn't want to blow the chance by making a wrong move. Bless the stars. Between moans, the holosex women always told him that he was a wonderful lover, but would a real woman react the same way? Would she welcome his caress?

Or tell him to blow it out an airlock?

DEEP IN HER erotic dream, Sara cuddled into the source of heat, her mind fuzzy from the shot and drugs, her thoughts unfocused. But that was okay. Because dreams were safe. Arching her breasts, belly and thighs into the penetrating warmth, she sighed in sleepy satisfaction. Rolling to her side, she curled a thigh and calf around the heat source, like a cat soaking up sunshine.

"Nice," she murmured, her throat husky.

Her head pillowed, her body nestled securely, she opened her eyes and stared into violet eyes. Eyes of a stranger. A face like his, she would have remembered. The bold nose. The dimple as he smiled at her. The sexy trace of beard that indicated he hadn't shaved that day. But what she liked best was his scent. He smelled of fresh air and a spring forest that reminded her of a favorite beach, where powdery white sand and sapphire waves lapped her feet. But never had she shared that fantasy with a man so gorgeous. This was the best dream she'd ever had.

"I'm Kendar."

"Sara," she introduced herself. The analytical part of her brain kicked in, telling her this stranger shouldn't be in her dream, shouldn't be holding her so closely, shouldn't be comforting her with his heat. Yet alarm barely registered in her consciousness. Tilting her head back, she gazed at him, noting the intensity in his eyes and the sensual curve of his mouth. "I'm supposed to sleep alone."

"But now that I'm here, may I stay?" That he asked

her permission chased away all worries that he might be dangerous. And besides, it was only a dream induced by the hibernating hypomist drugs. She might as well enjoy him. What woman could resist sleeping in such warm, strong arms? Only her subconscious could produce such an attractive man with such an agreeable attitude.

And any woman in her right mind would adore that strong jaw, slanted at an angle that revealed character and sensuality. Any woman would want a man like Kendar as a pleasure partner. Even lying down, he seemed tall, well formed, muscular. His shoulder pillowed her head with a strength that fired her imagination and enticed her fancy. She'd intended to take a Martian lover. Indulging in such a vivid dream was good preparation. The experience might even fulfill her needs and let her concentrate on work.

Later she'd immerse herself in work. Now, seemed the perfect time to play and give her passion free rein.

She ran a hand over his broad chest, the whorls of dark chest hair tickling her fingertips, then tilted her head back and chuckled. "I don't want you to leave. But how did you get here?"

He raised a speculative brow, his eyes twinkling cool violet. "I was about to ask you the same question."

"Professor Dixon arranged for this chamber to open only to my touch. But you got in. How?"

"Did you say Professor Dixon?" Never before had

her dreams and her conversations in dreams been so clear, so coherent, which made the experience even more pleasurable as he ran his hand up and down her arm, as if to warm her. However, the motion was slow, studied, languid, almost as if he'd never touched an arm before, and the care he took pleased her. She noted that he hadn't told her how he'd gotten inside the chamber, but she couldn't summon any genuine concern, not when he stirred her senses into a caldron of interest.

"Well, now that we're colleagues and no longer student and professor, I suppose I should call him Dr. Dixon. He requested that I join him on the dig. Is something wrong?"

Kendar shook his head, but his hand never stopped caressing or shooting pleasant tingles. "Nothing. It must be a coincidence."

"What?"

"Dr. Dixon was the name of the archeologist who found this site."

She trailed her fingers down his chest to discover he wasn't wearing any clothes. Mmm. Interesting. More than interesting. "And?"

"Nothing." At her intimate touch, he sucked in an audible gasp of air. Her fingers closed about his rod and she laughed. "This doesn't feel like nothing."

"I please you?"

His question was sweet. She couldn't recall the last

time a pleasure partner had asked for approval. In fact, it had been so long since she'd taken time to enjoy a man that she couldn't remember if she'd ever been so relaxed. Usually, she found the getting-to-know-you process a chore and the removing-the-clothes procedure uncomfortable. But right now she resented her sleeping clothes that prevented her from pressing bare flesh against his heat. She wanted…wanted him with an urgency that startled her.

She wanted to go with the flow. Enjoy herself. And him. There was no reason to send such a delicious man away. After all, he was only a drug-induced dream.

Lifting heavy eyelids, she murmured, "It would please me if you kissed me."

CHAPTER TWO

KENDAR COULD THINK of nothing but pleasing her. He couldn't think about the apparent cave-in. He couldn't think about the missing security. Or why he hadn't heard even one rumor about a living, breathing woman on Mars. Sometimes a man had to go on instinct. And right now his instincts told him that pleasing Sara was the most important task on Mars—a task he intended to savor like a ten-course feast.

"Where do you want me to kiss you?" He bent his neck to nip her ear for a taste of succulent ambrosia, and breathed in a whiff of heaven. When he pulled back the magic of her eyes shone as bright as Vega. "Here?"

She reached up and threaded her hands into his hair as if it was the most normal reaction in the world. But the scintillating touch of her fingertips rocked him into a spin. He hadn't known that a touch could be gentle and urgent at the same time. He hadn't known her response would make his heart pummel his ribs or that his ears would rush with a roaring bliss far more turbulent than a rocket launch.

"Mmm." She tugged his head closer. Her blue eyes, wide and deep as Earth's Pacific Ocean, locked with his. "Kiss me on the mouth."

He almost complied, but stopped, recalling from some forgotten text, that anticipation increased desire. So as much as he yearned to bring his lips to hers, he kissed her brow, instead. Planting a row of tiny kisses across her face, he memorized the line of her forehead and eyelids, trailed kisses over her angled cheekbones, admired the slant of her straight nose. The dilation of her pupils and the pulse throbbing at her temple told him that waiting to kiss her delectable lips had been the right move.

And he was learning that anticipation increased desire not just for her, but for him, too. He hadn't known he could grow so hard. He hadn't understood that until now sex had been a purely mechanical, efficient, unemotional experience. He'd always suspected a life without women was lacking, and now he knew it to be true. With Sara, he felt things, not just desire, but a yen for companionship, a yearning for completion, a wish to make the experience the best it could be—for both of them.

With a mix of tenderness and lust, finally, ever so slowly, he lightly brushed her lips with his. His mouth tingled from her softness, spreading heat into his core as if he'd drunk fine brandy. And when her lips parted beneath his and the tips of their tongues tangled, he groaned as need whipped him into a frenzy of lust.

Torn between wanting her now and making the experience last as long as possible, he pulled back to give his whirling sensations a chance to recover. But Sara was pulling her sleeping top over her head to reveal tempting skin that glistened burnished bronze under the light of the oil lamps and invited his delving into every shadow. At the sight of her magnificent breasts, he swallowed hard. The coral nipples pebbled, and, riveted, he stared.

"You're beautiful."

She laughed. "Don't you want to touch me?"

"Absolutely."

She reached for his hands and placed them so that he cupped her softness. Never had he felt anything so supple. As she breathed, her flesh filled his palms and he felt as though he was holding a precious gift, a rare poem, an erotic song. Instinct told him to take the utmost care of such delicate skin. As he flicked his thumbs over her nipples, he watched her eyes darken, her breath come faster, and as she hooked her thumbs into her pajama bottoms to pull them down, he rolled her to her back, straddled her hips, trapping her hands against her sides with his knees.

Surprised, her eyes widened, her voice went low, vibrating with excitement. "My hands…are caught."

"I know."

And then he very gently pinched her nipples. Her

back arched and she released a low, encouraging moan. "Lick me."

"Soon," he promised, wishing to please her. He wanted to take her tender flesh into his mouth, and part of him felt that holding back was crazy, and yet the other part knew how much pleasure he was giving her. Besides, it turned him on. He liked keeping her guessing. Liked the way she seemed unable to keep her hips from bucking under him. Liked that she didn't seem to mind giving up control.

If this was insanity, he intended to make the most of the experience. So many times he'd dreamed of doing whatever he wanted to Sara. And now she was under him, her flesh sunny, sizzling, submitting. He couldn't explain it. He couldn't even question it. He had no idea what was going on, but he intended to take his fill. He wished for her to want him as much as he wanted her. Determined to wait for that cherished moment, he stroked light circles over her breasts and teased quiet caresses on her belly.

Leaning forward for another delicious kiss, he was careful to keep her hands trapped, noting she hadn't tried very hard to free them. When the tips of her breasts beaded against his chest, she moaned prettily into his mouth. "Kendar."

"Yes, sweet Sara?"

"I'm burning up."

"We're burning together." And then he took her nipple between his teeth, the other between his fingers and pinched.

"Ohhh…oh…my."

With his tongue he laved away her tiny prickles of pain, watched heat flush her chest, saw her breasts swell and her eyes grow languid with desire. She would have thrashed in pleasure but he held her firmly, carefully watching her blossoming reactions to keep her well tended and aroused.

"Tell me how you feel," he demanded as he lifted her breasts, tweaked her nipples harder with his thumb and forefinger.

"Please…" Her head shook from side to side. "I want to make love."

"We are." He caressed her neck, her collarbone, her belly, enjoying every quiver.

She thrust up her hips. "I want you inside me."

"I want that, too. I've been waiting a lifetime for you," he admitted.

"You sound…as if…you mean it."

"Of course, I mean it. It's not every day a man on Mars finds such a creature as gorgeous as you."

She arched her eyebrows, her mouth teasing, tempting, enticing. "You haven't seen my legs, yet."

"Or your back. Or your bottom. Or your toes. But somehow," he squeezed her breasts, "I find I'm quite… content."

Now that was an outright lie. How could he be content when every inch of him longed to be inside her? Ever so glad that he was no longer a lad and had excellent control, he was nowhere near his limit. His brow might bead with sweat. His heart might have pumped all his blood below his waist. But as long as he could hold out, he planned to explore every delectable part of her.

As a womanologist, he knew men often misinterpreted woman's signals. And while she was apparently urging him to go faster, contradictorily, she was clearly enjoying the wait, as well as the fact that he'd taken charge.

Kendar had no idea how long he could last, but one thing he knew for sure—he might never have another experience like this one, whatever the stars it was. Like a precious treat of which he wanted to savor each lick and every delectable flavor, he'd make this encounter erotic and exotic and so very good for both of them. Relishing the soft taste and sweet texture of her breasts, he learned the exact amount of playful friction to induce the most pleasure by monitoring her quick pants of need, the fluttering pulse at her neck, her fingers clenching at her sides, as well as the puckering of her nipples.

And when she pleaded with him for more, he finally released her hands, but insisted on removing the pajama bottoms. Tugging down the material, he revealed flaring hips and a flat tummy, the curls at her mons, her contoured legs, lovely plump thighs and smooth, feminine skin. Even her toes were sexy with their bright lavender-polished nails.

When he urged her feet apart to make room for him between her knees, she stiffened.

"What's wrong?"

"Nothing."

She was lying. He could hear it in the tremor of her voice. The idea that he had done something to cause her reluctance, that he would cause his sweet Sara a moment of discomfort, hurt him, shook him, gave him doubts. Had he done something wrong? Violated some taboo? Gone too slowly? Too quickly? He'd wanted to do this right. He wanted her to have pleasure.

Lightly, he caressed the inside of her calves and knees. "Despite what you may have heard about Martian men, we cannot read minds."

"Huh?"

"I'd like to know what's bothering you, but unless you tell me…"

"I'm fine. You're great. This is the best dream I've ever had."

Dream? What was she talking about? Was *dream* a euphemism for lovemaking? He trailed his fingers higher up her thighs and noted her trembling response. Her legs relaxed a bit, and he inhaled a whiff of her enticing, intimate scent. "But?"

"I've never done this with the lights on," she finally admitted.

He brushed a finger over her lips. Should he offer to turn them down? He would do so if she insisted, but the ache to see all of her was so powerful, he resisted. "But you're so beautiful." He stroked, caressed. "Every-where." In spite of her shyness, her knees parted another inch. "When you spread your legs, it's like a crystal showing off the most precious of facets."

"Uh-huh."

"Besides, there's no bashfulness allowed in dreams," he said, trying another tactic.

"If you say so." She sounded unsure, yet her body quivered with eagerness. "Are you a poet?"

"Usually, I'm…not much of a talker, but with you, I seem to be quite verbal." He delved between her thighs, pleased by her moisture, then peeled back lips as soft as Dedan petals to see…her nectar. As she sucked in a breath of air, he laughed. "I'm also quite physical."

Dipping his fingers into her dampness, he spread her wetness over her pink center. He had no idea if his words reassured her, or if his actions made her forget her strange shyness, but he was simply grateful for the lights that allowed him to watch the expressions play across her face. She'd closed her eyes, flinging one arm over her forehead. Her lips alternately pouted or tightened and tiny moans of pleasure came from the back of her throat.

The urge to replace his fingers with his mouth was overpowering. He ached to taste her, run his tongue over the nexus where all her nerve endings centered. Yet, he hesitated, concerned that her bashfulness would prevent her pleasure.

But as her body drew into sinuous tightness, her back arching, he sensed he'd pushed her beyond her normal boundaries. Parting her thighs wide, he placed his mouth over her sweet little bud. She tasted tangy and sweet, and he lapped her like cream, pleased by her soft coos of encouragement.

In fact, she had difficulty holding still. Her hands reached between the crook of her bent thighs, and he captured her fingers, holding her exactly where he wanted her. Her breath came faster and faster, she pumped her hips, twisted with her female desires. But no matter which way she gyrated, he kept his mouth firmly in place, licking, laving, loving what he was doing.

When she gurgled her pleasure and the spasms claimed her, his heart bubbled with happiness. He, Kendar, had given a real woman pleasure.

"Ahh…oh…good. No…not…good. Great. Fantastic."

Proud that he had satisfied her, he was reluctant to stop. After all, women could have multiple orgasms, and he wanted his Sara to have only the best from him.

So he kept his mouth in place, his tongue flicking. Her fingers clenched his. "What are…you…" Her head thrashed from side to side. "Don't…stop. Please, don't…stop."

She was tightening every muscle, her body arching, her fingers clenching his so tightly he was shocked by her strength, astounded at the power of her lust. It was almost as if electric jolts shot through her.

"Yes. Yes. Ah…yes." Again she spasmed, but this time she yelped. "Oh. Oh. Ooooh."

This orgasm, clearly more powerful, lasted longer than her first. She jerked, cried out, and he wondered how many times she could come. But unfortunately her taste, her scent, her uninhibited thrusting had him so hard and tight that he could no longer wait. As much as he adored licking her, shooting her over the edge, he couldn't wait one more moment before thrusting into her and claiming his prize.

Although he told himself to be gentle, at the first touch of her heat, her slick folds encasing his tip, he rammed into her. She didn't seem to mind. Immediately winding her legs around his hips, she rocked her pelvis, meeting him halfway.

Sara felt nothing like antiseptic holosex. She was tight and warm and her scent drove him wild with the need to pump into her.

He held on by only the slimmest of margins. "Don't move."

She shook her head, pumped her hips, reached for his

balls, and he knew he had to take control once again, or lose the moment completely. Capturing her slender wrists in one of his hands, he pinned them over her head. Then he sat up and kept perfectly still, using the moment to regain control. And he took that time to renew his acquaintance with her wonderful breasts that seemed much more sensitive this time around.

If her breasts were more sensitive, would other parts have an increased response as well? He couldn't wait to find out. Creative, he used his beard, then his lips and finally swooped his tongue over her breasts until she opened her eyes and demanded, "Move, damn you."

She squeezed her slick folds and he couldn't misunderstand her meaning. Yet, he shot her a wicked grin. "Not yet."

"What do you mean, not yet?"

"I'm not done with you."

She chuckled. "Promises. Promises."

That's when he reached between their bodies and found her slick center. Her mouth rounded into a surprised *O*. "Again?"

"Again." In almost no time at all, she seemed ravenous to move. Kendar couldn't recall ever having so much fun. She was burning with feverish need. Her body slippery with sweat.

And he held her still, his finger dancing, until he recognized that another of her explosions was near.

He stopped.

Her eyes popped open, her blue irises glazed with desire and melting confusion. "What…"

"This time, you have to wait."

"Why?"

"Because…" He released her hands, pumped his torso. "I can't."

At his admission, she clasped his hips. And then he was pumping, thrusting. And when she screamed her delight, he went with her over the edge. Afterward, breathless, heart pumping so hard, he could barely think, it took several long moments for him to recover. Moments when he held her tight, pleased that she clung to him so fiercely.

When he finally had the strength to pull back, she looked at him, her expression odd. "This isn't a dream, is it?"

SARA'S ORGASMS SEEMED to have cleared the last drugs from her system. Although she was once again thinking clearly and knew her low inhibitions had made her susceptible to Kendar's charm, she had no regrets. Instead, words like *awesome, wow, fantastic,* zinged through her head. She'd come to Mars for new experiences and so far, the out-of-this-world pleasure had left her relaxed and satiated.

"I'm as real as you," Kendar answered in a voice that

couldn't have been sexier if she had dreamed him out of a secret fantasy.

"The pod's lock was supposed to have been keyed to open only to my DNA," she repeated. Despite her languid limbs and her fully satisfied body, Sara couldn't stop her natural curiosity. If he'd gotten past the lock to her pod, could he also open her heirloom box that she'd had keyed back on Earth to open only to her DNA? No, the locksmith had assured her not even the best thief could break a DNA lock. He must have found another way inside her sealed chamber. She looked around in search of another entrance besides the locked door. But aside from the one doorway, she saw only solid reddish walls, a stone floor and alien machinery—just as Dixon had promised. As much as the artifacts called to her on a professional level, she put off a comparison to the holovisuals she'd seen of the relic on Earth and forced her attention to Kendar's puzzling appearance. She saw no way for him to have entered this chamber, unless he'd broken the lock.

"When I came in, the door was open, and I didn't shut it." Kendar frowned, marring the lines of his smooth brow, his expression one of concentration and confusion. "One moment I was peering at the alien machine and then I saw you."

Sara had studied the diagrams of the Martian site before she'd left Earth. "Then who shut the door?"

"Maybe the security guard."

"Security guard?" What was he talking about? There weren't any guards on the dig.

Kendar ignored his nudity and strode to the door. The sight of his muscular back and well-formed buttocks pleased her, but reminded her of her own state of undress. Despite their lovemaking, she didn't feel comfortable walking about without clothing—though not because Kendar was ogling her, because he wasn't. In fact he seemed just as puzzled by how he'd gotten here as she was.

She pulled a shirt over her head, grateful for the length that stopped at midthigh. When Kendar tugged on the door and it failed to open, she approached, slid her arm past his and keyed the lock with her DNA. The door slid open to reveal several other archeological sites amid the Martian landscape of reddish sand dunes. The air, thin but breathable, reminded her of her one trip to Denver, except the Mile High City's thin air had been clogged with carbon monoxide and this air smelled crisp and clean as the Sarinbium Mountains in the distance. Her first scenic view of Mars was as breathtaking as the man beside her and she drank it in like champagne.

"Stars," Kendar cursed, his reaction startling her. When he swung round to face her, his body tense, his eyes disclosing anger, his words revealed that he'd suffered a shock. "What year is this?"

Sara backed away from him. She'd heard Martian men could be peculiar, some of them living in the Outback and mining their gemstones without much human contact. Others lost their manners and civilized ways, but she hadn't thought a man who could have just made love to her so gently was one of them. She hadn't missed how he'd put her pleasure before his own. How he'd taken such care to ensure that she'd enjoyed herself.

However, while she could understand mixing up the days, even the week, how could he not know the year? "It's 2405."

"Sure it is." He let out a strangled chortle. "And now you're going to tell me that I came here in a time machine and that you're Dr. Sara Tolliver, right?"

"I am Dr. Sara Tolliver." She couldn't mistake his sarcasm and kept her tone nonthreatening. "If you doubt me, you can check my identichip."

"Stars! The machine must have pulled me back in time."

At his startling proclamation, Sara took a step back, the hair on her arms standing on end. Something was very wrong and she didn't think it was an alien time machine but a problem inside Kendar's mind.

Kendar stared at her, his serious expression conveying urgency. "I want you to think very carefully and tell me everything you've done since the moment you arrived."

She humored him. "I arrived in my pod—asleep. I didn't regain consciousness until you awakened me."

"Think again. Maybe you sleepwalked and now believe it was a dream."

She shook her head. "I'm not prone to sleepwalking, and if I did so, I don't remember."

"You're sure?" His violet eyes tugged at her and she had to tamp down her compassion. She couldn't allow his beautiful lovemaking to alter her impression that he didn't seem balanced. Had he spent too long alone in the desert? Would his former gentleness turn wild? Had he sought her out in that chamber because he'd known that after her trip from Earth, her inhibitions would be lowered? She didn't want to believe him capable of such duplicity, but she couldn't ignore her doubts about his state of mind.

She shrugged and pulled the neck of her collar together, revealing her nervousness. When Kendar noted her action, she forced her hand to her side and tried to stay calm. Just because the huge man standing before her vibrated with tension didn't mean he would hurt her. "What's wrong?"

Kendar ran a hand through his hair. "I suspect you turned on the alien time machine and the old relic brought me here."

"I turned on the time machine… Me? How?" She turned to look at the machinery embedded into the rock-

and-dirt wall. She had yet to touch it. Had barely glanced at it. But the relic was millions of years old. It couldn't still work…could it?

"When I entered this chamber, the year was 2705."

O…kay. Sara tried to remain open-minded. Perhaps people in the future had learned how to travel through time. Although Kendar had seemed shocked that he had done so, he easily accepted the concept—as if he believed time travel was possible and the alien machine was responsible. "Let me get this straight. You're from three hundred years in the future?"

"Yes."

She muffled a snort of disbelief. "Can you prove it?"

"That's not what's important. What happens next is."

"You're losing me."

"Sorry. It's difficult to believe that I'm talking to Dr. Sara Tolliver. That you and I…" He gestured to the sleeping platform, then strode over to it.

His story grew stranger by the minute, and he never did what she expected. She thought he would don his trousers, but instead, he ran his hands over the sleeping platform as if looking for a secret latch or a hidden compartment. "You have to figure this out."

"Me?" First he wanted her to believe in time travel and that an alien machine brought him here, and now he expected her to help him figure out the rest of his delusion?

"You're the archeological expert."

He wasn't making sense, but she realized from the shock and urgency in his eyes that he was suffering. After what they'd shared, it seemed only fair to humor him. "What exactly am I supposed to figure out?"

"First, you need to read the alien writing." His tone was fierce, his eyes gleaming with intelligent determination.

"I may be an archeologist, but I can't read those pictographs—"

"You will. The historical records say you were brilliant, insightful."

Using the past tense, he sounded so sure, so confident, and that made her feel worse for doubting him. But what sane person wouldn't? Either the man was delusional, or…or…or he was telling the truth. And despite all known scientific data that stated time travel was impossible, his belief in his story matched his reactions, which all seemed to ring true. "If I succeed, wouldn't your records mention how I learned to read the pictographs?"

He shook his head. "Many records of this time were lost during the Martian Revolt, but since you learned to read the pictographs before, I'm sure you can do it again."

"You know, I actually understood what you just said, and that scares me."

"Nothing scares Dr. Sara Tolliver."

"Excuse me?"

"You were a legend. A city was named after you. A

statue of you—never mind, we don't have time. You need to get to work. Immediately."

Sara couldn't miss the ring of command or the reverberation of sincerity in Kendar's tone, but, even if she'd wanted to play along in his fantasy world, archeological discovery took years. No one did anything in a rush, or critical details could be overlooked. She tried to calm him, using common sense, still certain his time travel story was bunk, unwilling for his wonderful lovemaking to influence her logic. "The ruins have been here for eons. They aren't going anywhere." She reached for her slacks. "And I'm starved. First, we need to eat, then I must check in with Dixon."

And she wanted Dixon to look into Kendar's background. She hated to think that the man who had made love to her so tenderly could be mentally unstable, but she couldn't deny that his story had enough holes in it to drive a rocket ship through.

Yet, it disturbed her that she also couldn't explain his presence in the chamber. How had he sneaked past the DNA lock?

Kendar seemed to understand her skepticism. "Look, I'm sorry. There's much more you need to know. But I suppose it won't hurt to eat while I explain," he conceded.

"Good." She headed for the pod that came stocked with food pacs, hoping a little distance between them might ease her conscience. While the scientist in her wouldn't allow her to believe him without proof, the woman she was needed to believe she couldn't have had such a wonderful experience with a lunatic. Kendar had made love to her with the skill of a man who knew his lover well. He'd instinctively read what she desired, or been sensitive enough to take clues from her. Sara might not be the most sexually experienced woman on Earth, but she'd had enough partners to know that Kendar was an extraordinary lover. The man hadn't just practically read her mind, he'd known what she'd wanted better than she had herself.

That kind of skill took powers of perception beyond the norm. Could someone be so caring of another, so gentle, so skilled, so perceptive…and then be so unbalanced he had the date wrong by three hundred years?

She glanced at Kendar. Most men would have taken the opportunity to dress, but he seemed disinclined to do so. Although she enjoyed looking at his powerful chest, his long limbs and sinewy muscles, she didn't want the distraction. Didn't want to think about how he'd worshipped her body, left her tingling with delicious tremors. Or that she wanted to get to know him better. She had to stay focused on his story, on helping him to see past his error.

So as she pulled out the food, she gestured to his clothes. "Would you mind…?"

He gave her an odd look, but complied, sliding into

trousers and a loose-fitting shirt that reminded her of an ancient pirate's while she also finished dressing. Unable to decide if he looked more delicious dressed or undressed, she then shoved a tray of food into his hands, hands that had strummed her body to perfection. Hands that had known when to apply pressure and when to stop. Hands that had driven her into a series of orgasms she'd never forget.

If Kendar hadn't started talking about time travel, she might have suggested a temporary, exclusive union—perhaps six months. Then again six months of making love only to him might spoil her for any other man. But he had to go and ruin things. She wished he would take back his words. Blame alcohol or a drug.

Now he seemed set on talking and that made her even more uncomfortable. She always kept things on the surface with her passion partners. She didn't want to know their history, their likes and dislikes or even much about their lives. That way she could stay detached.

They sat cross-legged on the sleeping platform, facing one another. She pulled the rip cord that would heat her food and he copied her action. But as she dug into her spaghetti and meatballs, he ignored his food, as if trying to gather his thoughts.

"In 2705," he began, "there are no women on Mars." She wanted to tell him to stop. That she didn't believe him and didn't want to hear more. But rudeness was not in her nature, especially not after he had treated her body with such reverence. So she ate her spaghetti and let him speak. "We believe the alien technology—"

"The time machine?"

"Yes. It's responsible for a corruption of the time continuum that alters the female chromosome, including humans and animals."

Whoa! Now that was some myth to swallow. First he expected her to believe he'd traveled through the alien machinery through time, now he was asking her to conclude that using the machine killed all females?

She wiped her lips and carefully kept her tone even. "How do you know that it wasn't a Martian virus that killed all the females?"

"Women in your time lived here without a problem. But when your pod rested beside the time machine, the alien machinery activated, causing small, but measurable changes in the electromagnetic spectrum of the time continuum."

Sara stopped eating. His continual use of the past tense, combined with his insistence that she had something to do with the disaster made the food congeal in her mouth. For the first time, she wondered if what he was telling her could possibly be true, and it scared her right to her bones. A time machine seemed like something created by a science fiction writer. Far-fetched. Impossible. Incredible. She'd come to Mars to make new breakthroughs, but not in her wildest imagination had she thought to discover that Dr. Dixon's ancient alien machine could cause people to travel through time. "You're saying my pod activated the alien time machine, brought you here and altered the time line?"

"Yes. And our medical scientists say the chromosomal effect is no virus. In my era, machines aren't advanced enough to change the continuum. And in your time…the science is more primitive, but it is sufficient to determine that the moment you activated the time machine, something happened to the electromagnetic spectrum to distort time."

"You keep saying I activated the time machine but I've been asleep for weeks."

"Then the chromosomal effect has already begun." Kendar leaned forward and gently touched her cheek. "While we were never certain if the machinery still worked, my coming back in time proves that it's a fact."

"And you aren't listening. How could I activate the machine while I was asleep?"

"Maybe your presence, your breathing, your scent or a stray thought or an emotion during your dreams triggered the device. Or perhaps it was your pod itself. We may never know for certain, since we have no idea how the time machine works. But it does or I wouldn't be here." He placed a warm hand on her shoulder, his eyes full of sympathy for what she would undoubtedly be feeling if she believed him—which she still didn't. His story was fantastic, but she slid her gaze to the alien machine, then back to him as he continued, "Somehow you triggered the machine's operation, and if we don't shut it down—every woman on Mars will die, including you."

"Wait. Wait. You're going too fast. Why assume I did something? How do you know you didn't activate the machine?"

"Because Mars began to blink in and out of time immediately after your arrival."

"What does that mean? Blink in and out of time?"

"Time passes differently on Mars than on Earth—or anywhere else in the galaxy. Think of a light that goes on and off. When it's on, everything is fine, but when it's off, it's as if the rest of the universe is passing us by."

"How do you know?"

"It's been happening for three hundred years. And if we don't work to counteract the effect, history will repeat itself."

"And the women will all die?"

He nodded. "To ensure we didn't do any more damage we used force fields to prevent human contact with the artifact in 2705. But apparently you triggered the device from your side of the time line."

She tried to push aside her doubts for a moment to wrap her mind around his theory. "You think if we find a way to deactivate the machine…we can stabilize time and change the future?"

He nodded, his eyes intense. "We must restore the balance."

CHAPTER THREE

SARA DIDN'T KNOW whether to laugh or cry. "Let me get this straight. You need me to decipher an alien language and figure out how the time machine works to keep Mars in balance, so the time distortion ends and all the women on Mars in 2705 will live."

Kendar nodded, his expression grim. "I believe you now understand."

She shook her head, confused, full of doubts and wishing that their relationship didn't need to end. However, as much as she would have liked to explore the sexual side of his nature, she found his bizarre delusion too strange. "You're insane."

At her insult, she expected him to bristle. To argue. To curse. He didn't react as anticipated, surprising her once again.

"Do you have a communicator?" Kendar stared at her as if his request made perfect sense, his emotions locked down tight. Sometimes he seemed to have more control over himself than she did, as if he understood how impossible she found his story and was not going to let her doubts upset him. How could the man stay so calm when his delusion was so disturbing?

He was accusing her of ruining the future of women on Mars. He claimed she was responsible for thousands, maybe tens of thousands, of deaths. No. She shook her head appalled and horrified. She should send him away, but when her gaze caught his, she saw empathy there, as if he understood how much his words were hurting her.

"Sure. I have a communicator." She lifted her wrist. "Locate a news channel."

Sara tuned to the desired frequency and an announcer's voice echoed through the chamber. "Please stay calm. Stay home. The doctors at our finest hospitals in the capital are working round the clock to find the cause of this unknown ailment affecting women. So far only those over sixty and those younger than five have shown symptoms."

Kendar commented, "The weak die first."

Sara clicked off the communicator, her stomach tightening with apprehension. No matter how far-fetched Kendar's story, she could no longer ignore the possibility he told the truth. With a combination of genetics and bioengineering marvels, mankind had wiped out the last known illnesses over a century ago. Hospitals were no longer filled with sick patients but by those who required bodily repair due to natural aging or accidents. For Kendar to arrive at a time when people were once again struck by an unknown ailment lent credibility to his statements and was too much of a co-incidence to ignore. Besides, from what she could comprehend, Kendar had nothing to gain from lying. And he wasn't asking anything more from her than to study the machine—which was what she'd come here to do anyway. She accepted his story. She'd activated the alien time machine and brought him back in time. That's why all those women were sick. Nothing else made sense. At the implications, she began to shake and her gut clenched tight. "How long do I have?"

"A few days to live, but at the end..." He hesitated to speak the unspeakable.

"At the end, I'll be too sick to work?" Sara concluded, her tone grim.

"I'm sorry."

No pity entered his tone and for that she was grateful. To think of her own death saddened her, shook her, upset her, of course, but to think that she might be the cause of the death of thousands... It was a burden so horrible, that for the moment, she didn't want to ask any more questions. She shoved aside her food, too sickened to eat, and she couldn't help thinking that if Kendar came from a future where she'd failed, that she was bound to fail again. Ice seeped into her bones.

Was the future already written? Had the Sara Tolli-

ver in Kendar's history ever met this Kendar? She had
no idea. The circular logic made her dizzy. It was like
wondering which came first, the chicken or the egg, and
she decided to ignore theory and concentrate on the
pictographs.

Her communicator beeped and she answered, "Yes?"

"Sara, welcome to Station 32," Dixon's hearty greeting warmed her frozen core. The normalcy of his tone
reminded her that while she lived, she could work, and
while she could work, there was hope. Perhaps Kendar's warning would give her a head start on the project.
Dixon went on, "I'm sorry I'm not there to welcome you
in person, but I was called to the capital to give input
on the women's crisis. If you need anything, contact my
assistant, Terry. Sorry, I have to go."

What else could go wrong? Sara had been counting
on Dixon's help. Now, she had no idea when he'd return. Under normal circumstances, Sara would have
studied the exposed part of the artifact for weeks, maybe
months, before attempting to dig out the rest. But these
were not normal circumstances. Time was of the es-
sence. If she hoped to decipher the alien language, she
needed access to as many pictographs as she could un-
earth, and that meant digging out the artifact as quickly
as possible without causing damage. Perhaps Dixon's
assistant might be of help.

Terry had been quite enthusiastic about Sara coming

to Mars. She'd helped make all the arrangements, sending a personal note of what to bring from Earth and what she would find once she'd arrived. From the friendly notes, Sara had the impression the girl was lonely and looked forward to some female company.

She and Kendar found Terry outside the chamber about a hundred yards away. On her stomach in the Martian dirt, she was busy taking holopics of a set of stairs that led into red sand. She looked up at their approach, her cute nose and round cheekbones smudged with dirt, a friendly smile of greeting revealing a crooked tooth that lent charm to her grin.

Terry dusted off her hands and knees, then shook their hands. A girl with leathery skin, a wide smile and intelligent eyes, she hugged Sara, but couldn't seem to stop staring at Kendar.

Sara didn't blame her. Kendar was gorgeous, but still she took a possessive step closer to him. More bothered by Terry's interest in Kendar than Sara wanted to admit, her voice came out sharper than she intended, and she skipped the small talk after making introductions. "Terry, we need an air pump, hoses and nozzles. Where does Dixon store his equipment?"

Terry rubbed her face, making the smudges worse, but somehow her face now looked twice as cute. "Dr. Dixon didn't plan to use that kind of equipment for several months. I'm not sure it's arrived yet, but all our gear is over there." She pointed to a shed and led them across the site with enthusiastic steps. "Come on. I'll show you."

Sara appreciated Terry's helpfulness, but after they entered the shed, she was appalled at the limited equipment that consisted of shovels, picks, brushes and buckets. Where were the thermoluminescence machines to help with dating the Martian artifacts? What about infrared, sonohistograms and geographic information systems computers on which to build holo-models?

"This is it?" Sara turned to Terry, her heart sinking. The task before her was enormous, and if this was all the equipment she had to work with, finding, never mind reading, the pictographs would be like trying to locate an intact meteorite in the Marebrium Crater.

"Funds are not as ample as we'd like." Terry's apologetic tone was tempered by a what-did-you-expect shrug that emphasized her slender body. She gestured to a bunch of mining junk, left over from the days before the atmosphere was breathable. "Dixon hoped to salvage a pump from one of the rebreathers, but he's never gotten around to it."

"Perhaps, I could…" Kendar wound his way through the piles of dusty spacesuits, wire, barrels and odd pieces of scrap metal and picked up an old air hose that had once been used to tether a man so he could breathe as he mined underground. With little trouble Kendar unscrewed the fitting from a battered suit, wound the hose over his shoulder and continued searching through the junk piles.

"What are you looking for?" Terry's gaze followed Kendar with curiosity and she self-consciously swept a lock of hair behind her ear.

"A working pump. A generator." Kendar didn't seem to notice Terry's attractive flush, his gaze sweeping over the metal parts and settling on a tool box.

Terry looked from Sara to Kendar and back, biting her lower lip as if trying to figure out their relationship. "There's a broken heater and pump out back, but it lacks fuel cells."

Fuel cells? Sara knew exactly where to get some—if the new ones would work with such old equipment. "My pod has fuel cells. If you can modify them—"

"I will try," Kendar cut in.

Terry stumbled and raised a hand to her forehead. "Whew. The dust in here must be getting to me. Anyone else feel a little light-headed?"

Concerned by Terry's symptoms, Sara took her arm, alarmed by her sudden pallor and her dilated pupils. "Let's go outside."

"Thanks. I'm so glad you came to work here." Terry squeezed Sara's hand. "I hope we can be friends."

"Me, too."

Terry gave Sara a piercing look. "I hope you don't mind me speaking frankly."

"Of course not."

"I'm not the kind of girl to cut in on someone else's action. No worries there, okay?"

Startled by Terry's openness, then pleased, Sara helped Terry walk away from the dusty shed, unsure what to say. "Kendar and I... We aren't... We just met."

Once Terry breathed the fresh air, she didn't feel better. She trembled and sweat beaded her upper lip. "The doctors told my mother that I don't have a strong constitution. If I'd been born a century ago, I likely wouldn't have made it past my teens." She breathed heavily. "Whatever that sickness is going round, I think I've got it."

Hoping Terry would recover soon, Sara helped her to her quarters, leaving Kendar to collect what he could. "It's probably just the dust still in your lungs." Or perhaps the power of suggestion.

Sara wished she could believe that but she didn't. Between Kendar's appearance in the chamber where he'd seemed to come through a solid wall and the strange sickness on Mars, she'd lost any remaining doubts about Kendar's story. Women on Mars had less than a week to live—unless she succeeded in turning off the alien machine. So she hadn't a moment to waste.

SARA RETURNED to the chamber, picked up a holocamera and photographed the pictographs that were already visible. She tried not to draw conclusions but noted facts. The aliens used no straight lines within the pictographs, nor did they align the pictographs in rows. Instead, the symbols appeared random and didn't remind her of anything recognizable. She suspected that while directions might be inscribed on the ancient machinery, the makers had assumed the viewer would already know how to read.

Earth's first satellite to leave the solar system had been fashioned to draw on basic mathematical principles to help build a common vocabulary. But this artifact wasn't designed that way. Nor was it like the Rosetta Stone where several languages told the exact same message. What she had before her was the equivalent to one page from a computer manual. Not only did she have to decipher the language, she had to figure out enough to balance the time continuum—whatever the hell that meant.

She might be alone, but her computer could analyze the symbols against every hypothesis known to man. However, the aliens might have based their language on, for example, a five-hundred-day calendar, or on how often their home world suffered an earthquake—random cycles that would mean nothing to the computer. Sara tried not to think about the next-to-impossible task before her, or about how scientists over the next three hundred years had failed to read the alien markings.

Instead, she sketched on her pad of paper, an antiquated habit she'd acquired during her schoolgirl days when she'd thought using ancient equipment had been cool. Later, she'd scan the data into the computer and decide where to dig next. Usually, several different types of machines processed the information to determine what was rock and what was an object. Other machines drew three-dimensional maps. Without them, any digging would be going in cold and could damage a critical piece of machinery. She wished Dixon was here and wondered if he'd return if she told him Kendar's story. Yeah, he'd probably come back all right, to kick her off the site and get her mental help for believing that a machine millions of years old could transport a man through time.

Lost in her thoughts, she jumped at the sound of footsteps and carefully put down her notes before turning around. Kendar entered the chamber carrying an assortment of hoses, fittings and a modified heat pump. After depositing his finds on the floor, he strode to the pod, removed the fuel cell and placed it into a slot. When the motor purred to life, he grinned a satisfied smile. And despite everything she'd learned today, her pulse raced.

It figured that the one time she'd finally found a man that interested her, she didn't have time to pursue him. Still, she could enjoy the sight of him as he welded the equipment with ease. At thirty percent of Earth's pull, the low gravity made it possible for her to lift much more, but that old pump must weigh a ton and he hefted it with one arm. Brawn and brains. A nice combination. Kendar's cleverness and intelligence combined with his positive attitude were exactly what she needed right now and she took a moment to appreciate him. With his bulging muscles, the man exuded masculinity, but as he went about his task with a matter-of-factness, he impressed her even more.

"Now, I can uncover the rest of the pictographs for you." Picking up the nozzle he headed toward a section of wall that appeared to be dirt.

"Wait a second." She was the archeologist. She should be making the decisions, not ogling his muscles. Perhaps the residual traces of the drugs weren't totally out of her system as she'd assumed. "It would make sense to start near the pictographs we can already see."

Kendar kept striding toward solid dirt and rock, his confidence radiating from him like the sun's corona. "You're forgetting that I have the advantage of having already seen the machine. This area is what you want."

Sheesh. Right. How could she have forgotten he was from a future where the site had already been fully excavated? Probably because although she'd decided to believe him, her reservations remained huge. Either that or her poor brain couldn't quite take in all the ramifications of time travel. Especially going forward.

Sara was accustomed to ruins, relics, studying the past. As a child, she'd immersed herself in her most precious possession, the journal of her ancestor Lady Amanda Pratt. At the memory, her fingers itched to hold the journal that had always comforted her during times of trouble, but watching Kendar airbrush the machinery, removing eons of rock and sand until patches of the machine shone through, mesmerized her.

She'd thought that Dixon had meticulously wiped the machine clean, but the newly revealed ancient metal gleamed as brightly as new. Kendar had obviously known the exact location to dig and she realized that squashed the last of her doubts about whether he'd really traveled from the future. The place he'd chosen to uncover hadn't been logical, and yet, he'd unerringly found the right spot.

Despite her fascination with the relic, she couldn't help admiring Kendar. After his initial astonishment that he'd traveled back in time, he'd taken the news with a surprisingly optimistic and practical attitude. He'd plainly said what needed to be done and then hadn't once complained about the primitive conditions or the lack of help or equipment, or about her asking him for proof. Nor had he expressed dismay at having been ripped from his place in time.

And he'd modified a machine so that not only could

it blast away dirt but it could suck the dirt outside. She couldn't help but admire his determination as well as his ingenuity. The air in the chamber remained clean and she marveled at both his inventiveness and the steady determination with which his powerful arms held the hose. She realized how lucky she was that it had been him who had come back in time.

As he brought each new area to light, she sketched, scanned, catalogued, holophotoed and entered data into her computer. She took only one break, to check on Terry in her quarters, who appeared weaker and sicker than before but was determined not to be a burden. Even if Terry had been up to making the trip, the overflowing hospitals were no longer accepting new patients.

"The doctors aren't holding out much hope," Terry told Sara the latest news, her tone gloomy. "They haven't seen anything like this before. Apparently the double X chromosome of females simply breaks down. Babies and old women are now dying, and when Kendar checked in on me over the communicator earlier, he told me why. He explained that he comes from the future and—"

"Rest," Sara cut in. She propped a pillow behind Terry's head, wondering exactly how sick she would get. She already liked the girl and fretted how little she knew about doctoring the sick.

Terry clutched her hand with a strength that stopped Sara from leaving. "I want to volunteer."

Was Terry out of her head with a fever? Sara placed a hand on her forehead. The girl did seem a little warm and she handed her a glass of water. "Volunteer for what?"

Terry sipped. "Kendar says you need to balance the time continuum."

"You're in no condition to help, but I appreciate the sentiment."

Terry shook her head. "To create balance for Kendar's coming back—you have to send someone forward. That's what Kendar told me. And I want to be the one to go."

Stunned by Terry's request, Sara rocked back on her heels. She hadn't thought that far ahead. "It's an alien machine. That means we don't know how it works. Even if I can learn to read the directions, I can't guarantee your safe arrival."

"Staying on Mars at this time isn't safe, either." As if sensing Sara's next protest, Terry held up her hand. "Do you realize if the machine works, I'll be the only woman in the future on a Mars filled with men?"

"And that appeals to you?" Sara didn't know if Terry was stupid or brilliant or feverish and cracking a sick joke, but she sure seemed serious—and dead certain.

"Here, I'm no one special. I never finished my schooling and anyone could do my job. I've never been very strong or healthy either. What I really need, and all I ever wanted, was to find a man—"

"Which shouldn't be difficult considering the man/woman ratio," Sara stated with a dry chuckle.

"But if I'm the only woman on Mars, I'd be treated like a queen. It's a once-in-a-lifetime opportunity." She shrugged sadly. "In fact, it may be my only chance at life. And you need someone to go to the future. Why can't it be me?"

As Sara returned to Kendar and the chamber, Terry's request reverberated in her head. To balance the time continuum, it seemed to her that Kendar, not Terry, needed to return to the future. Sending Terry might throw the time line further out of whack. And yet, the idea of Kendar staying here with her held its own appeal.

She hadn't known him long, but in less than one revolution on Mars, he'd made exquisite love to her, revealed unusual patience and creativity and convinced her of an impossible scenario. The man had intelligence and a great body, all wrapped in one supersteamy package. Damn—the uninhibiting side effects of the drugs must be knocking her good sense into a feedback loop. She couldn't stop thinking about him when she really needed to be focusing on work.

Terry's request was moot at this point, at least until Sara spoke to Kendar and had some idea of how the machinery worked. She entered the chamber disappointed to see that Kendar had uncovered no more of the relic. He'd taken off his shirt and squatted next to the pump, wrench in hand.

"An O-ring broke. I'll have to pull out the pieces and find another."

"Thanks." She placed a hand on his shoulder. "I don't know what I'd do without your help. Are you a mechanic?"

"I'm a womanologist."

"Huh?"

"A womanologist studies women, but I've always been good with my hands." He smiled, letting her know that his double entendre was deliberate, reminding her exactly of how he'd touched her and stroked her.

"And what did you think of Terry?"

"She's not special like you."

He'd misunderstood her, but good answer. If she had only one week to live, she was glad to spend that week with Kendar—she wished only that she needn't spend all of her time working and could spare some for more lovemaking.

Enough. She picked up a brush and headed to the pictographs. Maybe digging would take her mind off how yummy Kendar looked with that wrench in his hand.

KENDAR FIXED the O-ring problem and went back to work, clearing debris from the machinery. He'd hated telling Sara the truth about her role in activating the machine, and her pain touched him deeply. She was everything he'd read about her—smart, warm and adaptable—but so much more. He sensed a depth to her, a mixture of emotions that ran the gamut from playful and adventuresome to responsible and determined. He had no doubt that she'd give her all to finding a solution, but if she failed, she would die. And if she succeeded, he'd have to return to his time.

Either way Kendar would lose her.

He told himself he'd live a far richer life for having known her, but that didn't relieve the ache in his heart. Or the sadness swelling a lump in his throat. Could a man fall in love in one day? He'd read of instant chemistry, of love at first sight, but he'd thought these concepts of storytellers and poets and dreamers. Yet, his feelings for Sara ran strong as the Martian sunlight and just as hot. And like a star going supernova, this shiny new feeling was about to explode in his face.

Kendar gripped the nozzle tightly, blowing away an eon of erosion, grateful for the noise of the pump that prevented conversation. He needed time to regroup. Perhaps a man more accustomed to love might know how to accept the loss better than he did. He hadn't expected loving to hurt.

On edge, he worried about Sara, too. She seemed to work at a frenetic pace, her expression tight, her shoulders tensed. When he finally uncovered the last pictograph, she was busy capturing the data, and he took the opportunity to clean up in the fresher. When he returned, she stood in the exact spot where he'd left her.

He joined her, gently placed his hands on her shoulders and began to knead the knots. She tilted her hand back. "Mmm. That feels wonderful, but I should be giving you a massage. You must be dead tired after all that hard labor."

"It's kind of you to think of me, but I'm fine." Even weary from work, she looked beautiful. But she was pushing herself so hard that he worried about distracting her, then wondered if a distraction to lighten the moment might be exactly what she needed.

In the end, he simply couldn't resist her. Taking her tools, he set them down. "I know we should work, but I want to kiss you, again."

She instantly turned and faced him, then wound her arms around his neck. "We can take a break." And he delighted at her unhesitating response.

Her gaze had brightened from a moment before and he liked lightening her mood. "Good. I'm starved. What else is there to eat around—"

She tugged down his head and kissed his mouth. Stars, she smelled good. Felt better. As she pressed her sensual curves against him, he gathered her into his arms, wanting to give her comfort and companionship. He'd never realized that kissing wasn't simply foreplay to lovemaking but that kissing Sara could be so satisfying in and of itself.

Perhaps it was the way she gave of herself, or threw

herself so wholeheartedly into the gesture, sweeping him away as if she had no other thought except desire for him, but, one moment he'd been tired, and now all he could think about was loving her again.

Marveling at how right it felt to hold her, how wonderfully her curves molded to him, he tightened his arms and deepened their kiss. She responded, parting her lips, beckoning, welcoming, drawing him deeper.

Her kiss elevated his pulse and stirred protective emotions he hadn't known he had. Wishing he could wrap her up, carry her away and tuck her someplace safe where they could escape from their problems, but knowing he couldn't, he instead put himself wholeheartedly into the kiss. He might not be able to solve her problems, but for a moment he could chase them away, give her a break from the relentless pressure on her slender shoulders.

Her kisses, as enthusiastic as his, fueled his certainty that destiny had arranged for him to meet such a special woman. Fate and alien machinery had brought them together, and for now, that was enough. Almost enough. It had to be enough.

Yet, he could have held her, kissed her for hours. Her warmth, her scent, her unique mixture of work ethic and passion, had his heart slamming against his ribs, his breath ragged in his chest. His studies hadn't suggested she had such a passionate nature and although he told himself to be patient, that now was not the time to make love, he nevertheless yearned for more. As much as he enjoyed kissing her, his blood danced hot through his veins and demanded that he remove her clothes so they could be flesh to flesh and make love all over again.

She pulled back, breaking the kiss, her faced flushed, her lips swollen, her eyes dancing with excitement. "You actually made me forget for a minute—"

"That was my intention." He held out his hand to her and beat his torrent of passion down with painful determination. "Now, how about some real food? And we should check on Terry."

"You're right, but I don't want to share you. Every minute seems precious."

Her admission warmed him to his toes and his heart ached once more, for all that he might have had with Sara, and all that he would lose. The thought saddened him and as much as he tried to stay in the moment, it was next to impossible. How could he not think about losing her when he had such a special awareness of her every action? If only he could stay here, or take her to the future. But that selfish action might throw time more out of sync than it already was and the consequences for everyone else on Mars could be disastrous. As much as he wanted to keep Sara, the possibility of ruining other lives was not acceptable. However, just because they weren't certain how to activate the time machine, didn't mean they couldn't learn how to turn it off. Finding that off switch might be their only option.

CHAPTER FOUR

TWELVE WOMEN had already died and Sara feared Terry might soon join them. The girl's pallor made her eyes seem to bulge. She hadn't eaten one bite of her dinner and had barely sipped her water. The visit to Terry had put a damper on Sara's former ardor. Despite her growing feelings for Kendar, there was simply no time to waste on personal activity, no matter how pleasant, not with so many lives at stake.

Earlier, she'd been wrong to kiss him when she could have been working and studying the pictographs he'd uncovered. Kissing him only increased her interest in him, and considering what she had on her plate, for both their sakes, she shouldn't encourage a relationship that had no future.

However, she understood too well the compelling urgency to grab on to someone to love when facing death's door. She supposed it was human instinct to mate and propagate the species—especially if one didn't expect to survive. So, not only was she fighting the chemicals still in her system, but millions of years of natural selection.

As Sara had tucked Terry in for the night, the girl had whispered into her ear, "Hurry." And Sara's guilt mounted over thinking about her own feelings when Terry and many others like her were dying. And yet…Sara could only focus for so long without her mind going numb from the tremendous amount of input.

She and Kendar returned to the chamber. Before she checked the computer data, she tried to gather any helpful information from the future. "Did your archaeologists have any theories about the alien machine?"

"Sure. But no one ever figured out how it works, why it was built or how to shut it down. We didn't even know for certain that it was still working—until I ended up here."

"And no one ever figured out how to read the pictographs?"

"If I knew anything that would help, I'd tell you." Kendar stared at the wall, frowning, his arms crossed over his chest. "I'm not holding back. What would be the point? After all, we're trying to change the future."

She peered at the alien machine, but the curves kept grabbing her attention as she sketched. "Have you noticed that there are no straight lines in any of the markings?"

"Is that significant?"

"Probably. But we need to find out why."

SEVERAL HOURS LATER Kendar watched Sara toss aside her notes in discouragement. He ached to gather her into his arms, tell her that everything would be fine, but obviously, everything was far from fine. "You don't have to solve the problem today," he murmured.

Her eyes remained bleak. "If I don't figure out how to read the language, we can't shut down the machine. And then how many women will die tomorrow?"

"You didn't build this relic. It's not your fault."

She let out a long, low sigh. "But I may have inadvertently turned it on."

The chamber's door opened. Sunlight beamed inside and a gust of air blew Sara's notes to the floor as Terry staggered forward. Pale and weak, her skin almost blue, she shivered and stumbled. Was she too sick to remember she could have called for help on the communicator?

Kendar grabbed her arm before she toppled. "What's wrong?"

Terry's eyes brimmed with tears. "I don't want to be alone."

"Join us," Kendar helped the weak woman to a chair. Her skin, clammy beneath his fingers, trembled. She breathed in shallow pants.

"Yes. Come in," Sara invited, stooping to pick up her notes. "I'll fix you some hot tea to warm you up."

Kendar retrieved a blanket and placed it around Terry's shoulders. The poor young woman was deteriorating quickly, and he wished there was something he could do to at least make her more comfortable. The wind gusted and rattled the papers Sara had scooped up and he stepped toward the door to close it.

Sara had turned toward her food supplies when she suddenly stopped and raised her voice. "Don't move."

Kendar froze, except for his eyes that scanned the chamber for danger. But he spied nothing out of the ordinary. Nothing lurking in the shadows.

Sara held up her notes, her expression of concentration intense, her eyes narrowed. "With the light coming in through the door, its shining through my papers."

Terry lifted her head, her sunken eyes burning with interest. "So?"

"I think…I'm not sure…" Sara grabbed her papers with both hands and Kendar expected her to straighten them into a neat pile, but she kept the edges at odd angles to one another. "With the three pages overlapping, I see a pattern."

Terry pulled the edges of the blanket more tightly around her shoulders, her knuckles white. "A pattern?"

"I don't mean to be rude," Sara's voice rose in excitement, "but please, be quiet so I can…" She hurried to the scanner and held the papers up to the light, entering all three layers, one overlying the other, into the database. "From this one scan, the language and decryption program will search for patterns and maybe…"

Terry ignored Sara's request for silence. "Maybe you can send me to the future?"

Kendar stared at Terry. She wanted to go? But that wouldn't balance his coming back.

"Perhaps I can read the alien language," Sara corrected her without directly answering her question.

Terry reacted to Sara's words as if she'd just taken a blow, slumping dejectedly. Kendar supposed he didn't blame the dying woman for her impatience. At Sara's announcement that she might be making progress, hope had lit Terry's eyes and she'd looked at Sara with a serious case of hero worship. But now, she had a secretive, sullen look.

Kendar fixed the tea, his thoughts turning to Sara. While the possibility existed that turning off the machine would stop the effects, it was more likely that if she succeeded, he would have to leave, travel forward to his time. If Sara learned how to use the machine and balance time, he would have to go back where he belonged to correct the irregularity.

He knew that, in that scenario, there would be women on Mars in Kendar's future—but none of them would be Sara. None of them would have her extraordinary combination of brilliance, humanity and sensuality. She was unique.

The computer whirred. Sara tapped her feet impatiently, her eyes going from the monitor back to her notes. He set a cup of tea by her side that grew cool as she ignored it. Terry sipped hers, but the heat didn't seem to lessen her chills.

As for Kendar, he was torn. Torn between wanting to do the right thing and losing the woman he loved. The emotion might be new to him, but surely if his deep feelings for her hadn't swept him away with longing, he wouldn't be aware of the excitement in Sara's every breath and how she so very studiously avoided looking into his eyes. If she looked at him, he was certain he'd see pain and regret there for what success with the relic would do to them personally. The woman clearly reciprocated his feelings, and though hers might not be as strong or as certain yet, nevertheless, she was too intelligent to deny the bond between them.

"Well?" Terry asked.

"The computer's processing," Sara said.

"Is that good?"

"Maybe." Sara glanced at Kendar, her eyes blasting him with longing, compassion and frustration. He didn't think it odd that he could read her feelings from just a glance. Although they'd known one another for only a day, he felt as if he'd known her a lifetime. No doubt his years of studying Sara's life added to his knowledge, but this was more than book learning, this was a connection both emotional and physical.

Tearing her gaze from his, she peered at her computer and bit her bottom lip. "We might have something."

Kendar strode to her side, placed his arm over her shoulder and watched the spinning symbols on the computer align themselves, separate and realign, as if he understood the computer's processes. But his viewing the data was simply an excuse to touch Sara, and as he breathed in her scent, a longing for more time with her washed over him.

Sara pressed buttons, giving several directions and the computer kept altering the pictographs. She pressed a button and the markings decreased in size. But now under them was a translation of the alien message in English.

Stars! Sara had done it. She'd figured out how to read the alien language. Kendar was overwhelmed with pride for her and had to force himself to focus as she read aloud, "Warning. Only one being may utilize the portal at a time. Allow twenty," she paused and the computer displayed a series of symbols that meant it couldn't decipher the word, "Allow twenty of these things between cycles."

"How long is a cycle?" Terry asked.

Sara shrugged. "Perhaps once the computer translates the rest of the pictographs we'll have a better idea." Leaning forward, she studied her screen, her eyes bright and determined. "This is good." Next to the pictographs, simple words were written. *Up. Down. Turn.* And then a seemingly endless series of numbers. "My sleeping pod seems to have been placed directly on a platform for the time portal."

"Do you see a way to turn off the machine?" Kendar asked.

She shook her head. "Those are likely scientific calculations. I may have to…" She reconfigured her computer. "If those numbers match any formulas known to human science, we might soon have our directions."

"Surely it won't be that simple?" Kendar frowned and held her tighter.

"It might be. And we needn't understand how the time machine works to shut it down or use it. Imagine a flashlight. A child can follow simple directions to turn on a light without having any comprehension of electricity."

"So if the directions are complete, you can send me to the future?" Terry asked, her tone pleading, her skin a sickly bluish white.

Sara sighed. "Right now, all I know is that the dial there," she pointed, "seems to correspond to years. And it's set on three hundred."

"You're sure?" Kendar asked, hearing the uncertainty in Sara's tone.

"The computer estimates the probability of a correct translation at seventy-two percent." She shrugged and glanced at Kendar. "And it makes sense."

"I like those odds better than the ones if I stay here," Terry muttered. She shoved out of her chair and staggered toward Sara and Kendar. Before Kendar realized what Terry intended, she'd climbed onto the portal, the spot where he'd arrived next to Sara. "So where's the switch that sends me to the future?"

Sara shrugged. "That part seems to be missing."

The machinery hummed.

And then Terry disappeared.

One minute Kendar had been watching her, the next she'd vanished.

Sara hadn't looked up from her screen. "Terry, please. I know you're sick, but you must try to be patient."

Kendar found his voice. "Terry's gone."

"What?" Sara glanced around the room, her eyes puzzled. "Where did she go?"

"I suspect she went exactly where she wanted to go—to the future."

HORRIFIED THAT SHE had failed to balance the time continuum, Sara fought to hold back tears. She knew of military scientists who'd created weapons, engineers whose experiments had gone awry, but as an archeologist, she dealt with civilizations that had been dead for tens of thousands of years. She'd never expected to be directly responsible for the life of a human, let alone the future of all females on Mars. Since Terry had taken Kendar's place in the future, time hadn't been balanced, but Sara hoped that Terry at least had gotten what she'd wanted. Hopefully, she was now cured and the sole female in a world of men.

Kendar, normally so sensitive, understood Sara was upset. Concern darkened his violet eyes, but she also read confusion in his expression. Nevertheless, he took her into his arms and lent her what comfort he could. Gathering her against his giant chest, one hand rubbing her back, he murmured soothingly. "There was nothing you could have done to stop Terry. Whatever happens, it's not your fault."

Sara allowed his tone to calm her. She'd responded emotionally, not intellectually. And she might have to live with never knowing what had happened. She flicked on her communicator, listened to the news, but no immediate change in the status of women's health was being reported. However, a few spacers were claiming the Martian clocks had gone awry. Still distressed, she turned off the news and remained in Kendar's arms.

"Now what?" he whispered.

"Even if I knew how to turn off the machine, I fear it might make things worse. All we can do is wait."

"We wait?"

"Maybe tomorrow all the sick women will be well." She tried to remain upbeat. "Or perhaps, no one else will fall sick. Or maybe the rate of decline will flatten."

Kendar's eyes oozed sympathy and determination. "Maybe you should send me, too."

She shook her head. "I won't compound one mistake by making another. Sending both you and Terry could make the balance more lopsided than it already is. We need to wait, see if her departure changes the sickness here."

A smile played over his face and brightened his eyes. "You're sure you're not simply making excuses to keep me around?"

"I don't want to lose you," she admitted. "However, I also have no idea how long the machine takes to recycle."

"We also need a break. We can't go nonstop or we won't think straight. As much as we need to find out how to turn off the machine and put time back in balance, we have to pace ourselves. Exhausted people make dumb mistakes."

"You're right."

There was nothing more for her to do at this moment. All her life she'd kept her heart in check, afraid to get too close for fear of losing those she loved. But knowing she might die in a few days changed her outlook, made her bolder, more willing to reach out and take what she wanted. This might be her last chance, and instinctively she knew she'd been waiting for this man. For Kendar. Placing her hands on each side of his jaw, she watched his pupils dilate and his nostrils flare. "And while we wait, I see no reason why we can't…enjoy ourselves."

"Sara." He groaned, slanted his mouth over hers and kissed her with a passion that sizzled straight to her toes.

Sara didn't know if the trying day, the uncertainty of the future, or the drugs that might still be in her system caused every nerve ending in her body to sing greedily for his touch. And at the moment, she didn't care about reason. She knew that Kendar caused her to feel sexier than she'd ever felt, more alive, more certain of her own sensuality. She didn't know how or why, but she liked the way he made her feel about herself. Period. End of story.

She needn't rationalize her need for this man. Wanting him was enough. And she wanted with a blazing, brazen boldness that had her taking off his shirt, slipping off his trousers, leaving him naked and proud and waiting, as if he understood exactly how much she ached to take control of at least one part of her life. And she appreciated that he was confident enough to allow her to do what she wished. That inner certainty and self-assurance was as attractive to her as his violet eyes and the way he'd helped her all day as a true partner.

Oh, yeah. She wanted his bod, but that was because she now knew he had a generous heart and a wise soul. She'd never understood how some very intelligent women seemed to go gaga over a man and lose their center, but she understood now. Kendar made her feel things she hadn't known she was capable of feeling. Trust. Companionship. Lust. Love?

Her mind shied away from the big L-word. She didn't need a label, not when he was standing before her, allowing her to smooth her palms over his shoulders and chest. Not after she plucked at his nipples and his Adam's apple hitched. Not when she leaned forward to wrap her arms around him, placing her mouth even with his nipples and her palms over his tight butt.

"Damn, you feel good," she murmured. Tilting her head back, she looked him straight in the eyes, pleased when he held her gaze with a direct I-want-you look.

"I like you, too." He brushed his pelvis against hers. "All of me likes you."

"Yes, I can see that." Her fingers scampered lightly over where he was hard, teased where he was soft. "But I still remember what you told me."

"Huh?"

"That anticipation increases desire."

His voice deepened with need. "Darling, I have been waiting for you my entire adult life. I just didn't know it—until now."

His words sped her pulse and she kept her hands roaming, stroking, caressing. As much as she wanted him, no way was she going near that damn pallet from where Terry had disappeared. However, the chair should be safe. And interesting. Shaking a stray lock of hair from her eyes and grabbing his hand, she led him to the chair. "Please sit."

"Okay." He did as she asked and patted his thigh. "Join me."

"Not yet." First, she dimmed the lights and set her communicator to emit an upbeat tune. And then she let her hips sway.

His gaze followed her as if glued and his hands clenched the arms of the chair, holding him in place. "What are you doing?"

"Taking off my clothes."

"I wanted to do that." He sounded like a kid who didn't get to unwrap his own birthday gift, but his eyes glinted with fire and his lips curved upward.

She didn't say he could undress her next time. They might not have a next time. She shoved the thought aside. She would think only about now. Only about making this the most memorable experience of his life.

She raised her hand to the top button on her blouse. "You get to watch."

"And touch?" he added, his voice tight, hopeful.

She swayed closer. "Maybe."

He reached for her and she stepped back, taunting him with a grin and an enticing shimmy. "And maybe not."

If he was about to complain, the words died on his lips as she unfastened three more buttons and allowed her shirt to drift open until he could see the curves of her breasts over the lace of her bra. She held up a finger, licked it, then slowly teased her breasts until her nipples hardened beneath the lace. She'd never done anything so sensual and her heart sped, her hips gyrated. Judging from the fire in Kendar's gaze, he was mesmerized.

Good.

Time to mix things up. She shrugged out of her shirt. Turned and removed her bra. When she spun back to face him, her hands covered her bare breasts and she could tell he was practically panting to see more of her. He leaned forward, his head angled intently, his expression fervent, his lips parted. So she made him wait, stepped right in front of him, and without missing a beat of music, she lowered her hands, letting her breasts sway just inches from his mouth.

The moment he tried to capture her between his lips, she dropped to her knees and took his straining erection deep into her mouth. He tasted like pure male heat. Her action must have stunned him because his thighs and calves tightened. He clenched the arm of the chair so hard she wondered if it would break. And his groan of pleasure urged her on.

She nipped and kissed and sucked, teasing and taunting him as he'd done to her. Loving the power of keeping him exactly where she wanted him, aching to bring him literally to his knees with need, she played his body like a musical instrument, strumming a sensual rhythm with her fingers. And when she suspected he couldn't stand another moment, she stopped and regained her feet. He blinked, as if coming out of a daze. Loving his crazed-to-have-her look, yet determined to make him wait a little longer, she gave him a few moments to recover.

And then she unfastened the button of her pants, unzipped and let them drop. She stepped out of them and danced for him, and all that separated them was three steps, his determination to stay put and a triangle of lace. As she danced, her feet moving faster, her hips swiveling to the music, her temperature rose, higher, hotter.

His grip tightened on the chair, until the knuckles changed from bronze to white. Oh, yes. He wanted her, all right. Seeing him fight to keep his desire in check made her determined to see exactly how much he could endure. Exactly how hot could she fire his senses?

"You look...incredible." His voice was hoarse, husky, hard with need.

"Mmm. I can look better."

She eyed the water leftover from making tea, grabbed the pot, raised it over her head, tipped back her neck and poured, letting the now cool liquid sluice over her heated skin. Water droplets clung to her face, her neck, her breasts and Kendar's every appendage tightened, showing his appreciation. He took in all of her with a voracious gaze, and she arched her back, the water glistening on her flesh. When his gaze dropped to the dark, damp triangle of lace, moisture pooled between her thighs.

"Come here," he demanded, his tone needy.

"Soon."

She danced for him as if this was the only time they would ever have, as if she could brand his memory and his need for her into her brain. And when her breath came fast and furious, when her own craving for him demanded that she go to him, she forced her steps to be slow and sure.

As she closed the distance between them, she saw the strain in his eyes, the effort it cost him to wait. Licking her bottom lip, she tossed her wet hair over her shoulder, hooked her thumbs into her panties and yanked them off in one sensual move.

"Stars, you're beautiful."

"Like you have seen a lot of naked women to compare me to," she teased, but he must have realized that although she said the words in jest, there was genuine concern there, too. She *was* the only woman he'd ever seen naked. He couldn't know how he'd react to anyone else. But, she knew she'd never felt this way about any man.

Letting go of the chair, he tugged her forward until she straddled his knees. "Sara, you're special. I want you. Only you."

He seemed sincere, but he was a man. He was primed to make love. He'd say anything at all to have her. And even knowing that, she wanted him, ached for him.

She began to inch forward, lowering her hips to take him inside her. Gently, he clasped her bottom, she thought to guide her over him, but he sat her on his lap, slipped his hand between her parted thighs and found her center, moist and ready. His clever fingers seemed to know exactly what she liked and she closed her eyes as he caressed her and the friction consumed her. She pumped her hips, wanting faster, harder, more.

"We need to talk," he said, though his hand never stopped stroking.

Her eyes popped open. "Now. You want to talk now?"

"Yes." He brushed her nether lips with his fingers, teasing and taunting.

She gritted her teeth, forced herself to concentrate as if he wasn't fondling her with sensual intimacy. "What?"

"You're special to me. Not because you're the first woman I've seen or made love with, but because you're the first to touch my heart."

"You can't know that," she protested, finding it so very difficult to talk while he caressed her.

"Sure I do." He locked gazes with her, his finger slipping into her, then sliding slowly in and out. "I know that I want to know you better. I know that no matter how much I learn about you, I'll still want to know more. And no matter happens, there's a place inside me that will always belong only to you."

God, how could his talk be so sweet while his fingers were so wicked? He had her head spinning, her blood singing. And she understood that he believed what he was saying. For now, that was so much more than she'd ever thought she'd have that joy swelled within her.

She locked gazes with him, wondering if the tenderness in her heart showed on her face. "I need you."

"I'm glad."

"Damn it. I need more of you inside me."

"I'm not a play toy, Sara." He sounded hurt, but his thumb kept doing marvelously imaginative things to her and her breasts ached so much for his touch that when he finally took her into his mouth, she had to…she had to…. "Yes. Oh, yes."

She was so close.

And then he trailed his fingers upward to her breasts. His tone soft, he said, "I love you, Sara."

"What!"

"I love you."

He couldn't love her. They'd only known one another a day. But the way she felt right now wasn't exactly the time to be thinking. He'd kindled every cell of her body into a wildfire and he was having this impossibly sincere conversation. But she couldn't talk. Her mouth had no moisture. Her lungs were starved for air.

"Please, Kendar." She lifted her hips, attempting to take him inside her. "We can talk later."

"Okay," he agreed but then he pushed her bottom back onto his knees, captured her breasts in his hands, his words soft and sexy, holding her somewhere between bliss and outrage. "Tell me you feel the same way I do."

"I...can't."

"Ah sweet Sara. I want more from you." He nuzzled her neck with his lips, blowing a waft of cool air below her ear. She leaned into him, tried to kiss him, but couldn't quite reach his mouth.

She frowned at him, confused. From his physical state, there could be no doubting that he wanted her. Apparently, he wanted more from her emotionally than she was willing to give. She placed her hands on his shoulders. "You didn't mind casual sex yesterday."

"I'm smarter today."

"Or more stupid." Furious with him for making her hot enough to shatter and then asking her to face issues better left alone, she yanked away from him, spun on her heel and bent to pick up her clothes. His hand snagged her waist and he yanked her against him so that her back was to his chest. His hands closed over her breasts, cupping her.

She tried to twist free. "Don't touch me."

"Why not?" he asked, his voice calm, albeit a bit hurt and puzzled.

"Because," she sputtered, so angry she was shouting, "I am not made of stone."

He smiled. "About time you admitted that."

She was about to attempt to twist away again, but he tweaked her nipples, shooting sparks of pleasure to her center. "Kendar…please."

"Please, what? Please press all the right buttons so you can have an orgasm? Please distract me while we wait to see if the experiment worked? Please don't think?"

"Would that be so bad?" As fast as her anger had washed over her, it subsided. She simply couldn't stay angry with the man when he was so logical. Reasonable. Sexy. She leaned back and enjoyed what his hands were doing.

"I want more than an orgasm."

"How about two?" she teased, unable to hold on to even annoyance when she wanted him so much.

He groaned. "I want a relationship. Is that so wrong?"

"This is ridiculous. I may be dead in a week. You may have to leave tomorrow."

"All the more reason not to deny our feelings now," he countered with a logic that made her heart pound and a lump form in her throat.

"Okay…Okay. I'll tell you my feelings as soon as I figure them out."

"Sara, give me something of yourself that you've never shared with anyone else."

"That will satisfy you?" she pleaded.

"For now. Then I'll make love to you. All night if that's what you want."

All night? Yes, she wanted him all night and tomorrow night and the next one, after that, too. She closed her eyes, enjoying his gentle caresses that soothed and fired her up all at the same time. Enjoying even more that he wanted to really know her. "When I was a little girl, my parents died. They left me alone. And it hurt. It hurt so much that I swore I'd never let myself love again. I wouldn't risk loving someone for fear of suffering the pain of losing that person. I studied the past, because the past was safe. Everyone was already dead and gone. Then I met a guy and my resolutions went out the window. But he died in an accident, left me just as my parents had."

"I'm sorry."

"After that, I was done with love. So you see, Kendar, I can't love. I'm damaged. And the fact that you may have to leave me, makes it impossible for me to have more than superficial—"

He angled his mouth over hers to cut off her words and kissed her deeply. She melted into him, her breasts absorbing the warmth of his chest, his heart beating next to hers. The intensity and tenderness of his kiss stole her breath. And then he jerked back and gasped, "If you tell me you felt nothing, then you're a liar."

"I'm disappointed that you stopped. I'm disappointed that you're upset with me."

"I'm not upset. I thought you had more courage."

"I don't. I'm scared."

"Of what?"

"Losing you."

His arms closed around her, his mood turning quiet and gentle. "Listen to yourself. You wouldn't fear losing me, not unless you cared."

She hated him for pointing that out. "Damn you." But his mouth closed over hers again, and the smart man that he was didn't give her a chance to say another word. He lifted her hips and she straddled him, and they ended up against the wall, making love upright.

And when she exploded, lights and sunspots bursting in her head, she shattered, fragmented, barely noting that he fell apart right along with her, and when he did, he shouted her name. It took long moments before the fragments settled and her head stopped spinning. Long moments during which she clung to Kendar in support, wondering what the hell had just happened between them.

CHAPTER FIVE

THE HUMMING in Kendar's ears had to be the aftermath from the rushing orgasm, didn't it? But no, he'd fallen asleep in the chair, holding Sara in his arms. The hum had awakened him.

It was coming from the alien time machine.

Gently, he kissed Sara awake, enjoying how she clung to him in sleep in a way she wouldn't when awake. As her eyes opened and she regained awareness, she turned her head toward the machine. "Something's happening."

They both dressed and he'd barely finished fastening his pants when a light flashed. And Terry suddenly rejoined them.

Sara rushed to the other woman, her face full of concern. "Terry, are you all right? How do you feel? What happened?"

Terry swung her legs over the stone pallet and sat up. Still looking sick, her face pale, she shuddered. "I went to the future but I couldn't stay. Scientists there believe the machine is broken in the *on* position."

"Broken?" Sara exchanged a long, silent, painful glance with Kendar.

"They aren't sure but they said that if I got pulled back to 2405, it would confirm their theory."

"Did they say what we should do?" Sara frowned, and Kendar's heart went out to her.

"They said not to try to shut it off. Instead, they want you to send Kendar to them, but if that doesn't work, and they don't think it will, they want you to look to the past."

Huh? That made no sense to him. What did Sara's past have to do with fixing the future? Kendar helped Terry to her feet and guided her back to her quarters.

Meanwhile, Sara checked her communicator and gave him the news when he returned. "More women are sick and it's spreading." She gazed at Kendar. "I hate asking—"

"You don't have to ask." He climbed onto the pallet, his heart full of sorrow. Either he would go to the future and lose Sara, or he would stay here and lose Sara. Either way, he lost.

And from the desperate look in her eyes, she'd feel the same loss. Reaching out he took her hand. "I'm not sorry I've known you."

She bit her bottom lip. Her eyes brimmed and then she flung herself into his arms. "I'll miss you."

"Maybe not. The scientists don't think this will work.

We don't even know how long it takes the machine to recycle."

"We'll wait as long as it took for Terry to leave and return."

"While I'm gone, do as Terry suggested and look to the past. Since you're the one who apparently changed the time line, it makes sense to study your history to search for anomalies."

"I'll look. I know time is supposed to have a ripple effect. The future can be changed by altering the past." She shook her head. "But I don't know what I'm doing."

He kissed her goodbye, wishing he didn't have to put her through the possibility of losing someone else whom she'd come to care about. However, he believed he was going to return. He had to. She meant too much to him for them to spend the rest of their lives apart. "You'll figure it out, Sara. I have confidence in you. Now, set the dial and let the machine do its job."

SARA HAD HAD no choice but to do as Kendar asked. And in a beat of her aching heart, she sent him back to the future. Then the tears flowed and the pain knifed through her. Why did this keep happening to her? Every time she found someone to love, she lost that person.

Come on, Sara. There's no time for a pity-party. Terry's dying. So are others.

Get a grip. Look to the past.

Brushing away her tears with the back of her hand, Sara eyed her computer, which was full of notes, history and ancient civilizations she'd studied. However, if she had changed the future with her actions, it made sense that she had personally altered the time line. And if the solution was to modify her own past, then she needed to look at her life and the lives of her ancestors.

Striding to the chest she'd brought with her from Earth, she retrieved the heirloom and carried it back to the chair. She'd always kept her journal inside the box and she now hoped the words she'd written might provide a clue. But hours later, she was frustrated, worried and hungry. With no idea what to look for, she was stumped. Without Kendar to steady her, she had trouble keeping down the panic—because she was failing and had no idea what to do.

Was she supposed to go back into time and convince herself not to travel to Mars? If she convinced her yester-year self not to go to Mars then she wouldn't have activated the alien machine and women on Mars wouldn't be dying. That was assuming her presence had turned on the machine—they weren't even sure of that. She eyed Lady Amanda Pratt's journal. Perhaps Sara was supposed to prevent her ancestor from meeting Maxwell Wolford, Earl of Dorsey, her husband. Then Sara would never be born.

But if her ancestors didn't meet, then Ryan Kinsey

wouldn't be born to create the fuel formula that brought people to Mars. Not only wouldn't she have ever been born and live to go to Mars, neither might Kendar, or thousands of others.

The endless possibilities made her head ache, her stomach growl. Deciding she needed food and that she should check on Terry, she left the chamber. Minutes later, she returned in a dejected stupor. Terry had been so weak she couldn't swallow and Sara had had difficulty holding back tears at another imminent loss. She didn't know Terry well, but she was too young to die and the possibility that Sara was responsible for her illness sickened her.

Sending Kendar back clearly hadn't helped change anything for the better. Sara worried that he wouldn't return, but supposed he was better off in his own time than staying here to watch her die, too. Besides, unlike Terry, who the machine had sent back, he belonged in the future and perhaps the machine might sense that and leave him there.

Concentrating on her own life was difficult, but the discipline she'd learned in college helped her work her way through years of notes. As the time neared when she expected Kendar to return, if he returned at all, she found it harder to sit still and keep reading. She missed Kendar's steady encouragement, his reassurance and his belief in her. And she missed his warmth. Her limbs had felt icy since he'd left and no matter how many clothes she'd donned, she couldn't seem to get warm. She made tea and still shivers racked her.

Eventually, she realized that she wasn't ill from missing Kendar. She was in the early stages of the same sickness Terry had, which reminded her once again that time was running out. She had to find a solution, but was no closer to doing so when the machine hummed.

Dropping the journal, she rushed to the time machine. And suddenly, Kendar was there, looking so good her knees almost buckled. Selfishly, her heart lifted at the sight of him. He took one look at her face and held out his arms. "I'm back."

When his strong arms and familiar scent wrapped her up safely in his cocoonlike embrace, she felt as though she'd come home. She could have stayed right there for however much time she had left, but he broke the embrace. "According to scientists in the future, the time line in 1820 needs a repair."

"1820?"

His gaze searched hers. "Do you know the significance of that date?"

"It's the year two of my ancestors met, Lady Pratt and Maxwell Wolford. I guess I should have been reading Lady Pratt's journal, not mine." She started to fetch it, but he held her back, his expression tender, concerned.

"You look exhausted."

"I'm sick."

"Then rest."

She shook her head. "I'm going to get weaker, not stronger. Poor Terry is...I'd better read while I still can."

Sara opened the lid of the chest, her eyes alighting on the journal, the paper pages yellowed, frayed and fragile from age. Her knuckle grazed the box's lid. Where was Ryan's formula? The one he'd carved into the box?

"The formula is...gone." Making sure it wasn't a trick of the light, she ran her fingers over the lid to find it smooth and unmarred.

"Formula?"

"My ancestor carved a formula into the lid of this box. It was here when I came to Mars. Now it's disappeared."

And then it hit her.

"What?" Kendar must have seen the glimmer of excitement in her eyes, the one she always got when puzzle pieces clicked into place.

"Using the portal has altered the past. Time has changed."

"You're certain?"

"This box has been in my family for generations. I played with it as a child. It's not the same and that may mean it's the key. Using the time machine has changed the past and every moment we delay might be tearing apart the past further, and therefore upsetting the future."

If she'd been cold before, now she was ice, ready to shatter.

Kendar took a seat, made a place on his lap, and then after she settled against him, tucked a blanket around her. "Better?"

"Thanks." She opened the journal's leather cover and her hands shook. She didn't just fear she might tear the delicate paper but that the words that she was supposed to read might have altered or vanished like the fuel formula.

"Why don't I read to you?" he suggested and she adored the way he always tried to help her without mentioning her shortcomings.

"I'd like that."

The story he read was old and familiar and helped her rioting nerves settle down. Not only had she altered the future, now she had messed with the past. Who knows what the ripples in time would do to the fabric of history?

In a voice strong, yet gentle, Kendar retold the story of Lady Amanda Pratt, how she'd crossed paths with Lord Maxwell Wolford, who'd bought an unusual heirloom chest right out from under her nose from Gibson's Antiques and Curiosities shop, and how they'd subsequently discovered that the heirloom would only open to Amanda's touch.

"What!" Sara straightened so quickly, she knocked the blanket to the floor. "Did you make up that part?"

"What part?"

"About the box opening only to Lady Pratt's touch?"

"Of course not. I read it right there." He pointed, guessing at the reason for her upset and displaying a keen intelligence. "What's different now?"

"I've read that story dozens of times and I don't recall that detail." Her eyes narrowed. "Or maybe I didn't realize the significance until now."

"I don't understand."

"Before I came to Mars, I asked a locksmith to install a lock on the box so it would only open to family members who shared my DNA. Back in 1820 England that kind of technology didn't exist."

"You had the lock altered before you came to Mars, but according to the journal the lock would open only to your ancestor's touch."

"Exactly. After I altered the lock, I must have sent it back to my ancestor. There's no other explanation for the box only opening to her touch. The box is the key!"

"So now what?"

"I think to balance time, I must take the heirloom back to 1820 and place it in Mr. Gibson's shop so Amanda can track down her earl."

"Stars! You don't know that!" His arms closed around her and he pulled the blanket back up, but not even his heat stopped her shivers.

"We don't know anything for certain, but this heirloom is also supposed to have the fuel formula to Mars etched in the top. I've seen that formula but now it's gone. Look," she smoothed her hand over the lid, "there's no design. I think *I'm* supposed to put it there for Ryan to find."

"This time loop is very confusing."

She forced herself to leave the warmth and security of his lap, determined to do what she must. "I need to look up the formula and engrave it on the box's lid before I take it back to Cardiff, United Kingdom, 1820. That's how I'm going to make time whole again." She was certain. Although she hated the idea of leaving Kendar, and she didn't much like the idea of living in 1820 either, she couldn't allow her feelings to interfere with what she knew must be done.

Sara now believed it was her fate to find love and lose it. Each time she lost a loved one, it seemed as though a piece of her heart went missing. Soon, she wouldn't have one left. But she couldn't dwell on how much she would miss Kendar, or how little time they'd shared together. Or that airplanes hadn't yet been invented in 1820. "Women are dying. I need to get busy."

He snagged her wrist and tugged her toward him. "Sara, there's no rush. If the machine sends you back and you fix the problem, no one will die."

"We don't know that," she countered. "There may only be a small window of opportunity before you and

I and everything we know ceases to exist. Waiting would be foolish. Risky."

"And I still don't understand how my coming back here means you have to go back there to balance things."

"Maybe the aliens made the machine that way. Maybe it's broken. I don't know. But we have too many clues inside my heirloom to ignore them…or to delay." She hugged him, her throat tight, tears welling in her eyes. "I have to work. And then I have to leave. I'm sorry."

"I understand." But he held her closer, until she could feel his heart racing, and only with the utmost reluctance did he loosen his hold. "Do you suppose I could go with you?"

She wished with every cell in her body that it was possible. "The machine says only one person can travel at a time." She saw the longing in his eyes that matched her own yearning to be together. A yearning she had to deny.

"And you mustn't try to follow me. We can't change the time line to suit our whims. As much as I would love to be with you, as much as I'd like to stay in my own time, we can't take a chance of altering history."

"By going back, you *are* altering history."

"I'm supposed to alter history. I have to place this box in the attic of Gibson's Antiques and Curiosities shop because the journal says it was there with a lock that will open only to Lady Amanda's touch." Sara kissed him then, a desperate prelude to a goodbye that would come all too soon. It didn't take long for her to look up the fuel formula in her computer and carve it into the top of the box.

Heart heavy, shoulders sagging under her sorrow, she headed to the pallet, the box in her hands. Unable to speak past the tightness in her throat, she nodded for Kendar to set the time dial to 1820, the place dial to Cardiff, England. Instead, he brushed his lips over hers one last time, a tear falling onto her cheek. One of his tears.

"I love you, Sara."

"And I love you," she admitted as he set the dials and she climbed onto the pallet. The machine hummed. Kendar's tears fell freely, and Sara closed her eyes knowing that the sorrow of losing him would haunt her for the rest of her life.

And then light flashed. Sara had no reason to be certain of what time or place the machine would send her to. She hoped the damn aliens had calibrated their device to direct her to the right place and that she didn't end up on Mars before mankind had colonized it. But if she landed somewhere without oxygen or air pressure, her death would be instantaneous, and then at least her heart would stop its awful ache.

Finally, after taking a few deep breaths that proved she had enough air to survive, Sara found the courage to open her eyes. And blinked. She was still on Mars.

Kendar was turned away from her, as if he hadn't been able to bear watching her vanish. His shoulders shook with deep sobs, and he had yet to realize she was still there. That he cried over losing her touched her deeply, but she had to block out how much she wanted to comfort him. She had to find out why she had failed.

She spoke softly, "Kendar."

His head jerked up. His reddened eyes found hers. "Sara?"

"Something went wrong." Yet, her chills were gone and she felt strong once again.

Kendar's beautiful chiseled tear-streaked face broke into a wide grin of happiness. "Something went right."

He was in denial. Had he accidentally set the dial incorrectly? No, he was too careful to make that kind of mistake. "We should try again. Unless you think we used the machine too soon?"

"The machine worked." He stepped to her and scooped her into his arms. "You're well. Your color is back. Your cheeks are pink and the dark circles under your eyes are gone."

He sounded so certain, and oh, how she loved being in his arms. Yet she was afraid to hope. "But I'm still here."

"Yes, but your heirloom isn't. The machine sent the box back. Apparently, your presence wasn't required."

History only required that the box go back in

time—not her? Could he possibly be right? Could she be that lucky?

Heart racing, hopes brightening like a soaring comet in the Martian sky, Sara flipped on her communicator to the news channel. The DJ made no mention of the women's illness. It was just as Kendar said—as if nothing had gone wrong.

She certainly felt well and sent a signal to Terry, who soon answered in a normal voice, "Yes, Sara?"

"How are you feeling?"

She yawned. "You woke me in the middle of the night to ask how I'm feeling?"

Grinning, Sara couldn't hold back a happy laugh. "Sorry, Terry. Go back to sleep."

Smiling through his drying tears, Kendar twirled her around the chamber. "Satisfied?"

Sara flung her arms around Kendar's neck. "We did it. And you know what the best part is?"

"I get to kiss you?"

"What else?"

"I get to stay here?"

They were going to have a future she'd never thought possible. She had fully expected to return with the heirloom to her ancestor's time. She'd never been happier to be so wrong. This was her time. She belonged here and the alien time machine had made the necessary calculation to keep her with Kendar.

"Mmm. What else?" she snuggled closer.

"You tell me."

"We can spend time together. Days. Months." She nestled her head under his chin, pressed her cheek to his chest, close to his heart. "Years?"

"Decades, Sara." His arms tightened around her and his tone told her that this man was here to stay. The time machine had brought him to her and she thanked her good fortune. "And if I can talk you into a century that would be even better."

"One hundred years has a nice ring to it." And then she kissed him, knowing they had all the time in the world.

*Everything you love about romance...**and more!***

*Please turn the page for Signature Select™
Bonus Features.*

Bonus Features:

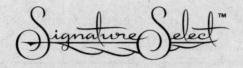

BONUS FEATURES

THE HOPE CHEST

Conversations with the authors of The Hope Chest

Jacquie D'Alessandro

How did you begin your writing career?

My writing career sprang from my love of reading. I grew up loving mysteries and romances, and one day it just struck me that I'd like to follow in the footsteps of the authors I admired and write my own book. I began scribbling on napkins and various scraps of paper. I soon invested in some notebooks, and eventually I had notebooks placed in every room of the house so I could jot down ideas as soon as they hit me (a big improvement over those napkins!). After purchasing a computer, I started compiling all those notes into stories. When my son began school full-time, I started writing full-time.

Do you have a writing routine?

Yes. After seeing our son off to school, my husband and I take a walk and have breakfast together, then I head to my home office and write. I have a set number of pages that I try to accomplish each day. Some days I

make it, some days I don't. The number of pages I
need to produce each day depends on how close to
deadline I am. Some days (good days) it takes six to
eight hours to get the pages done. Other days (not so
good days) it takes twelve to fourteen hours. I've pulled
some all-nighters getting the pages finished.

When you're not writing, what do you love to do?
So many things! Our son is in a marching band and we
love to attend his performances. I love reading,
shopping, going to the movies, spending a relaxing day
at the lake, playing tennis (I'm not very good, but it's a
great calorie burner!), preparing family meals and
traveling. We like having "house picnics," where we'll
spread a blanket on the living-room floor and have an
indoor picnic while watching a movie.

What or who inspires you?
My family inspires me. They are incredibly supportive
and proud of me, and that gives me such incentive to
keep going, to keep trying, to keep doing my best.

If you had a hope chest, what would be in it?
I actually do have a hope chest—the one my parents
bought me as an engagement present. It's filled with
things that are special to me—some beautiful baby
items my mother knitted and crocheted for both me
and my son, favorite baby outfits my son wore, my
husband's and my high school and college yearbooks,
and lots of photo albums. My hope chest is filled with
happy memories that I'll pass along to my son
someday so he can look back and smile.

What are your top five favorite books?

The Prince of Tides by Pat Conroy, *The Bronze Horseman* by Paullina Simons, *Pride and Prejudice* by Jane Austen, *Something Wonderful* by Judith McNaught, *Rising Tides* by Nora Roberts.

If you could travel across time, what time period would you whisk yourself off to first?

Definitely Regency England. I love writing about that period—to me it's just so romantic, with the lords and ladies and balls and country estates. I'd love to spend a day in the period that Jane Austen immortalized in her wonderful books, and if I were given the opportunity to meet Jane herself—what an incredible honor that would be!

Julie Kenner

How did you begin your writing career?

Honestly, the real question is what took me so long to begin my writing career. Until last summer (June 2004) I was a practicing attorney. Prior to that, I studied film instead of creative writing. But I can't remember a time when I didn't want to be a writer. I used to sit in my dad's study and pound out "books" on the typewriter. This was before I could really read, and long before I could type, so the books were, of course, gibberish. And then I used to do the same thing on an IBM Selectric. Now, that was a thrill (really, a computer keyboard just doesn't compare). I guess I'm just addicted to stories...and always have been.

When I was living in Los Angeles I wrote a few screenplays with a friend (unproduced, though one is still occasionally shopped around!) and tinkered with writing a legal thriller. But it wasn't until a friend hooked me up with romance novels that something in me clicked. I tried my hand at an historical novel, realized at about ninety pages that I was failing miserably, then tried short contemporary, specifically Harlequin Temptation, because that was my favorite line. My first manuscript didn't sell, but my second one (which became *Nobody Does It Better*) sold to Harlequin Temptation. And a new career was born!

Do you have a writing routine?
Before I quit my day job, I had a strict routine of writing in the evenings (and in the evenings *after* my daughter went to bed once she was born in 2001—that made for some pretty late nights.). Now that I've quit, I'm still working on developing a new routine. Mostly, I write during the day while Catherine is in day care, then pick her up relatively early and spend the afternoon with her until her dad gets home. I'm trying to wean myself off working on the weekends so that I can spend time with my family!

When you're not writing, what do you love to do?
Play with my daughter! Travel with my husband and daughter! Shop! Watch movies! Rummage in flea markets and thrift stores with my mom! And always, read, read, read!

What or who inspires you?
Oh, lots of things. A fabulous sunset or a view of the mountains inspires me, but not to any particular goal. But it still fills me with a deep sense of respect for beauty and creation. A movie like *Star Wars* inspires me (and makes me think I'm a hack!) because of the brilliant (in my opinion, anyway) way in which mythic structure melded with enduring characters. My critique partners, Kathleen O'Reilly and Dee Davis, inspire me with their wonderful characters and plots and writing styles, and make me grateful every day that we found each other. And of course, the arrival of the monthly bills inspires me to write, write, write!

8 **If you had a hope chest what would be in it?**
All of my favorite children's books, the ones that I stayed up late to read when I was a kid, or that kept me glued to the couch when my friends were outside playing. I'd collect them all and keep them nice and pristine for my daughter and her daughter, and so on and so on.

What are your top five favorite books?
This is an incredibly hard question, and on a different day you might get a different answer. Let's see: *A Wrinkle in Time* by Madeleine L'Engle, *Harry Potter and the Sorcerer's Stone* by J. K. Rowling, Shel Silverstein's *Where the Sidewalk Ends, Gone with the Wind* by Margaret Mitchell.

If you could travel across time, what time period would you whisk yourself off to first?

Hmm. Well, here's where my paranoid, analytical side peeks out. Because the answer is, I can't think of an answer. Go to the past, and I no longer have my daughter or my husband. (I'm assuming I'm traveling by myself, and it sounds dangerous enough that I wouldn't take my daughter! I mean, I'm paranoid just flying her to California this Christmas.) And what if I accidentally changed something and messed up the future (my present)? Or what if I got stuck? The past sounds all well and good, but go too far back and you don't have indoor plumbing and allergy meds and the Internet. And life without a cell phone? Without Starbucks? I managed in the eighties, but, really, I'm not sure how. And the future's not much better. Again, it's the getting stuck thing. Miss watching Catherine grow up? I don't think so.

I guess I'm a content-in-my-own-time kinda gal. I'll take my time travel in novel form! A good book, a nice bright lamp, and I'm all set to go anywhere you'd care to take me. And so long as I've got my coffee and my phone and my plumbing and my electricity, then I have to say that life is good.

Susan Kearney

How did you begin your writing career?

I'd always been a reader, and when I read *Warrior's Woman* by Johanna Lindsey I thought it was a great book. And I was so excited that I wanted to try to write stories like hers—ones that combined romance and other worlds. I've written historical romance, contemporary romance and futuristic romance and I admit that although I love them all, the ones set in the future are my favorites. So I was so excited to write this story for Harlequin.

Do you have a writing routine?
Six pages a day, six days a week is my writing routine. All the extras, proposals, revisions and copyedits are completed after I write those six pages.

When you're not writing, what do you love to do?
I've always liked sports, especially the kind that require concentration. In college I was a three-time all-American diver for the University of Michigan. Later I earned a brown belt in karate. Currently I've taken up figure skating and hope to land my first Axel soon.

What or who inspires you?
My inspiration comes from internal motivation. I've discovered that striving toward a goal makes me happy. It's not so much achieving the goal, but attempting to attain it that gives me pleasure. So although I try to plan to go to great destinations, it's the journey that's the fun part, and celebrating the little steps along the way to my goals with my family keeps me going.

If you had a hope chest what would be in it?
Books and chocolate.

What are your top five favorite books?
Atlas Shrugged and *The Fountainhead* by Ayn Rand, *Time Enough for Love* by Robert A. Heinlein, *Warrior's Woman* by Johanna Lindsey, *The Challenge* by me.

If you could travel across time, what time period would you whisk yourself off to first?
I'd like to travel to the future. We already know what's happened in the past, and a life without indoor plumbing, restaurants and air-conditioning sounds like a hardship to me. I'd like to go to a time when we can readily visit other planets, a time where we've discovered other life beyond ours. Soon we will have cars that are fueled by hydrogen batteries, armor that's made with nanotechnology to repel bullets and medicines that could keep us alive for centuries. Just thinking about an extended lifetime and what we could accomplish with those extra years excites me.

Marsha Zinberg, Executive Editor of Signature Select, spoke with Jacquie, Julie and Susan in the fall of 2004.

The Legend of the Hope Chest

Hope chests have been in existence as long as furniture itself. The "hope" revolved around a young woman's future as a wife. The tradition involved her collecting items such as clothing, linens, china, silverware and other valuables in the hope of marriage. These items were lovingly stored in the chest, and when she married, the chest was taken to her new home and life. In order to preserve the delicate materials, many chests were constructed of cedar. Decorations on the outside varied, from plain to ornate, and inlaid wood designs. In some instances the hope chest was considered a dowry, the contents used as a way of enticing a man into marriage.

Because of the number of bulky items stored in it, hope chests were large, often doubling as a place to sit in many homes. So if we happened upon a chest that was only the size of a loaf of bread, our first thought wouldn't be that it was a hope chest.

But we all know that things are not always what they seem....

Such as a loaf-sized box displayed in the window of an antique shop. With its unusual glossy surface, intricate inlaid wood design and silhouette of a mysterious woman on the lid, the box appears to be nothing more than an attractive decorative piece. Except for some unusual carvings on the inside, the box is empty. Or is it?

Certain things—like hope—don't always take the form of clothing, linen, china, or silverware. Sometimes it's invisible, intangible and seemingly just beyond our reach. We know we're hoping for *something,* but we're not always sure exactly what that something is. Until we see it. And then, in a heartbeat, we know that what—or who—we've been hoping for has been found. And if the desire to purchase a decorative box in an antique shop brings two people together—a man and woman who otherwise would never have met, a man and woman both lonely and searching, hoping for *something*—well, then I think we'd see that hope comes in all different shapes and sizes. It can dwell in boxes, but the most important place it lives is in our hearts.

All in a writer's life...

We asked all three authors to tell us a bit about why they write in the time periods they do. Their answers might surprise you...

[14] Jacquie D'Alessandro

I write in the Regency period because I think it's very romantic, and since I write romance, that works very well! The thought of a faraway place with lords, ladies, fancy balls, magnificent country parties, horse-drawn carriages and spies (those wars, you know!) is utterly fascinating to me and a huge inspiration to my imagination. I like working within the strict confines of England's Society, especially the strict limitations placed on women. My stories explore how those limits affect my characters' lives, and how they overcome the difficulties imposed upon them. Yet after spending several months immersed in the past to write a Regency historical, I then like to switch gears completely and write a contemporary story. It's a rhythm that works well for me, and so far I've managed not to have my historical characters end up with a cell phone or my contemporary characters dancing the quadrille.

Julie Kenner

I took the contemporary tale in the anthology because, frankly, I tend to write stories set in contemporary times. In this case, though, the real thrill for me wasn't the time-setting so much as it was the NASA trappings I was able to bring to the story. That element came into being when Susan, Jacquie and I were brainstorming the overall story thread, and we realized that Susan's story was taking place not only in the future, but on another planet. Jacquie's story was in the past, and mine was a bridge. I saw it not just as a bridge in time, though, but also as a bridge from the earth to Mars. And what better way to hit that topic than to have one of my characters somehow involved with NASA?

So why is that such a thrill? Well, because I've always been fascinated with the space program, not in small part because my parents used to work at NASA in Mountainview, California (where I was born, though I don't remember it, since we moved to Texas soon after). My mom was a secretary (until I came along) and my dad was an aeronautical engineer. I'm pretty sure a satellite he worked on is still up there, circling in some endless orbit.

Without giving away my exact age (ahem) let's just say this was during the space program's heyday, but before Apollo 11 (I was little, but I actually remember watching Neil Armstrong's historic step onto the moon on our television; we were in Texas by then). At some point when I was a little kid, my dad gave me a NASA folder. I still have it somewhere. It's filled with eight-by-ten glossies of astronauts, moon rocks, a view of earth from space. It also has some maps of the moon and other stuff I don't specifically remember.

I think my grandmother must have shared my fascination (or maybe she was just proud of her son, my dad) because bits of NASA and astronaut-related things made it into our family mythology. For example, from the time I was a very small child, my grandmother told me that Al Bean (one of the Apollo astronauts) used to baby-sit me. Naturally I thought this was pretty cool. And it even made sense after I got older and realized that the astronauts did not, as a rule, hang out at the Mountainview NASA office. Houston was really more their domain. But the reason it made sense is that my dad grew up in Fort Worth and went to school with Al. Thus the story had an air of respectability and I ate it up.

Alas, my illusions were recently shattered. I happened to mention this bit of family history to my dad, and he looked at me as if I were nuts. Yes, he knows Al (he even visited him at his Houston home not too very long ago), and yes, they went to school together. Mr. Bean probably even met me at one point or another in my youth. But he never baby-sat me. That honor was usually reserved for teenage neighborhood kids, not my dad's old school chums, and certainly not astronauts.

And that's why I never asked my dad to confirm or deny the next bit of Grandma Ebby's NASA family mythology. I've bought in to this one fully, and no one is gonna tell me it ain't so.

From before I was born, my parents had a wonderful cat named Sammy. (By wonderful I mean that he put up with little me dressing him in my doll's clothes. No scratching, biting or hissing. He'd just put up with it until he had enough, then go hide under the couch. I adored Sammy.) I learned from Grandma that Sammy was short for Sam-somethingorothermythologicalsounding. And that Sam had a brother named Rom-somethingorothermythologicalsounding.

My parents acquired Sam in California while they were working at NASA. He was born to a cat who belonged to a guy in the astronaut program, and when the guy's cat had kittens, he named them Sam-etc. and Rom-etc. It turned out that Sam-etc. and Rom-etc. were the code names for two top secret projects that the astronaut had been assigned to. No more. He was reassigned (to Alaska, the story goes) and the cats stayed behind with my dad's best friend, who turned out to be allergic, and my dad got Sammy, a king among kitties and, if the rumor is true, with an Eyes Only name.

True? Not true? Beats me. I've believed it for thirty-something years, and Daddy, if you're reading this and it's *not* true, please don't tell me!

So you see, my fascination with spinning yarns about NASA is genetic. And in fact, I actually have an idea for a thriller involving an Apollo astronaut. Maybe someday I'll give Al a call. Just for research purposes, you know. I mean, surely he'd talk to a little kid he used to baby-sit....

Susan Kearney

Stories have always come easily to me; however, writing them is quite difficult. That's probably because I didn't like English classes in school. Grammar is boring, boring, boring. And studying business at the University of Michigan wasn't exactly the right background for becoming an author. I had one thing going for me: I'd always loved to read. Growing up I loved biographies, mainstream fiction and science fiction. When my grandmother gave me my first romance to read at age ten, *The Wolf and the Dove*, I was hooked.

I've read romances for years. Back in my teens the romances I read were all historical and my favorites were the hot and spicy ones. And then I read a futuristic romance by Johanna Lindsey and was fascinated. I tried to find more romances set in the future, but they were few and far between back then. So I figured the publishers must need more of them. I was so wrong—the futuristic market simply wasn't that popular. But in my ignorance I happily went about writing three love stories set in the future. Along the way I made a bunch of great new friends and discovered I didn't know squat about writing. Editors expect you to know where to put those pesky commas. And they expect the book to be broken up into chapters.

Luckily, I didn't know how much I had to learn. I wrote five books in eighteen months, then sold my first two books, historical romances, to Zebra's Heart Fire line. I told everyone I'd sold a book. Lots of people didn't believe me, but I didn't worry, because soon I would have a book in print to show them. Only, Zebra canceled the line and those books were never published.

Determined to sell a book, I decided to write a contemporary romantic suspense for the Silhouette Intimate Moments line. But the fit wasn't right. However, the book, *Tara's Child,* found a home with Harlequin Intrigue, and after that sale I was on my way and wrote another twenty or so books for Harlequin Intrigue.

However, I'd never lost my love of science fiction, and Charlotte Douglas and I wrote a *Star Trek* book, *The Battle of Betazed,* that made the *USA TODAY* bestseller list.

Meanwhile, Harlequin had begun a line of books called Blaze—hot, sensual and spicy books that sounded like fun. So I started writing for Harlequin Blaze, too. I enjoy creating different kinds of stories, and the simmering sensuality of Blaze was a challenge I relished.

And then I heard about a publisher who was looking for paranormal romance and I sent my very first futuristic story idea off to them. To my delight they were interested in my paranormal romance—which needed a complete rewrite. After some forty books, after ten years of writing, I'd learned a lot. So my very first story, *The Challenge*, was released in February and the sequel, *The Darè*, will be out in July.

However, I've never lost my love of suspense. Harlequin Signature Select allowed me to write a paranormal romantic suspense, titled *On the Edge*, which will be in stores in May.

Writing has kept me extremely busy. The fun part is that I can sit in my home and create to my heart's delight. I've been fortunate to combine creativity with a career I love. You can read excerpts from all my upcoming books at www.SusanKearney.com.

Here's a sneak peek...

ON THE EDGE
by
Susan Kearney

*Some dreams are all too real...how much did Kaylin
Dancroft really know about her sister's disappearance?*

PROLOGUE

IN THE GLOOM of the late-night storm, rain pinged on the roof and the wind keened as if in warning, bringing realism to Kaylin Dancroft's nightmare, in which warped branches twisted like arms rising out of a tree trunk in search of prey. In search of her.

She had to wake up.

Had to get out of bed.

Hide.

Still more than half-asleep, she rolled off the mattress, stumbled into the walk-in closet and shut the louvered door. She crouched shivering, teeth chattering, filled with the conviction that the evil lurking outside was stalking her.

Terror clawed up her gut. Fear squeezed her throat tight, and she couldn't mutter as much as a yelp. Though she told herself she'd experienced only another ugly nightmare and should climb back into bed, her feet might as well have been encased in hardened cement. Wedged in her closet by her subconscious, she couldn't move. Couldn't breathe.

Thunder boomed. Her window squeaked open. Damp air and the scent of rain saturated the room.

Oh, God.

This wasn't part of another bad dream. Someone was here. In her room.

She peeked through the slats of the closet door. A man's silhouette hovered over her bed. Lightning bolted against the black clouds, and for a split second Kaylin glimpsed a swarthy shape against the stormy sky.

For a moment she hesitated, indecisive. Maybe he was meeting a lover and had climbed into the wrong window of the wrong house.

Yeah, right. And she was Xena, warrior princess.

No matter how much she wished otherwise, the gun in his hand, as much as his ominous hulk looming over her bed, convinced Kaylin that he meant business—nasty business. Menacing malevolence clung to him like the stench of foul garbage. She sensed a monster beyond her worst nightmare. Without remorse, without humanity. Without a soul.

He turned from her tossed-off blanket and vacant pillow to check the bathroom, but still blocked her chance to flee. After assuring himself the bathroom was empty, he trod back to Kaylin's bed and slicked his hand over her bare sheets. *Oh, God.* He was checking for warmth, assessing how long ago she'd left. Lightning flashed again. With his face in total shadow, enough light glinted for her to see him raise the finger that had just touched her bed to his mouth for a long lick, an obscene gesture. Shuddering, she prayed he wouldn't find her.

And her prayer was answered. The intruder retreated from Kaylin's bed and padded over to Jenna.

She's not the one you came for. Leave her alone. She's only sixteen, too young to know that evil like you exists in the world.

Twenty-two-year-old Kaylin knew this man had willfully targeted the Dancroft home. And Kaylin. Although she couldn't pin down the specifics of her dream, she'd sensed that he was coming for *her*—but dear God, not for Jenna.

This time God didn't heed Kaylin's prayer. And when the monster nudged Jenna with the gun, Kaylin's terror kicked into high gear.

Blissfully asleep, Jenna was unaware of the menace focused on her. Kaylin had to protect her sister, had to stop the predator. But how? He had a gun. Calling out to her parents down the hall could get them all killed.

She had to save Jenna.

Kaylin's fingers skimmed over a shoe box, a tennis racket, a backpack. *Damn. Damn. Damn.* Where was a golf club or a baseball bat when she needed one? Adrenaline rushing, she settled for an umbrella, clenching it with both hands.

Wait for the right moment.

Wait until he's vulnerable.

Wait…

He turned his back.

Now.

Pulse speeding, palms sweaty, Kaylin slowly and silently shoved open the closet door with her foot. Barefoot, she advanced with quiet steps.

Again he poked Jenna with the gun, but, as usual, Jenna didn't want to wake up. Her sister groaned and turned onto her stomach, one hand flung over her head.

Almost there. One more step.

The man wound his arm around Jenna's throat and yanked. She let out a short, muffled curse.

And Kaylin pounced, smashing the umbrella on the arm of the hand holding the gun. Although she had lunged silently, the intruder spun to meet her attack like a wild jungle animal focused on survival, his mouth spewing obscenities. With an upward swing of his arm he blocked her blow as easily as he'd have brushed off a flea, then slammed her into a wall.

Her head burst with hot pain that caused her legs to buckle. She fought to push back to her feet, but her muscles refused to work.

Kaylin's world went black.

26

CHAPTER ONE

Four years later

Shane Lynch eyeballed the woman sitting by herself in the dark movie theater. If she'd glanced his way just once, he would have smiled, flirted, charmingly used one of the dozen pickup lines he'd kept handy for this mission, but Kaylin Dancroft looked neither right nor left. Her hair had fallen forward and half covered her cheek. Watching her run along Tampa Bay this morning, he had thought it pure golden; now in the light from the screen he noticed auburn tints, a rich warmth that contrasted with her too-pale cheeks and the dark shadows under her eyes. As the trailers ended and credits for the feature rolled, she stared straight ahead, almost transfixed, her don't-approach-me vibes obvious to anyone. To a man with Shane Lynch's extraordinary perceptions, her aura was in shut-down mode, a condition that wasn't just unusual or rare, but unique.

Even if work hadn't required him to get to know Kaylin Dancroft, Shane would have gravitated to her like a collector of rare art to a newfound Renoir. In search of a casual way to meet, he'd tailed her since before dawn when she'd jogged along Tampa Bay, her sneakers tapping a swift staccato on Bayshore Boulevard's sidewalk. Her stride, a sassy sway of trim hips mixed with her own brand of feminine swagger, had shaken him up and restarted his engines. Until that moment he hadn't known how much he'd looked forward to a new challenge. Or how tired he'd become of Middle Eastern countries—it had been too long since he'd seen bare legs. And Kaylin's were tanned and toned, incredibly shapely. However, great legs and a fine-looking woman alone would have held his interest for only a short time. Shane had known many beautiful women, their auras ranging from quiet green to blazing scarlet. None of them had Kaylin's strength of mind.

28

Self-contained, Kaylin hadn't given him one opening to approach her with a casual greeting. How did one meet a woman who was so isolated? All day she'd hurried from one task to the next. She'd never stopped moving until she'd entered the movie and sat in her aisle seat.

Apparent exhaustion caused her head to droop. Her eyelids fluttered. As if to counter the sleepiness stealing into her shoulders and softening her stiff posture, she gripped her thighs, her fingertips leaving indentations in her slacks. Still, her chin declined another notch. She jerked in her chair, as if making one last-ditch effort to avoid slumber, before her jaw went slack, her eyes closed and she succumbed to sleep—once again squelching all opportunity to introduce himself.

Like men exhausted from arduous Special Forces training, Kaylin twitched, jerked and spasmed. She remained oblivious to Schwarzenegger's on-screen entrance in the nude as she slumped into deeper sleep.

During REM sleep most minds were exposed, vulnerable, yet even in sleep Kaylin kept tight control of her aura. However, not even she could prevent several low-level leaks in the violet end of her spectrum.

Finally. Something Shane could work with.

Until today, he'd believed he'd already seen every possible aura variation. Shane had worked as chief assistant to the ambassador in Afghanistan, gone undercover and infiltrated cells in Iraq and Kuwait, employing his special talents to reroute tempers and passions into positive directions. But Kaylin's aura was different from any he'd encountered. Finally, as she dreamed, she exposed a thin crescent, reminding him of a lunar eclipse, the gray penumbra a muted violet that shadowed the surrounding light.

Kaylin moaned, and the feral, guttural intensity coming from those coral-glossed lips startled Shane. He wouldn't have thought a slender throat could emit such a splintered cry. A man in the back of the audience hissed for quiet. Someone else cursed. Unaware of the commotion she was causing, Kaylin let out a piercing wail that sliced like a garrote. Even as he gathered strength to help her, her pent-up pain reverberated through him, heightening his desire to go to her.

Shane leaned forward until his mouth neared the shell of Kaylin's ear and her citrus fragrance teased his nostrils. He kept his words clipped, his tone easy. "Wake up."

For all the response he received, he might as well have been talking to the robot on the screen.

Again she screamed, this time in a stubby burst that seemed artificially cut off and all the more shocking for ending in an insufferable gurgle. Shane noted the additional shouts of annoyance from the peanut gallery, but his immediate concern was for Kaylin, clearly caught in an unbearable nightmare. As badly as she needed sleep, he had to wake her before the security guard entering through the double doors identified who was causing the disturbance.

By the flickering violets of her aura, Shane knew she'd finally yielded to deeper sleep. He hurdled over the row and took the seat beside her. Lightly he placed a palm on her shoulder. With a violent wrench she rejected his touch, pitched forward and let out a full-throated shriek, drawing the guard's attention.

The security guard strode down the aisle, stopped at her row and aimed his flashlight at Kaylin. "What's the problem, ma'am?"

With her fingers now clasping the chair in front of her and her eyes wide open, she appeared to be awake. But she didn't turn her head toward the bright light or alter her expression.

Shane spoke quietly to the uniformed guard. "She's having a nightmare."

The guard's light revealed Kaylin's dilated irises, her too-tight grip and her unnaturally stiff bearing. "Looks more like she's on something."

Shane had run into his share of security personnel. This one, with his middle-aged belly hanging over his

30

belt and his kind eyes, seemed like a guy inclined to take the easiest way out. If Shane could extract Kaylin from the premises, he didn't think the guy would call the cops. But if she shook off Shane a second time, he feared the guard would make a move.

With swift decisiveness that had earned him a Silver Star during his stint in the army and presidential commendation after a classified assignment in an African nation, Shane dropped to one knee, scooped her up, gathered her against his chest and strode out of the movie to the applause of the entire audience.

She was thin, so he hadn't expected her to weigh so much. Her delicate facial features and slender body disguised a muscular frame, but her weight was not a problem for him. Shane had carried full-grown men off battlefields and he'd dragged an injured partner through a muddy rice paddy to safety, but those men had placed their trust in him. Kaylin was a stranger, and lifting her into his arms seemed an invasion of her privacy.

She screamed again, and he winced. There was nothing fragile about her voice or the pain the nightmare had brought out.

Striding quickly through the exit and the lighted foyer into the lobby, he noted from her disappearing violet aura that she was rousing slowly from her frightening nightmare. She blinked a few times, tucked her cheek into his shoulder and muttered a few muffled words he couldn't understand. Lifting her hand, she skimmed her palm along his cheek, caressed the line of his jaw, trailed the pads of her fingertips over his shoulder.

"You'll be fine," he murmured.

Finally she opened her eyes and stared at him, strength evident in her eyes, her green irises flecked with golden sparks of confusion. Waking in a strange man's arms must be disconcerting. Another woman might have slammed her fists between his shoulder blades or kneed his ribs or screamed hysterically, but she took in the people around them in the brightly lit lobby, then focused on him.

"Why are you holding me?"

He chuckled, pleased by her logical question. "You had a bad dream."

"I always have bad dreams. But no one has ever carried me out of a theater before." Taking a deep breath, she stared at him, her perfectly arched eyebrows drawing together. "Please put me down and tell me what happened."

Casual on the surface, her tone was threaded with steel. He set her on her feet, and with her aura again locked down tight, she gave away nothing, not even a dim glow from the embers he sensed beneath her caged emotions. Not good. Especially when his goal was to get her to talk.

"You fell asleep, screamed and disturbed the audience." He jerked his chin over his shoulder at the security guard who'd trailed them into the lobby. "I carried you out."

Her lips tightened, then twitched, revealing she was both wary and amused. "Why didn't you just wake me?"

He shrugged. "I tried."

32

She laughed, her tone throaty and low, and she surprised him yet again by her seeming acceptance of his explanation. Shane had been out of the country so long that he'd forgotten the effect a sophisticated, confident and successful American woman could have on his senses. The memory of carrying her, the feel of her trim thighs under his arm, her hand reaching to touch his face, her slender waist beneath his hands as he'd set her down intrigued him. But it was her aura that fascinated him.

"Kaylin Dancroft." She offered her hand, her tone friendly. Her grip was firm, the nails bitten down to the quick, but smooth and straight and polished, as if she'd tried to repair the damage. "Thank you for getting me out of there."

"Shane Lynch, and you're welcome." Sensing the cool composure she'd wrapped around herself as a self-defense mechanism to keep him at a distance, he tried his charming smile. "Do you want to go next door for a coffee or a bite to eat?" He spoke softly, his voice inviting, allowing his interest to come through. If he remembered correctly, a woman usually responded by reciprocating with a brightening of the eyes, a luminous smile, or by letting him know that she was unavailable. Kaylin did none of the above.

Cocking her head, she drank him in with a lingering appraisal, examining him from the cut of his hair to his casual sport coat and open-necked shirt to his ultra-comfy but slightly scuffed loafers, without revealing a clue to her thoughts. Shane rarely came across a civilian good at hiding her feelings.

"Coffee sounds good," she replied, but with a measure of reserve that told him he had opened a mere sliver in her armor. If he'd ever seen a woman who needed to relax, it was Kaylin, and as he searched for a topic that wouldn't alarm her, he sent feelings of soothing calm her way.

Shane had the advantage of knowing Kaylin's background, thanks to her father. General Dancroft had briefed him last week when he'd requested Shane's help. Apparently Kaylin had good reason to shut down. She'd been through hell since Jenna's kidnapping. Wary of doctors, hypnotists, psychics and strangers, who'd poked and prodded her memory in an attempt to make her recall the kidnapper's identity, Kaylin would likely oppose cooperating with a man who specialized in reading auras and transferring emotion. So her father had insisted that Shane approach her covertly and earn her trust before they attempted to reconstruct the image of the kidnapper's face together.

Privately, Shane had questioned if deception was the right way to go. Gaining her trust by lying seemed like a bad tactic. Yet Shane didn't want to second-guess the wily general who'd been known as a brilliant strategist before his retirement. He'd agreed to Dancroft's plan— with the understanding that he could alter it as he saw fit.

Giving a firm nod to the security guard to signal the situation was under control, Shane led Kaylin out of the theater's lobby and into the shop next door. The rich scent of coffee enveloped them, and the Rolling Stones played on the speakers. The only other customer lounged in the back, drinking coffee and using the wireless Internet service. While hoping the setting—with its aroma of exotic coffees, and pastries and confections enticingly displayed—would reassure Kaylin, Shane appreciated the smooth marketing angle of having related accessories and equipment for sale.

It was good to be back in the States with all the comforts of home. And working with an interesting woman instead of infiltrating terrorist groups was a bonus long overdue.

He ordered a cappuccino and she the espresso con panna. After taking a booth, he savored the first rich sip and noted her fingers tightly clutching her hot cup. She neither relaxed nor chattered to fill the silence with small talk.

After allowing the caffeine to kick in, Shane tapped in to more of his calm, then wrapped her in a soothing cloud of relaxation, sympathy and compassion, and she rewarded his effort with a pink flickering flame in her aura. Like a survivalist dependent upon that fire for heat and warmth, he tended that pink with care, feeding it with dry twigs of tranquil energy.

"How long since you last slept?" he asked.

"Seventy-eight hours." When he raised a skeptical eyebrow, she added, "My record is ninety-six. I'll reach the walking-zombie stage soon. So please don't hold that against me." She plucked a napkin from the holder and dabbed at her lip. "Enough about me. Tell me about yourself."

She'd told him almost nothing about herself, but he let it go, sensing if he pushed too soon, she'd shut down again. "What do you want to know?"

She eyed him a bit warily. "You came to the movie alone?"

"Yes." Habit kept him from saying more. He didn't want to spook her by admitting he'd gone to the movie for the express purpose of meeting her. Then he realized that even if she wasn't digging for information to satisfy her curiosity, he might help his cause and get her to relax by giving her some personal details. "I'm not currently seeing anyone. I've never married. Guess I haven't stayed in one place long enough."

"And your family?" Her eyes bored into his, and he caught on quickly to what was important to her by how her question homed in on family, not what he did for a living.

"There's just me," he said, "and my sister, Eileen." And their sordid family history.

He didn't let himself dwell on what might have been. Now was not the time to think about Peggy Robards. He shoved down hard on the churning anger that filled his gut every time he recalled her rejection of his marriage proposal. She hadn't wanted to marry a man who'd inherited such a violent nature, and he shouldn't blame her. If he hadn't learned to control himself most of the time he'd probably have ended up on death row—like his father, the bastard. Shane hoped he rotted in hell. Death had been too good for the son of a bitch who had abused his mother and Shane for years.

36

He shouldn't blame Peggy for her unwillingness to take a chance on him, but he did. Yes, he'd lost control. Yes, he'd used more force than he should have, but he'd had good reason—at least in his mind.

Fortunately for Shane, his sister trusted him, even with her children. And that gave Shane hope. If Eileen could trust him, surely another woman could, too.

Although Shane knew Kaylin was single and free, he pretended otherwise. "What about yourself? You with anyone?"

She shook her head and shot him a wry grin. "Most men are more frightened of my nightmares than I am."

With another woman he might have suggested that he'd awaken her if necessary, then make her forget her nightmare. But he didn't tease Kaylin. Although she was talking to him about personal things—score one for him—Shane's legendary charm was far from chipping away at her solid walls. Besides, he had too much compassion for what she'd gone through after the loss of her sister to make light of her nightmares.

"You have these nightmares often?" He kept his voice casual, but sensing that she wouldn't be honest with a stranger unless he maintained a balm of security wrapped around her, he sent out soothing calm and extra sympathy.

She shrugged and licked a dab of whipped cream from her lip. "Sometimes..." she said, the words slow and hesitant, and he nudged his compassion up a notch to encourage her. "Sometimes I go for months without a dream. Sometimes I can't close my eyes without..."

SNEAK PEEK BONUS FEATURE

The pink that had brightened suddenly faded. Shane refused to let her ability to open up to him wither—not after she'd begun to be honest. He packed encouragement and tranquility around her, nurturing the flickers that brightened and multiplied. "Can't close your eyes without…what?"

"Dreaming." She shook her head. "I don't usually talk to strangers about… Tonight was especially bad."

He softened his tone, didn't let up his mental soothing. "What did you dream?"

Shadows in her eyes, she stared into her coffee so long he wondered if she would answer. Finally she raised her pain-filled gaze and he wished he could take her into his arms. Instead, he forced himself to be patient and sent more psychic empathy her way.

In contrast to her visible pain, her voice was strong. "Four years ago while I was home from college on spring break, my sister Jenna was kidnapped. She was never found."

He shook his head. "That's horrible—to lose a loved one in such an awful way. Were you close?"

"She was much younger than me and we were nothing alike, but yeah, we were…friends. I'm the typical first child, the one who wanted the parents' approval and played by the rules, but Jenna's middle name should have been rebel. She loved life, feared nothing and raised hell. She adored bad boys and fast cars…yet I admired her spirit of adventure, her zest to live every moment fully, and she envied my dedication." Her voice filled with fondness. "We shared everything and I tried to keep her out of trouble. The one time she needed me…really needed me…I didn't come through."

"What do you mean?" He kept his tone nonjudgmental and pushed comfort her way. He might be able to take the edge off her pain, but the wound was still too raw for him to heal. Shane often took missions where he felt sympathy for the people he helped, but Kaylin's quiet strength combined with her suffering tugged at his heart, and he hoped he could lessen her pain.

"Jenna's kidnapper was coming for me that night. But when I hid, he took her instead."

"Sounds like survivor's guilt."

"So over half a dozen shrinks have told me. Too bad they don't have a clue how to cure it." Disgust smoked up her voice. She sipped her coffee and stared over his shoulder, but he could still see the agony in her eyes.

He couldn't let her remain silent, especially now that he understood that keeping her past bottled up was her natural inclination. As an expert at persuasion, Shane drew upon his talents, again infusing her pink auras with encouragement.

"Why did you hide from the kidnapper? Did you hear him coming?"

"I dreamed it." She thrummed her fingers on the tabletop. "You see, my dreams aren't normal. Mine come true."

"Your dreams come true?" Shane repeated Kaylin's words as if deciding if he liked the flavor. There was no doubt in his tone, no snide patronization, just acceptance and a compassion that she rarely saw in others. He spoke without the skepticism she'd come to expect from people, and maybe that's why she found talking to him so easy. Still, she couldn't believe she was opening up to a total stranger. Shane was affecting her oddly and she didn't understand why she wanted to talk about such personal things. Perhaps it was simply because she'd kept her fears and thoughts contained for so long that at the first sympathetic ear, she'd opened up. Or maybe she'd spoken so freely because he had no ulterior motive. She could speak to him like someone beside her on an airplane, knowing she wouldn't see him again.

She had no idea how he could accept such a preposterous phenomenon as her clairvoyance without knowing more than she'd told him. From the moment she'd opened her eyes and seen him, he'd seemed so much a what-you-see-is-what-you-get kind of guy that she'd just enjoyed the moment, relaxed in his support.

What woman wouldn't? She swallowed a grin of pleasure at the memory of him cradling her easily against his powerful chest. After a tough day at the real estate office where she'd lost what would have been a lucrative listing to another saleswoman, then had to convince a home seller that the current buyer's market required him to repair his roof in order for her to sell his home, she'd gone to the movies to watch Arnold Schwarzenegger and ended up with her very own action-movie hero. Shane might have that larger-than-life demeanor, but he also seemed gentle, considerate. And if he had trouble swallowing her claim of clairvoyance, he had the impeccable control not to show it. His gray eyes seemed open, warm and compassionate.

On the surface, Shane appeared a man's man with muscles and chiseled bones and honed edges. He seemed the kind who judged someone a friend or a foe with little room between. So when he followed up with another question, she was pleased to hear genuine curiosity, not skepticism, in his tone.

"Have your dreams always come true?"

"For as long as I can remember." Although she couldn't recall the last time she'd admitted her clairvoyance, it felt good to air her secret, the relief like lancing a boil.

His eyebrows narrowed. "You sound as though you don't appreciate your gift."

"Gift?" She snorted. "It's more a curse."

"I don't understand."

Of course he didn't, but his lack of comprehension didn't surprise her. It was his seeming belief in her clairvoyance that brought her up short. Kaylin's job involved meeting many people, but the nature of real estate entailed a steady stream of buyers and sellers coming and going, none of whom she got to know well. Her job suited her. She liked the freedom to set her own hours. She liked the contact with people—people who never knew her well enough to know she was different. People who would have thought she was crazy if she'd told them what she'd just spilled to Shane.

Yet he believed her.

She didn't know why, but he did, and his belief in her must be what had allowed her to set aside her normal wariness of strangers. At the most primitive level of her psyche, Kaylin recognized Shane had an edge that made him see or accept what others didn't or couldn't. Something elemental was allowing her to overcome her customary suspicions. Something she couldn't nail down. Something that she found damn attractive. Almost irresistible.

She felt compelled to explain, to make him understand. For once she didn't overanalyze the connection they seemed to share and went with her gut. "When I was eight, I dreamed that my puppy had gotten loose. As a result, for weeks I didn't let that dog out of my sight. When a neighbor accidentally left our back door open and the dog escaped, I cried and cried that I'd failed to protect him."

"Did he get struck by a car?"

She shook her head. "That's what I feared, but that night he finally returned home safe and sound. But because of my dream, I'd spent weeks worrying over him…for nothing."

"Does that happen a lot?"

"The dreams are never clear. I get haunting flashes, distorted images, and have no way of knowing what the dreams mean. The most frustrating thing is how little control I have. When I was about six years old, I dreamed about drowning. I saw thrashing, arms slipping under the water, then a body floating, facedown, on the surface. But I never saw the child's face."

"You knew him?" Sympathy oozed from his tone, but no pity. Pity would have stopped her, because she hated that more than the people who didn't believe her. Even more than her mother's belief that her clairvoyance came from some evil part of her.

She saw only reassuring interest in Shane's eyes. According to all the shrinks she'd seen, talking was supposed to help her survivor's guilt, yet despite the difficulty she had finding people who could converse rationally about an irrational subject, she didn't understand her almost compelling need to spill her story. "The following week I learned that a neighbor, Bobby Becker, had drowned. I became hysterical—because I'd seen his death, but not enough of the details to warn him."

"You were a child…"

She sighed. "It never gets easier. Too many of my visions turn out correctly for me to ignore them. The bad ones haunt me, as well as the harmless ones. The timing is always a bitch."

"The timing?"

"The most frustrating part of my clairvoyance isn't that people don't believe me—it's that sometimes they do."

"You're losing me."

"Last year I dreamed that my friend Leslie would break her arm in a car crash. So of course I cautioned her not to drive, and she didn't for a week. Two days after she began again, a drunk driver smashed into her, and she broke her arm."

"You envisioned the crash, but not the date." He caught on quickly.

"Yeah. Leslie couldn't give up driving for a lifetime. So not only is my foreknowledge useless, the inability to change what I see is no gift."

She'd already opened up more to Shane than any man she'd ever met. The late hour and the lack of other customers made the conversation intimate and easy. And perhaps she knew that Shane wasn't going to remain in her life, since she'd never dreamed of him.

Talking about her dreams usually bothered her as much as having them. Her dreams often left her with a depressing awareness that she didn't have much control over her life. Besides fighting her constant dread of the inevitable, Kaylin also had to cope with the draining physical aftereffects of her dreams—violent headaches and dizzying nausea, plus a punishing weariness as if she hadn't slept at all. But strangely, talking about her dreams to Shane eased the tension in her gut, the knots in her shoulders, the ache in her heart for the sister she missed so much.

"And tonight? What did you dream?" Shane asked, revealing a sharp memory, which retained the fact that she'd never answered his earlier question.

44

"I saw Jenna's face and her breath on a window. It was raining outside and dark. Car headlights flashed by. I saw no road signs, no trees, nothing to indicate her location. And it may have been a memory from seven years ago, or four. In the dark I couldn't tell her age. But I still hope we'll find her."

She rubbed her temple, willing to suffer the extreme aftereffects of a nightmare—if she could only dream the right clues. She'd never give up hope that Jenna was still alive, unless evidence was found to the contrary.

"Are you hurting now?"

She liked the way he asked the question with sympathy, yet without pity. She hadn't told him about the physical suffering after her nightmares. Perhaps he'd seen her rubbing her temple. If so, Shane was damn observant. She turned her coffee mug in circles. "You woke me before I suffered any ill effects. After I dream, I often feel ill."

"You've always had…"

"Always. That's why I don't like to sleep," she admitted, her tone bleak. "It's my fate…and my curse."

…NOT THE END…

Look for On the Edge *in bookstores May 2005, a Signature Select Spotlight book.*

LOGAN'S LEGACY

Because birthright has its privileges and family ties run deep.

The long-awaited Logan's Legacy conclusion is here!

THE HOMECOMING

by *USA TODAY* bestselling author

ANNE MARIE WINSTON

Sydney Aston is determined to reunite Danny Crosby with his long-lost son. But she soon finds herself falling totally in love with this tormented man—and realizes that this could be a homecoming for all three of them.

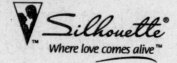

Where love comes alive™

Welcome to Courage Bay, California...
a community founded on bravery.

CODE RED

Two former flames become suspects
for murder in an electrifying new
Code Red episode...

CRITICAL AFFAIR

by

M.J. RODGERS

When food poisoning contaminates
a wedding rehearsal dinner, the entire
wedding party is rushed to the E.R.
Only the bride, Jennifer Winn, is
unaffected. And now the groom
is dead....

Coming in May!

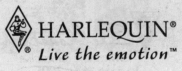

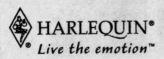

Silhouette
BOMBSHELL

**BRINGS YOU THE THIRD
POWERFUL NOVEL IN**

LINDSAY
McKENNA's

SERIES

Sisters of the Ark:

Driven by a dream of legendary powers,
these Native American women have
sworn to protect all that their people
hold dear.

WILD WOMAN

by *USA TODAY* bestselling author
Lindsay McKenna

Available April 2005
Silhouette Bombshell #37

Available at your favorite retail outlet.

If you enjoyed what you just read,
then we've got an offer you can't resist!

Take 2 bestselling love stories FREE!

Plus get a FREE surprise gift!

Clip this page and mail it to Harlequin Reader Service®

IN U.S.A.	**IN CANADA**
3010 Walden Ave.	P.O. Box 609
P.O. Box 1867	Fort Erie, Ontario
Buffalo, N.Y. 14240-1867	L2A 5X3

YES! Please send me 2 free Blaze™ novels and my free surprise gift. After receiving them, if I don't wish to receive anymore, I can return the shipping statement marked cancel. If I don't cancel, I will receive 4 brand-new novels each month, before they're available in stores! In the U.S.A., bill me at the bargain price of $3.99 plus 25¢ shipping and handling per book and applicable sales tax, if any*. In Canada, bill me at the bargain price of $4.47 plus 25¢ shipping and handling per book and applicable taxes**. That's the complete price and a savings of at least 10% off the cover prices—what a great deal! I understand that accepting the 2 free books and gift places me under no obligation ever to buy any books. I can always return a shipment and cancel at any time. Even if I never buy another book from Harlequin, the 2 free books and gift are mine to keep forever.

150 HDN DZ9K
350 HDN DZ9L

Name	(PLEASE PRINT)	
Address	Apt.#	
City	State/Prov.	Zip/Postal Code

Not valid to current Harlequin Blaze™ subscribers.

Want to try two free books from another series?
Call 1-800-873-8635 or visit www.morefreebooks.com.

* Terms and prices subject to change without notice. Sales tax applicable in N.Y.
** Canadian residents will be charged applicable provincial taxes and GST.
  All orders subject to approval. Offer limited to one per household.
® and ™ are registered trademarks owned and used by the trademark owner and or its licensee.

BLZ04R   ©2004 Harlequin Enterprises Limited.

JACQUIE D'ALESSANDRO

Growing up on Long Island, New York, **Jacquie D'Alessandro** fell in love with romance when she was introduced to the delightful bygone era of Regency England in Jane Austen's novels. She dreamed of being swept away by a dashing rogue riding a spirited stallion. When her hero finally showed up, he was dressed in jeans and drove a Volkswagen. They married after both graduating from Hofstra University and are now living their happily-ever-afters in Atlanta, Georgia, along with their very bright and active son, who is a dashing rogue in the making. Jacquie loves to hear from readers! You can contact her through her Web site at www.JacquieD.com.

JULIE KENNER

Julie Kenner's first book hit the stores in February 2000, and she's been on the go ever since. A *USA TODAY* and Waldenbooks bestselling author, Julie is also a former RITA® Award finalist, and winner of the *Romantic Times* Reviewer's Choice Award for Best Contemporary Paranormal of 2001. She retired in June 2004 from law practice and now lives and writes in Georgetown, Texas, with her husband and daughter. She loves writing contemporary romance because she gets to read trendy magazines and call it research.

SUSAN KEARNEY

USA TODAY bestselling author **Susan Kearney** used to set herself on fire four times a day. Now she does something really hot—she writes for Harlequin Blaze, Signature and Tor. A business graduate from the University of Michigan, an all-American and professional diver, dabbler in the martial arts, sailor, real-estate broker and former owner of a barter business, she has recently taken up figure skating and is planning a trip to New Zealand. You can visit her Web site at www.susankearney.com.